I0628518

GODS OF TALERA
THE TALERA CYCLE, BOOK 5

THE TALERA CYCLE
Swords of Talera
Wings Over Talera
Witch of Talera
Wraith of Talera
Gods of Talera

GODS OF TALERA
THE TALERA CYCLE, BOOK 5

CHARLES ALLEN GRAMLICH

WILDSIDE PRESS

Copyright © 2016 by Charles Allen Gramlich
All rights reserved.

Published by Borgo Press,
An Imprint of Wildside Press LLC.
www.wildsidepress.com

CONTENTS

WHAT HAS GONE BEFORE

Ruenn Maclang was born and grew to manhood on Earth. On the planet of Talera, he was reborn a swordsman and a leader of warriors. He began as a man lost and alone on an alien world of savagery and beauty, but he found his path. He found friends who fought with him, and for him, and he found a woman to love. That woman was Rannon, a princess who became Queen of the island kingdom of Nyshphal after her father was murdered.

Ruenn and Rannon married in a bloody throne room after a desperate battle and narrow victory against the Witch Vohanna and her allies. But as soon as the Witch's War was over and Vohanna destroyed, an even more deadly threat arose.

Vohanna had called herself an Asadhie, a member of the ancient and alien race that created Talera. In Talera's mythology, Vohanna was wed to another Asadhie named Vessoth, who had been imprisoned for trying to cleanse the planet of all life. Ruenn and Rannon were skeptical of the myths, but in *Wraith of Talera* they found out there was far more truth in them than they'd imagined. Vessoth *had been* imprisoned—on the Taleran moon of Nimeru. And he'd broken free.

With allies old and new, Ruenn travelled to Nimeru to confront Vessoth, who considered himself a god and was worshipped as such by many of his followers. Ruenn found Vessoth and defeated the Asadhie's greatest warrior. But once more the sorcerer escaped. Ruenn was left paralyzed.

At the end of *Wraith of Talera*, Ruenn was offered a chance to regain the physical skills he'd lost. It required a dreadful risk, one that could change Ruenn forever, or kill him. But Vessoth still had to be stopped before he destroyed everyone and everything Ruenn had come to love. For Rannon, for Talera, for himself, Ruenn took the risk. So begins, *Gods of Talera*.

CHAPTER ONE

REBIRTH OF A SWORDSMAN

Broken.

Shattered. In agony.

The pieces of me shrieking in a thousand voices.

Chalathar, the Asadhie sorcerer who had joined in the war against Vohanna and Vessoth, had said the Asadhie transference process would hurt. He had lied. I had hurt before. This was far beyond any experience that could be called hurt. My mind, my spirit, my soul—my khi as the Talerans call it—was being torn up by the roots from the bed of my body.

I could not bear it.

I could not stop it.

Unless I give up, I thought. *Death will stop it.*

My eyes were closed but something within me could see. My body lay stretched infinitely across a black heaven. Cracks of light shone through my spread-eagled form. A dagger storm of purple lightning struck at me, and every strike carved the cracks deeper. With each moment, the pain ratcheted higher.

Give up, a voice whispered. *Scatter into the blackness. Claim peace.*

I would not. I pushed back against the pain, trying to seal the cracks ripping me apart. At first it was no more than the animal urge to live that drove me, the beast's instinct to fight when cornered. It became something else. It became a face with dark hair framing it like a silken scarf.

Rannon.

The pain snarled in response to that thought, bit deeper like a predator determined not to lose its prey.

Rannon!

Whatever is stretched far enough must eventually snap. It was as if all the pieces of me that had been straining for cohesion suddenly achieved it. Except for one piece. The piece that made me Ruenn Maclang tore free. A last crescendo of pain caressed me. Then came surcease. All around it was dark, but I felt like a wind rushing across a great silence.

Rushing. Rushing.

Stillness followed.

I opened my eyes on a brightness that stung.

Rannon?

There was no Rannon. I looked upon an enclosed amphitheater of dark stone. Weapons hung on the walls: swords, spears, axes, war-hammers. Light globes embedded in the ceiling painted both walls and weapons with a satiny sheen. Some sixty bodies stood in three tiers of glass cases around the room—men and women, human and alien and even those who appeared as beasts. They looked asleep but I knew they were all empty—empty and waiting. These were surrogate forms that Chalathar, or any Asadhie, could inhabit at will.

At the front of the amphitheater, at the lowest point of the room, rested a long obsidian altar, and behind it stood Chalathar himself. At the moment, he wore human guise. He appeared as a tall, powerfully built warrior, with long hair of a reddish-blond and eyes as colorless as gin. His was a compelling figure, but it was not he that held my gaze. Upon the altar lay the body of someone who was not a sorcerer but merely a man—Ruenn Maclang. Except that, *I* was Ruenn Maclang and that body was no longer mine. Like the surrogates, it too was empty, a shed husk with legs that would not move.

After the strike of the blade that severed my spine, after Vessoth had escaped the moon of Nimeru and fled we knew not where, Chalathar had brought me here to his home. He'd offered me hope that I could walk again, fight again, love again. He would transfer my personality, my very nature, into one of his alternates, into a body that worked.

Those surrogate forms stood in this room and it seemed the transference of my spirit into one of them had been completed. But who was I now? Or what?

CHAPTER TWO

A LOOK IN THE MIRROR

Looking out at Chalathar's surrogate room, I reached to press the latch to open my own glass chamber. I stopped.

My hand!

It looked…almost human. Four long fingers, a thumb. The skin had a faint yellowish cast, like a faded tan, but with a dusting of copper flakes throughout that resembled embedded snake scales. I quickly lifted the hand to explore my new face. Strange fingers met prominent brows and cheekbones. The jaw was angular, the nose sharp, the lips thin. The features felt human but strangely sleek.

I looked down along the body I wore. Boots and breeks of light brown leather encased it from feet to hips. A long-sleeved shirt of black cotton hid the upper part of the form. *My new form!* The usual number of limbs lay beneath the clothing. The contours of the muscles seemed correct. Everything was in proportion but nothing felt quite right.

With my new heart beating rapidly, I unlatched the case and stepped out. Chalathar heard the sound and looked up. He was smiling, though the smile faded almost imperceptibly when he saw me. I strode cautiously toward him, aware of the need to choose my steps carefully to keep from stumbling over my unfamiliar feet. I stopped across the altar from him. The abandoned body of Ruenn Maclang lay between us; the eyes of that figure were closed and the chest did not rise or fall.

My gaze met Chalathar's. His irises glinted like chips of ice, though his face held an expression of warmth.

"Who am I?" I asked, and even my voice sounded strange, with a rasping note it had never contained before.

"Ruenn Maclang," Chalathar answered. "Warrior of Talera. King of Nyshphal. My friend."

"Are you sure?"

"It is the khi that makes the man. Not the shell he wears."

"Still, I would know what shell this is."

"Its name is Baadon," Chalathar said.

He lifted a finger, sketched an oval in the air that began to glow gray. The glow cleared in another moment to form a floating mirror. I saw my newly acquired form. It stood inches taller than my old one, and broader shouldered. Above those shoulders loomed a brutal face. It was humanoid but built of all sharp planes and angles. The nose was knife-edged, the mouth a colorless line.

The skin lay tight over the prominent cheekbones, almost without pores, and in each cheek were three ragged grooves that looked like scars left by the talons of a tiger. They were too regular for scars, though, and each was coated in metallic looking scales of copper, silver, and gold. The short hair on my scalp was snowy white and clung close to the skull almost like a covering of feathers. The eyes were faintly slanted and deep-water green. At least that color was familiar from my old face.

"Tell me about Baadon," I said.

"I know little," Chalathar replied. "I have never inhabited that body. It was not originally one of my surrogates."

"Whose then?"

He did not answer.

"Whose?"

He sighed, a very human-like response, though his inner self was far from Human.

"When Vessoth was imprisoned," he said, "all his surrogates were taken from him. They were distributed…to others."

I nodded. "That would explain the reptilian qualities."

"Yes."

"Of what race is Baadon? I've never seen the like before."

"Of no race. You know the Asadhie bred whole races such as the Llurns and Koro from Humans. But they also bred exotics for various purposes. Either aesthetic. Or, like this one…for battle. There are no others like Baadon. At least that I am aware of."

Studying Chalathar for a moment, I wondered if one of his statements had indeed been a slip of the tongue, or merely a poor choice of words. He'd said, "you know the Asadhie," as if he weren't one of them himself.

I had become increasingly suspicious of the Asadhie. Vohanna originally. Vessoth next. Even Chalathar now. The beings who had condensed Talera from the heart of a gas-giant planet and set an artificial sun and artificial moons around it would have had immense powers, far beyond anything I'd seen wielded by those who called themselves the Asadhie today.

Perhaps it was time to confront one of them about that discrepancy. I opened my mouth to ask a question that Chalathar would probably not want to answer, but it was he who spoke first. His words forced my thoughts in another direction.

"It seems unlikely that your khi chose the body of Baadon by accident," he said.

I frowned. "What do you mean?"

"The spirit seeks that which is compatible with it. It makes a *choice*. I do not believe it is a conscious one, but it is a choice all the same. And there are reasons behind it." He jerked his chin in my direction. "In the selection of Baadon by your khi, there is both danger and promise."

"Maybe you'd better explain that."

His gaze met mine steadily. "Vessoth has inhabited that body you wear. I don't know how frequently. Vessoth was never one to seek physical battle but he trained for it just in case, in that body. The more often one uses a surrogate, the easier the process of transference becomes. A residual connection is left after a single use, but can strengthen with repetition. The body you see me in, for example—Chalathar—is by far the easiest for me to inhabit. That is one reason I call upon it so often."

"Are you telling me that Vessoth could take this body away from me?"

He shook his head. "No. But it might just be possible for him to trace you in some way while you're in it. Of course, he has no idea that you're inhabiting it. He can't see what he isn't looking for."

"I guess that's the 'danger' you mentioned. What of the 'promise?'"

"The opposite is also true."

I felt an eyebrow arch. "You mean I might be able to trace *him*?"

"Perhaps. I'll have to spend some thought on it. But first, I need your help with something else?"

"What?"

"I told you before that there's a traitor among my people. I'm not sure who. But this might be the moment to find out."

"How so?"

"Whoever the traitor is, he or she stole the machine from me that Vessoth used to create the Jedik Ver Lha Yed clone so recently used against you."

I well remembered that awful battle with a version of my old friend Jedik at the heart of the Taleran moon called Nimeru. Jedik had taught me most of what I knew about the sword. It is unlikely that I could have beaten him under normal circumstances. Fortunately, I'd not faced the man who'd been my friend and mentor, but rather a corrupted being given life and hate through a combination of advanced technology and Vessoth's blackest sorcery.

"What does the incident with Jedik have to do with now?" I asked.

"Vessoth had to have used a sample of Jedik's flesh to create that clone. How much more would he like to have a clone of Ruenn Maclang? And here," he waved his hand over the altar where my old body lay, "we have plenty of flesh for such a process."

I glanced toward the altar, took in the stillness of my abandoned form. "Ah," I said.

"Just so. We extend an invitation to the traitor. A vacant body cannot offer any resistance to having a sample of its flesh stolen. And if Vessoth builds a clone from a piece of an emptied body, he can easily place within it whatever spirit he might wish."

I shuddered at that thought, but smiled at the possibility of trapping a traitor. "Tell me what to do."

CHAPTER THREE

SMOKING OUT A TRAITOR

Carefully, we laid our trap. We first selected and hid another of the sorcerer's surrogates—a Nokarran named Chaiden. Then Chalathar cast an illusion of an animated Nokarran, which would leave this room beside him as if it were real. If someone were watching us, he'd seen two beings enter this room and needed to see two exit if our trick was to work.

Finally, Chalathar handed me a sword pulled from the chamber's walls and left me with a few words nearly as sharp as the steel of that blade. "This sword is a precaution; I hope you won't have to use it. Whoever comes in here to look at your former body will be our traitor, but the most *important* thing is to identify them. If you show yourself, they'll almost certainly flee thinking it's a trap. You don't need a confrontation while you're still learning how your Baadon form works. No one here can open a sphere gate except for me. Find out who they are and we can capture them later."

I opened my mouth to protest, then shut it again. He was right. My pride was not the issue. Nodding my agreement, I returned to the glass fronted case where I'd awakened as Baadon such a short time before. There, I strove for stillness while Chalathar left the surrogate room with an illusion striding beside him.

Time passed. Half a dhaur or a little more. I'd finally had to scratch my nose and had just put my hand down again when a suspicious clicking sound froze me. A second click came, as of a door being closed. Stealthy footfalls slipped down the corridor leading to this room. The lights had been dimmed but were bright enough for me to see a skulker in robes and hood steal into view.

The figure's face was concealed—and its body. I could tell only that it was tall. I peered intensely, as if sheer will could pierce the gray cloak the being wore. It could not. The figure moved toward the black altar, toward the still form of what had once been Ruenn Maclang. It leaned forward, studying the emptied body. A glint of light flashed in its hand.

A knife!

Surely the skulker did not intend to cut a lifeless throat. It wanted a sample of flesh. And if it got that sample and escaped without being identified.... Well, that could not be allowed. Grabbing the sword leaning by my side, I leaped from my hiding place. The figure heard me, looked up. The hood slid back far enough for me to recognize the face beneath it.

No! Surely not!

It was Shai's face looking back at me.

Shai? A traitor? How could it be?

I'd not known her long but we'd bled in battle together. I'd come to trust her. She'd piloted our sky ship to Nimeru so we could face down Vessoth. Only days ago we'd fought side by side across that jungle moon, had faced the Snake God's best warriors with our backs against the sea. I would have died without her. And she without me.

"Shai!" I shouted, perhaps with a note of despair in my voice.

She turned and ran.

The chamber that I was in rested among the third tier of bodies in this amphitheater. Marble steps led down through the tiers toward the obsidian altar. I rushed down them as Shai fled back into the corridor along which she'd come, her cloak whipping at her heels.

I stormed past my abandoned body and into the corridor myself. The light here was much dimmer but I could still see well enough. No Shai, only a few statues and display cases. The door to the outer hall was closed. I'd not heard that door open but Shai *must* have gone out. I followed, into a wide hall of brightly lit stone. Left and right, I looked. The passageway lay empty of any cloaked figure. Or of anything else.

How could she have moved so fast?

I rushed back into the hallway of the surrogate room. The display cases were all open and empty. There were four statues, one of the goat-like taverel, another of the predatory reeth, then a wading bird, and some kind of fish. None were big enough to hide a person of Shai's size behind them, or within a hidden chamber inside of them. The circle of surrogate bodies and the black altar were as I'd left them. The former body of Ruenn Maclang still rested as before.

Shai had escaped. I did not know how. But perhaps it didn't matter. We had a name for our traitor now—hard as it might be to believe. I had to find Chalathar, let him know. It was no chore to relish. I'd seen how fond he was of Shai. He trusted her. As had I.

Though Chalathar had been closer to Shai than I, we had both been betrayed. To my thinking, all of Talera had been betrayed. And such an act could not be allowed to go unpunished. Even for someone I'd judged a friend.

CHAPTER FOUR

WHEN THINGS ARE NOT AS THEY SEEM

Leaving Chalathar's surrogate room once more, I locked the door behind me and returned to the main passage, heading left along it. I'd traveled this way once before, though that had been while lying in my old body on a wheeled table pushed along by another.

The corridor did not run straight but curved gradually. Little in this whole place ran straight. Whoever designed it must have been uncomfortable with right angles. I did not think that designer was Chalathar, though at some point he'd claimed the place as his own.

Following the hallway, I soon came upon a long, wide set of windows that looked out from the building. While passing here before, Chalathar had stopped to let me see more of his home base. I'd been stunned at my glimpse through the glass.

Straight out of the windows one could see a warren of white buildings. They were polished to a high shine beneath the emerald spring light of the sun and appeared to be built from marble. That was not the image that stunned me, however.

Dominating the sky above the buildings, hanging like a painting of stark imagination, a golden mass filled almost the entire horizon. The mass curved like an orb, though I could not see the whole of it, nor make out any details of the surface against the bright glow. It was Tisiminna, one of the four moons of Talera.

I have spoken before of Talera's moons. Vessoth's prison had been inside Nimeru, the smallest of the four. I had visited that world. Its exterior consisted of an interweaving of giant tiles that emitted the gloaming blue light of the "Little Dreamer." A riotous jungle full of strange, wonderful, and awful things filled its interior. Now I looked upon another Taleran moon, one known by many as "The Beauty." Her light is not blue but gold, a delicate shade like the finest and richest of Starkayan silks.

To see Tisiminna in this way, I could not be upon its surface. Instead, my feet must be treading upon one of the two much smaller orbs known to circle Tisiminna. They are typically named the "courtiers." Chalathar agreed when I mentioned this to him. He said that we stood upon the larger of the two orbs, which is called Nald. The other is Hael.

Although *I* knew that the moons had been constructed by the Asadhie, various Taleran legends offer more romantic explanations for Tisiminna's origins. In some tales she was a beautiful maiden in love with a great warrior who died in battle. She could not bear her loss and pined away for her lover, even though many rich and handsome suitors tried to woo her. The gods eventually took pity on her and made her into a moon. To keep her from being lonely, they set two of her courtiers in orbit around her forever. In other variations, Tisiminna's warrior lover also became a moon, the one known as Rath, the largest of the four and a bloody crimson in color. In that version, the courtiers are said to be their children.

Not slowing this time for the view through the windows, I hurried on past to find Chalathar. I'd gone only another fifty paces when footsteps rang out ahead of me and there came the very man I sought. At his side walked a tall and easily recognizable warrior.

I froze. "You!"

Shai's gaze met mine, confused yet apparently guileless

"What?" she asked. "Who are you?"

"I saw you!"

She looked at Chalathar with curiosity; the sorcerer stared at me with the same.

"What did you see, Ruenn?" he asked.

"Ruenn!"Shai exploded. She glanced back and forth between the two of us. "What by all the hells is going on here?"

Chalathar held out his hand toward me but spoke to Shai. "I used the Asadhie process to transfer Ruenn's khi into this body. We will need him in our battle against Vessoth. And he'll need the use of legs."

Shai looked at me with apparent wonder. She had to be faking it. Did she not realize I'd seen her face in the surrogate room?

"She knows who I am already," I snapped. "Or at least she knows that the body of Ruenn Maclang is emptied."

Shai frowned, and the first signs of irritation crossed her face. She was not the most patient of women. "I don't know what you're talking about. I knew nothing of any of this until Chalathar's words of a moment ago."

"Yes, Ruenn," Chalathar said. "Please explain."

I turned my gaze toward the Asadhie. "It was Shai who came to the room after you left. She wore a cloak but I saw her face. She had a knife. To take a cloning sample of my old body. I tried to stop her and she ran. I'm not quite sure how she eluded me."

Shai had been leaning belligerently toward me. She suddenly straightened her shoulders and took a step back. "Sae Yaal shei! This is insane. I haven't seen you in this form at all. I've been—"

Chalathar interrupted. "How long ago was this, Ruenn?"

"Moments," I said.

Shai started to protest but Chalathar laid a hand on her shoulder. "That's not possible, Ruenn," he said to me. "She has been with me for much longer than that."

My mouth opened, clicked shut. I glanced at Shai.

"But...." I shook my head. "It must have been some sorcery then. I saw her clearly."

"Not sorcery," Chalathar said. "I would have detected it."

"So how?"

"Follow me," he barked, as he strode swiftly past me and back the way I'd just come. I fell in behind him. Shai hurried along beside me but did not look in my direction. It was impossible to tell if she was angry or hurt, or perhaps just completely confused. 'Confused' summed up my own feelings quite well.

Quickly, we reached the door to Chalathar's surrogate chamber and entered. In the hallway there, where I'd lost sight of the skulker I'd thought to be Shai, Chalathar passed his hand over a glass square in the wall and the light globes in the ceiling brightened.

"Do you notice anything different here?" he asked me.

I looked around at the statues and display cases. "I'm...not sure. I looked to see if anyone were hiding behind the statues. I don't remember paying any close attention beyond that."

"Behind the statues?" he asked. "Were there the same *number* of statues here before?"

I felt myself frowning. "Let's see. There was a taverel. A fish. Uhm...." My eyes widened. "There was a reeth." I pointed. "Right there. But it's not there now."

Chalathar nodded. "The reeth is known for its mocking smile. A predator that never attacks from the front but always by surprise. We have a shapeshifter among us."

"A shapeshifter?"Shai asked.

"It probably raced into this corridor and disguised itself as a statue. Ruenn ran right past."

I looked at Shai and this time she met my gaze. "I'm sorry," I said. "I could not believe you were our traitor. But my eyes...."

"Understandable," Shai said. "We all believe what we see. But why did the thing choose *my* face?"

"No doubt because you would be recognized and considered safe if anyone saw you outside this room," Chalathar answered.

She nodded.

"I should not have missed such a thing," I said, angry at myself.

"Not your fault," Chalathar said. "I did not suspect either. Though it explains much."

"It means we still don't know who the traitor is," I added.

"We have a clue. It did not use sorcery to shape shift. I would have known instantly. That means it's a fhaze."

"Never heard of such," I said.

"Nor should you have. They were bred ages ago. As far as I know there were only three, and all were destroyed long before you came to Talera. Their ability to shift form is based on their biology and not on magic. It would appear that at least one of them has survived much longer than anyone thought."

"Or been recreated," Shai added.

Chalathar shook his head. "That knowledge is lost."

My heart suddenly began to pound. "If that thing was here. After I left...."

Chalathar's mouth spilled an oath. He turned and rushed down the short corridor into the main room of the surrogate chamber. Shai and I followed swiftly at his heels. As we came into the big room, Chalathar suddenly slowed. His shoulders slumped. I looked past him to the black altar.

The body of Ruenn Maclang was gone.

CHAPTER FIVE

QUESTIONS WITH FEW ANSWERS

"I'm a fool!" Chalathar snarled. His face flushed red. "I thought to trap the traitor and instead played into his hands."

"I'm the one who was fooled," I said. "I should never have left the room unguarded."

Shai interrupted our self-flagellations. "There may yet be time. The shifter escaped with Ruenn's body but it hasn't escaped this planetoid." She focused her gaze on Chalathar. "If the creature has some way of using a sphere gate, you'll know. You'll track it. Until then, we can initiate a search of everyone's quarters here. We might have luck."

Chalathar took a deep breath. His flush slowly receded and finally he nodded. "You're right. I have things I can do. As for the search, the people I trust most right now to handle it are in Ruenn's group. None of them have been here before. They could not have been responsible for stealing the cloning machine, which first revealed a traitor among us."

"They'll still need help from some of our own," Shai said. "Even if just as guides through the buildings."

"You and Rence," Chalathar said. "I trust you both implicitly."

Shai nodded.

Chalathar turned his gaze to me. "Do you need me there when you speak to your brother and friends? Can you convince them that *you're* Ruenn Maclang?"

"I think so. I know their secrets. And they know mine."

"I'll gather them," Shai said. "It'll give you time to figure out what to say. We can meet in the room where you first awoke here. Say half a dhaur."

"Good. Just tell them I want to talk with them."

"Just so," she said.

She turned to go after taking one last look around at the glass chambers holding Chalathar's surrogate bodies. She understood that Chalathar and other Asadhie could assume alternate forms, but I thought it must have been the first time she'd seen this place for herself. She looked awed, but also strangely disquieted. I knew from spending time with Shai that she was in love with Chalathar. I wasn't sure she understood that herself. Chalathar was certainly fond of her as well, though whether that feeling could be called love was open to question.

As an Asadhie, was Chalathar even capable of loving in the way that most natural races of Talera were—such races as Humans, Nokarra, Kaldi, Klar, Ss'Korra, Vhichang? In his current guise he looked so Human it was easy to forget that inside he was far more alien than any of those others. I could *not* forget. I'd seen the true form of other Asadhie, of Vohanna and Vessoth. They'd more closely resembled some mixture of insect and mollusk than anything else. And neither of them had seemed capable of true love, although they'd been quite adept at hate.

Shai had also seen an Asadhie's true form—Vessoth's, not Chalathar's. But it made me wonder. Had the experience triggered any concerns in her regarding the nature of the being she loved? That question was soon replaced as Shai left to gather my friends and Chalathar spoke.

"I wonder how long this fhaze shapeshifter has troubled us. And how it infiltrated my people?"

"How many work with you here?" I asked.

"Around thirty. It varies. But not much. Of course, many will be gone on missions at any given moment. There are only eleven here on Nald now. Besides *your* people, that is."

"So, most likely, one who left at some point on a mission came back as someone else."

Chalathar nodded. "Yes, I suppose. Though such an impersonation would not be easy. I know well those few who are invited here. The fhaze must be very adept to mimic such a one." He sighed. "It must mean that someone who was once a good friend of mine is now dead."

"Likely," I agreed. "Too dangerous for the shifter to let them live. But tell me, are there any permanent residents here?"

Chalathar frowned. "Basinj. He cooks, among other things. He was badly injured in my service and no longer goes on missions. There are a couple of others. Why do you ask?"

"Because any permanent residents are probably *not* your fhaze. For the shapeshifter to carry out its acts of theft and treason, it would need to travel to and from this place."

Chalathar arched an eyebrow. "Yes, of course."

"And you have no way of telling through Asadhie means who the shapeshifter is?"

"Through what you call 'Asadhie' means, I would only be able to detect alterations produced by sorcery. The fhaze do not use such. But

I may be able to consider other facts. Who has been here at what times. Whether certain individuals have shown anomalies in their behavior."

"Circumstantial evidence," I said, nodding.

"What?"

I smiled. "It's a term from Earth. It means that you don't catch a criminal committing a crime, but are able to infer that they must have done so by looking at other information available to you."

Chalathar nodded. "Yes. I need to consider the...circumstantial evidence." He met my gaze. "Can you find your way back to your original room from here?"

I nodded, and we both departed the surrogate chamber. At the main corridor, he turned right with a brief goodbye and I went again to the left. While walking, I contemplated the risks involved in revealing my identity to my brother and our friends.

How would they accept it?

Could they accept it?

I would have to make them.

CHAPTER SIX

A REVELATION

I came once more into the room where I'd first awakened at Chalathar's base on the planetoid called Nald. I'd still worn my original body at that time, with its crippled spine. My brother and my friends had worried for me. I'd seen their pain. Now I walked into the room on two working legs, and gathered before me were those same beings. They were all like family to me, but they did not recognize me now.

Bryce, of course, *was* family. My brother stood a touch under six feet and was as lean as a strip of rawhide. His hair was cotton white, not unlike *my* new hair color. Once, his hair had been dark brown. Before Vohanna. But at least his eyes had returned to the grey color I'd known when we'd grown up together in the state of California, in the United States of America, on Earth. Such a lifetime ago, it seemed.

Valyan waited in this room, too. Though not my brother by blood, he was as close as one emotionally. He was not quite human, but a Green Llurn, a Nakscherii. All Llurns, and there were several types, had been modified in ages past from the basic Human stock. Valyan's skin held the emerald hue of his people; his eyes were yellow as beads of amber. Even here in relative safety he wore a bow and quiver of arrows slung upon his back.

Next to Valyan stood Diken Graye, once a mercenary with sword for hire, now a good friend whose blade was dedicated to the service of those he cared for. He was as Human as Ruenn Maclang had once been. His long brown hair hung in warrior braids at the sides of his head. A pale scar marked his chin. His black eyes studied the new me curiously.

There was Rence, with his shaved head, mescal-colored eyes, and the twin short blades called kahnnas that he carried over his shoulders. I had known Rence for a much shorter time than the others but we had fought side by side through many terrors. I considered him a friend as well.

Finally? Shai! I was very glad this warrior woman with her bone armor and her gold-flushed skin was not the traitor we sought. I remembered too well the blood we had spilled together on that battlefield of white sand beside a black ocean within the moon of Nimeru. Her bravery had been matched only by her skill with a blade.

But now Bryce questioned me. "We were expecting my brother," he said. "Who are you?"

Before answering, I saw a scabbarded sword leaning against the bed I'd lain helplessly in not very long ago. Striding over to it, I picked it up. Every eye in that room narrowed; every hand shifted toward a weapon. Tension thrummed like a harp strung too tight. I had their attention—as I wished it. But for just a moment I ignored them all and studied the blade in my grip.

The sword's metal haft was wrapped in rough leather to give a sure hold for the hand. A knob of ivory from some unknown creature formed the pommel. The cross-guard curved slightly away from the hilt and at the tip of each quillon was carved the snarling head of a beast that resembled a wolf. The three-foot blade, hidden inside a leather scabbard, gleamed like silver and yet was as hard as any metal I'd ever seen. That blade was etched in strange runes no human hand had carved. I had first taken it from a being I'd killed in the jungles of Vohan, in the land of Nyshphal. I'd carried it against many foes since.

"That is my *brother's* sword," Bryce said. "You have no right to touch it."

I gazed at him; he gazed back. Suddenly he seemed confused.

"I ask again," he said, "who are you?"

"Do you remember, Bryce," I said, "a big sow pig called Raisin? When you were about eight, she had piglets and you were told to leave them alone. But you wanted to pet one and climbed into the pig pen. Raisin knocked you halfway across the pen, into the fence. You got a face full of splinters."

Bryce's pale face went paler. "How could you possibly know that? Who *are* you?

"You didn't want your Pa to know about the piglet. Well, you didn't want *our* Pa to know. I lied for you, Bryce. You still owe me for that."

"Ruenn!" my brother exclaimed, his mouth agape in shock.

I smiled. "Yes."

Shai quickly added her own words. "He is indeed Ruenn Maclang. I know it."

Suddenly, everyone in the room except Shai and Bryce seemed to be chattering questions. I held up my hands until they quieted. Without mentioning quite yet that my old body had just been stolen, I explained what Chalathar had done and why, and that the plan was to reverse the process in a year and restore me back into the form of the Ruenn Maclang they knew.

For a long time after I finished, the silence lay unbroken. Bryce still seemed in shock. He believed me. I could tell. But he did not know what came next after that belief. As for Valyan and Diken, they still had questions. So, I spoke to them in turn, giving each a word or mentioning a deed that we two had shared alone. Afterward, Valyan came and clasped my arm in the Taleran fashion. I took his in return. And Diken stood nodding.

"So your khi will eventually be returned to the Ruenn Maclang body," Diken said.

"Yes."

He grinned. "I should hope so. Ruenn was ugly but at least his face didn't make you want to gag."

I laughed. Everyone laughed.

Then Bryce said: "But what is Rannon going to say?"

For that there was no answer.

CHAPTER SEVEN

NO SAFE HAVEN

As I imagined how Rannon might react to my altered form, Shai began speaking of the search that Chalathar wanted us all to undertake. Perhaps we could find the traitor before he or she—or it—could escape with the body of Ruenn Maclang. For the moment, I put aside thoughts about my wife and began to consider the best way to conduct such a search. Even as I did so, a loud gonging rang through the room.

Shai's words faltered. Rence, who had been sitting, leaped to his feet.

"What is that?" Bryce demanded.

"It's...." Shai's voice held surprise, and what might have been a note of fear. "I haven't...heard it before. But I know it's—"

"A warning!" Rence interrupted. He'd drawn his kahnnas.

"Warning of what?" I demanded.

"Something that's not supposed to happen," Rence said.

"An attack," Shai added. She looked at Rence. "Chalathar," she said to him.

Rence nodded, loped quickly from the room. I glanced at my friends. Valyan stood very still; Bryce frowned; Diken swore an oath under his breath and drew his own sword.

"We'll go to the roof," Shai said. "See what is happening."

I nodded and slung the rune-blade over my shoulder by its strap. Shai headed for the door; the rest of us followed. Just beyond the room, Shai turned swiftly down a corridor I'd not noticed before. It led to a set of marble steps and we pounded up them.

None of the buildings I'd seen on Nald rose more than three stories high. Nor did this one. We quickly came to another door and went through it to find ourselves on a long, wide rooftop. The gongs clanged louder than ever here in the open.

Clay pots of various sizes dotted the roof, holding bushes and flowers of many hues. Beyond this roof were others, a whole city of white buildings with broad, winding streets and many open courtyards between them. But Shai was staring into the emerald sky and I turned my gaze after hers.

Huge airships were curving down out of that sky, with the golden bulk of Tisiminna looming behind them. These were sailed ships—battleships not unlike my own warship, *Khiang*, but half again as large. There were four of them, each painted dark purple, with flags flying from their masts bearing an image I could not make out at this distance.

"I don't know those ships," Shai said.

"Do you have defenses?" I demanded. "Preparations to meet such an attack?"

Shai shook her head. "Our defense has been our inaccessibility. None of the civilizations of Tisiminna are capable of building sky craft like those. And I could not imagine such a fleet would have been able to reach us from Talera."

"Yet these ships are here," Bryce stated flatly.

"We thought this a safe haven," Shai protested.

"In a world of sorcerers such as Vessoth, there are no safe havens," I replied.

The ships began landing between the white buildings, disgorging their passengers, which numbered about forty per ship. Any thought that our visitors might be peaceful was dispelled as light flashed from bronze helms and armor, and from swords and axes already held in the hands of the disembarking warriors.

"Chalathar will know what to do," Shai said.

"He'll run and take us with him," Bryce said. "If he has any sense. We have no chance against so many attackers."

"We'd better do something," Diken said. "Those rucking things are coming fast."

They were indeed. The strange warriors moved on all fours, like charging gorillas on Earth. They covered the ground swiftly and some-one among them must have sighted us. Our building seemed to be their target.

"I sent Rence," Shai said. "When he finds Chalathar they'll signal—"

At that moment, an explosion of yellow-gold light went off in the air to our left. The gongs fell silent. Beneath the coruscating light stood a building somewhat taller than the others around it.

"The temple," Shai said.

She turned, started toward the steps leading back down from the roof. Abruptly, she stopped and cursed. I knew why. Four more of the great purple ships had already landed in the city behind us. They too were emptying warriors onto the streets.

"Looks like we'll have to battle our way through," I said. It was not something to relish.

Shai snarled. Clearly, she *wanted* to fight. But she was no fool to fight and die if there were another way.

"Not yet!" she said. "Follow me. And let's hope you can all jump."

For a moment I had no idea what she meant. Then she turned toward the direction from which we'd seen the golden light and took off at a dead run across the roof. I saw what she intended. The buildings leading in the direction of the signal-light stood in a long white row, with only narrow gaps between them. Shai took that pathway, leaping from our roof to land on another. She turned and waved us toward her. I looked at the others. I looked at Bryce.

"Can you make it?" I asked my brother.

He growled an answer and took off running toward roof's edge. Diken followed at my nod. I looked at Valyan and him at me.

"You," he said.

There was no time to argue. I broke into a sprint, and the movements came easier than I'd feared. The legs of the Baadon body were long; they ate the ground and the large muscles in my new legs bunched and released as I leaped. I landed well past everyone else on the second roof. Valyan landed just behind me a moment later. Shai tore off again, leaped to a second building, a third. The rest of us followed.

It was from the fourth building that the gold light had risen. The roof there slanted upward and at the apex stood a kind of steeple with a small door leading into it. That door was locked. Shai kicked it in and swung into the building. Everyone else followed. We found ourselves in a kind of open loft with stairs to our left. Below us in the building, I saw Chalathar and Rence, and close to a dozen others, including Tuunshin, the phoros who had treated my wounds when I'd first arrived on Nald.

Chalathar stood in the center of the building between four tall, rectangular panels that seemed to be made of translucent ruby. He did not look up at us, though surely he'd heard the crashing sounds of our entry. Instead, his fingers danced rapidly over columns of gold hieroglyphs that inscribed the jewel-like panels. Every glyph he touched sparked immediately into glowing life. Rence stood near Chalathar and did look up at us. He beckoned, his gestures urging us to hurry. We rushed down the stairs to join the milling group below.

"Just in time," Chalathar said. "We go."

We all understood what he meant. He was going to open a sphere gate, take us away from this place. He lifted his hands from the ruby panels, sketched a different kind of symbol in the air.

The main door to the temple was thrown back and a dozen beings poured through. They saw us, howled a challenge as they rose onto their hind feet and clashed their weapons together. Chalathar said a word. The world fogged over as a sphere gate began to swirl into existence around us.

I recognized our foes. I'd fought some of them before in the jungle of Vohan. From one of them I'd taken the sword that hung over my shoulder. Only, then they had been corpses resurrected by the sorcery of Vohanna in her war against my homeland of Nyshphal. I had thought of them as Bull-men, as minotaurs, and had not realized how truly powerful they would be in life.

These were eight feet tall or better when standing erect. Their bodies were largely humanoid, though massively muscled and covered with mats of rough, reddish hair. Their hands resembled normal human ones, though their feet were hoofed. Their heads named them. There they resembled bulls, with blunt muzzles, broad nostrils and wide-set eyes. Copper rings pierced their large, bovine ears. Most also had horns that appeared to have been deliberately sawn off close to the skull.

One monster slung an axe at us just as Chalathar's sphere gate took us. The temple around us disappeared. A new place began to materialize.

A scream rang out.

CHAPTER EIGHT

REFUGEES

I spun at the sound of the scream. Chalathar stood with his face and the front of his shirt splashed with blood. His arms held Tuunshin up against him. She was dead. The axe thrown by the Minotaur warrior had sheared away half her head. I stepped toward them but Rence got there first and took Tuunshin from Chalathar's arms.

The Asadhie's eyes raged but his voice remained calm. "I have to open another gate," he said. "We must pass through three such portals to ensure our foes cannot track us."

His hands sketched symbols in the air. His voice muttered unknown words. Again the gray swirl of a sphere gate coalesced around us. I barely noted that the first gate had deposited us on a golden plain of tall grass before the next gate tore us away. This time our gate opened on the barren shore of a dark lake. Waves lifted across the waters; a cold wind slapped my face. Almost immediately, the lake disappeared and we were in the dark.

The tingling that always shocked my body during transitions through sphere gates disappeared. I thought the third portal had closed but still could see nothing. Then a hundred shades of delicate light began to bloom around us: lavender, mauve, pearl, ruby, saffron, umber. They brightened.

"Do not panic," Chalathar's voice said. "We are safe."

For a moment I thought the light must come from some kind of plant growing on the walls of a cavern. Then I saw its true nature. And panic suddenly seemed a real possibility. The same incipient panic filled the murmuring voices of those around me. We were underwater, inside some spherical room of glass. The light came from thousands of luminescent creatures swimming or drifting in the depths outside our translucent cell.

I'd seen the wakes of ships filled with phosphorescence, with the multicolored flow of tiny plants and animals that churned the water to liquid light. I'd admired such beauty. But I'd been standing on a dry deck safe above the sea. Here, the sea surrounded us. It teemed with creatures much like jellyfish and worms and giant shrimp. I glimpsed swimming things that looked like spiders and moths, and many others that resembled nothing ever seen on Earth.

"Where are we?" I asked, and wondered if a faint tremor distorted my voice.

"I'd prefer to explain later," Chalathar said. "Just be aware that there's a network of rooms and tunnels here that will keep us dry. There's food and other materials stored in case this place were ever needed as a bolt-hole. Unfortunately, I did not plan for an attack on Nald such as we experienced today. I don't have everything I'd like. We'll have to improvise."

"What about your traitor?" Bryce asked.

The word "traitor" landed with a thud that brought everyone to silence. All eyes turned toward Chalathar. Clearly, most among his own group had not yet heard of this traitor. Only Shai and Rence did not look surprised at the word.

Chalathar held up a hand as if to forestall questions that had not yet been asked. "That's one reason why I don't want to reveal *where* we are. But it's likely that I'm being overcautious. We don't know if the traitor is still with us. But if he, or she, is, they can have no way of reaching through the depths around us to contact their masters. Or of telling them how to find us. Even if they knew where we were and could get the word out, our enemies would still find it difficult to open a sphere gate here without risking drowning. Certainly not while I'm able to counter them. We'll be safe.

"As for the traitor," he continued. And he spoke primarily to those who had been with him on Nald when my friends and I arrived from our battle with Vessoth. "I'd suspected one for quite a long time but was not sure of its nature until today. It's a shapeshifter. That is how it has managed to hide itself so easily among us."

Chalathar's people still remained silent, but began casting suspicious gazes upon one another, and particularly upon me and my friends. Other than Shai and Rence and the dead Tuunshin, I did not know any others among Chalathar's group. Three were Humans; three were Kaldi. The other two were a Vhichang and an Ss'Korra. One of the three Humans limped about on a peg-leg and had a twisted arm. I imagined he was the one Chalathar had named to me as Basinj—the cook.

"How long do we remain here?" Bryce demanded. "We can do nothing to stop Vessoth if we're living like refugees."

Chalathar had been under immense strain for many days. Most of us had shared some part of that strain but Chalathar's role had been the hardest one. His thinning lips made clear that Bryce's question angered him, but he controlled himself well and spoke softly when he answered.

"A little patience is all I request. Some things require time."

Bryce started to retort but I grabbed his wrist and he fell silent. Chalathar was right. Too, I suspected that much of Bryce's impatience had more to do with being cut off from Ahrethane than it did with stopping Vessoth. Though important to my brother, Ahrethane was not our main concern at the moment.

"What about Tuunshin's body?" Rence asked.

Chalathar sighed. "There are rituals for the dead among her people." He nodded toward the Kaldi members of his group. "But we have not the materials we need." He strode over to Rence and held out his arms. The mescal-eyed swordsman laid the physician's broken form across them. Chalathar continued: "I have a place where her body can be stored and preserved until we can hold the proper ceremonies. Please follow me."

Chalathar's command to "follow" him confused me for a moment. I could see no sign of the "network" of tunnels he had mentioned. Where was there to go in this place? Then, as the Asadhie walked away from us, I detected the outline of a glass corridor leading off from the open area where we'd materialized. We followed Chalathar along it, with sea creatures lighting our way.

I walked tentatively at first, worried about the strength of the nearly transparent floor to support us. No problems arose, however, and soon we exited into a rocky grotto sealed off on three sides from the water. Light globes took over the illumination duties here and it was a relief to see their familiar bright sheen rather than the ghostly glow of the underground sea.

Bales of leather and cloth, and barrels full of unknown contents were stacked around the grotto. There were tables and chairs of wood. Three stone corridors stretched off from the area and Chalathar stopped before the middle one.

"The barrels contain food and drink," Chalathar said to us all. "Help yourselves. I'll return in a few dhorrin. After placing Tuunshin's body in a safe place."

"I'll go with you," I said.

"And I," added Shai.

Chalathar considered for a moment before nodding. We proceeded down the corridor he'd selected. A few tunnels branched off from the main one but we continued straight onward until we came to an iron door. It opened at Chalathar's prodding and inside I was surprised to find another room of surrogate bodies. Several of the glass chambers for holding the surrogates were empty and the Asadhie sorcerer placed Tuunshin into one and closed it.

For the first time, I noticed that the chambers were engraved with odd symbols. They were largely invisible until Chalathar called my attention to them by stroking his fingers across the ones on Tuunshin's chamber. A faint snick sounded as the casket-like structure sealed. A bluish mist filled the chamber for a moment before dissipating.

"This will preserve her until we can treat her death properly," Chalathar said.

I nodded. Then: "We have to talk."

Shai seemed to be watching everything intently, but said nothing. Chalathar smiled, though I saw no corresponding emotion in his gin-pale eyes.

"I imagined you wished it so," he said. "What is it?"

"You keep many secrets," I said. "You did not even tell most of your own people about the traitor among them."

Shai started to protest my words but Chalathar held up a hand to silence her. His gaze burned. "Such secrets are mine to keep," he replied softly.

I nodded. "Just so. "But there's something else you're keeping secret. And it impacts my friends. It impacts Rannon and Nyshphal. When that happens, it's not yours to keep anymore."

"Speak plainly!" he snapped.

"Vessoth has help," I said. "Far more than could be provided by any fhaze shapeshifter. Or by any Thye Vessoth priests. He has Asadhie help. Doesn't he?"

"What makes you think such?"

"In Teleur, on the coast of Nyshphal, when the moon Nimeru first cracked open to free Vessoth from his prison, a sphere gate opened and two monstrous creatures called Quattles came through. It seems to me that Vessoth could not have been responsible for that gate."

"Why not Thye Vessoth?" Shai interjected.

I glanced at her, then back to Chalathar. "Because the gate they came through was huge. Far bigger than any I've ever seen. And I just don't believe a Thye Vessoth wizard would have that kind of power."

Chalathar puffed a breath of air through his mouth. "What else?" he asked.

"The ships that attacked us today. Big ships. They could not have reached the moon of Tisiminna from the surface of Talera. And Shai told us there are no civilizations on Tisiminna capable of building such vessels. So, unless you've been keeping secrets from her, that means our attackers must have come through a sphere gate. A very large one."

Chalathar glanced at Shai, let his gaze linger for a moment before looking back to me. "You're right," he said. "Vessoth has Asadhie help."

Shai sighed, as if she'd expected Chalathar's answer but hoped not to get it.

Chalathar continued: "Other than the Asadhie, those who have the power to open sphere gates are extremely rare." His gaze locked on mine: "Ruenn, your brother Bryce had such power. But it was Vohanna who created that in him in her attempts to make him her Bane-thrall. Vohanna also implanted the specially prepared milkstones in your friend Diken Graye that turned him temporarily into a wild gate (see *Witch of Talera*). And Asadhie have, at times, implanted milkstones in other beings to be activated by specific triggering events.

"Too, the efrinoire—your Ahrethane—has the ability to open gates now. Though I do not understand how. It must have been through some transference from Bryce when he was a Bane-thrall. The *only* Thye-Vessoth who I've known to be capable of opening gates were also Bane-thralls. And certainly there have been other such beings on Talera in the past. All of those are either dead or have been transformed almost beyond recognition. It has served the purposes of some Asadhie to let Talerans believe that a Human, or a Thye-Vessoth, or a sorcerer of some other race might open sphere gates. This is largely untrue. Except, as I have indicated."

I protested. "But I knew a man named Tovaris in Nyshphal who could open such gates. He did it for me. When I was still fresh to this world. He let me return to Earth to see about my parents, *and* brought me back to Talera."

Chalathar gave a faint chuckle. "I am Tovaris."

A hundred thoughts tried to churn their way into my mind at the same instant. I struggled to put order to them. Finally, I was able to speak.

"Why the misdirection? Why let people think that sorcerers other than Asadhie related ones could open sphere gates? What do the Asadhie gain from that?"

"It's the game," Chalathar said.

"You mean the game the Asadhie 'First Gods' played with Talera? Where they treated the people and nations of this world as nothing more than pawns to be used or tossed aside at a whim?"

Chalathar's voice turned grim. "Yes. And for beings like Vohanna and Vessoth that game never ended. The sphere gates are an important move in the game, a move that most Asadhie would not give away freely."

"So, is there anything I know about sphere gates that is, in fact, true?"

Chalathar shrugged. "I will give you truth. You believe that most sphere gates are fixed in one physical location, and that they open only to a limited number of other sites. There are some such, but not many. Some of these *have* opened spontaneously in the past. And things have come through. It is not a common event. Fixed gates can be large or small, though most are only big enough to pass a few beings such as you through at the same time. They also tend to cycle open and closed rapidly, though larger gates take longer to both open and close.

"With some restrictions, the Asadhie can open gates to and from almost anywhere. As long as they can locate the destination mentally. They can generally open bigger gates. And keep them open much longer. You have seen such from me and from Vohanna. However, there are also constraints on how big sphere gates can be. The one I opened for us today was close to the typical Asadhie limit. Except...."

"Except what?" Shai asked.

"Except that, for reasons unknown, there is one Asadhie who is able to open much bigger gates. When I heard of the gate in Teleur that passed the Quattle, I began to suspect this Asadhie of helping Vessoth. Today's little adventure confirms my suspicions. In fact, I'm surprised he played his hand so clearly."

"Heshval," I said, guessing. "Vessoth's brother!"

Chalathar smiled but shook his head. "A good guess. But no. I believe it to be Urthrik."

I frowned. I'd read much of the mythology concerning the Asadhie. I knew Urthrik was one of the twelve so called First Gods. But from what I could ascertain he had lost most of his powers.

"Wasn't he supposedly trapped forever in the body of one of his surrogates?" I asked.

"He was. But contrary to the stories that have spread from that event, it did not cost him his powers. It seemed even to amplify some. In particular, his ability to control sphere gates."

I frowned. "So the fact that he can open larger sphere gates was the giveaway?"

"That and one more thing."

"What?" Shai asked.

"The surrogate body that Urthrik is trapped in. In that form he is known as Kamrack the Bull."

"A minotaur," I said.

CHAPTER NINE

A MISSING PIECE OF THE PUZZLE

As we returned toward the grotto where our companions-in-exile waited, Shai asked Chalathar another question.

"Do you think you should tell Ruenn where we are?"

I glanced at Shai with some surprise. I'd figured this was another secret Chalathar was keeping even from those who followed him, but apparently Shai knew it. I looked at Chalathar himself.

The Asadhie sorcerer seemed to consider for a moment before nodding. "We're in the interior of the Hael planetoid," he said. "Nald's sister world. I found the place largely through accident. It's not very big. The unflooded section that is. I've explored it all. I've been moving supplies here for some time in case of need. Shai knows about it. The rest do not."

"You figure this was someone's bolt-hole before?" I asked.

"I don't think so. I believe it was someone's aquarium."

The term he actually used was marinia-ost, which literally translates as sea-home. Aquarium is its practical meaning. The word startled me.

"Aquarium? Truly?"

"Yes. The glassed in sections are extensive. And they pass near some very interesting phenomena."

"Such as?"

"There is an intelligent race of water dwellers living here. Some of the glass tunnels run near their cities. And there are even benches in those areas where observers can sit. The glass, by the way, can only be seen through from inside. From outside it looks opaque."

"How do you know that?" I asked.

"I've taken a swim or two," Chalathar said, smiling. "There are exits. And entrances. Specially built to exchange water and air. Whichever you need."

"Talera continues to surprise me," I said. Glancing at Chalathar, I added, "The *Asadhie* did amazing things here." But if Chalathar caught the meaning of my emphasis, he made no comment. Instead, he began telling me about the members of his group who I did not know. It was important enough information to demand my attention.

Not long after that we reached the grotto where our companions waited. Rence and Basinj and a few others were eating. Others were sharpening weapons or pacing back and forth in apparent frustration. Only two still seemed in shock, a paunchy Kaldi who everyone called Semish, and a pale-haired Human woman named Lyra.

According to Chalathar, most of his people were hardened fighters, beings like Rence and Shai who had joined him in the life or death struggle to preserve Talera. Semish and Lyra were exceptions. Apparently, Semish had once been a fine warrior who lost his nerve after barely surviving a particularly grueling mission. Lyra had been a slave girl who'd helped save a tortured and feverish Semish on that mission. He'd brought her back to Chalathar's base because during his fever he'd let slip far too much information about the cause and the being he served. Even though he'd healed physically, Semish had never left the base after that. He'd taken on the role of gardener. Lyra had become cook's help and general housekeeper.

Chalathar stopped for a moment to speak with the two, who were sitting together. Shai and I continued on to the table where Bryce, Diken, and Valyan were drinking verhlis tea and nibbling on passal, a Taleran equivalent to pemmican. I picked up a strip of passal and had just taken my first bite when Chalathar exclaimed:

"Where is Tesluc?"

Everyone looked around. Shoulders lifted into shrugs. Shai and I exchanged glances. Had our traitor revealed herself, or itself, already?

"She was here when you three left," Rence said to Chalathar. "I took a head count. She probably just went looking for the cohr." Cohrnex, often abbreviated as "cohr," is a Taleran word for bathroom. Rence was suggesting that his missing companion had gone to pee.

As for Tesluc, she was the lone Ss'Korra among Chalathar's people. The Ss'Korra are one of the 'natural' races of Talera, meaning they developed normally on their own planet rather than being the product of genetic manipulation by the Asadhie. Most people describe the Ss'Korra as wolf-like. They are certainly mammalian, though bipedal like most other intelligent races of Talera. To me, they more resemble baboons, although much bigger. Their feet are paw-like but their hands are very human. They have many variant fur colors. Common ones are black and gray. Tesluc's fur was red.

"We need to find her," Chalathar stated. "I'll take Semish and Lyra with me back down the middle corridor to explore its branches. Ruenn, Shai, Rence. Divide everyone else up and explore the other two stone corridors and the glassway we came down after first arriving here. No matter what, let's meet back here in a dhaur. If we haven't found her by then we can make plans for a further search."

I beckoned to Bryce, Diken, and Valyan. We took the stone corridor on the far right and moved cautiously along it. Our hands never strayed far from our weapons. No branches exited off that corridor to its right hand side. In fact, it seemed to parallel the underground sea because in places the stone walls were pierced by long, irregular windows of glass through which we saw the strange glow of the "aquarium's" underwater creatures.

At a corridor branching off to our left, we stopped. Asadhie light globes do not cast shadows, but I sensed some kind of darkness here. The others seemed to feel it as well, and I did not discount their wariness.

"Bryce, Diken," I said. "Stay here in the main corridor in case Tesluc comes back this way. Valyan, we're going up there." I nodded my head toward the side tunnel.

"Right," Valyan agreed.

"Be careful," Bryce said.

I did not reply but dropped my hand to the pommel of my sword. Valyan drew his bow over his shoulder and strung it. We stalked forward together. About a hundred paces in we found the cohrnex. It smelled only slightly of urine. It reeked of something else. We stepped through the doorway.

My boots found blood.

My gaze found our missing Ss'Korra.

Tesluc's hands had been tied behind her and roped tightly to her ankles, forcing her body into the shape of a bow. Her throat had been cut so violently that the neck was nearly severed. The murderer had then twisted the head around so that the corpse's open eyes stared back over her own shoulder with horror.

The murder was bad enough, but the positioning of the body indicated a cruelty that went beyond just killing. It seems our shapeshifting traitor had a vicious streak and had found a chance to indulge it.

CHAPTER TEN

SUSPICION

I stayed with Bryce to watch over the body and sent Diken and Valyan to fetch Chalathar. I paced while we waited. Bryce stared for a long time at the corpse before looking toward me with a faint shudder.

"I want to close her eyes," he said. "No one dead should still have their eyes open."

"I know," I agreed. "But leave them. We don't know what Chalathar might find important."

Bryce walked over and leaned against the wall. "You know this won't be the end of it," he said. "We'll have more bodies like this before we're through."

"Likely," I agreed, stopping beside him.

"Any suspicions so far?"

"Too many. I can rule out Chalathar and Shai. And our own group. I feel pretty sure it's not Rence. Other than that…." I shrugged.

"What about Semish and Lyra? Their 'shock' could be an act? It would be a perfect cover to throw us off the scent."

"Chalathar told me that Lyra, Semish, and Basinj no longer go on missions. That seems to point suspicion away from them. Whoever we're looking for would need to leave the base on occasion to carry out their sabotage."

"Maybe they don't go on missions for Chalathar anymore," Bryce said, "but he isn't at his base every moment to observe them."

"True. I guess we can't completely eliminate them either then."

"Still," Bryce said, "that seems to leave us with four primary suspects. One Human, a Vhichang, and two Kaldi."

"Right."

Bryce chewed his thumb for a moment, then sighed. "I don't know enough about any of them to judge."

"Maybe Chalathar will have some thoughts."

"Let's hope."

I leaned against the wall next to him. We both fell silent, although it felt as if Bryce were studying me surreptitiously. Finally, with a tinge of irritation, I asked him, "What?"

He shook his head. "Sorry. Your face is taking some getting used to."

"Hnnh," I said. "Harder for everyone else than for me. I'm not looking at myself every moment. From in here it doesn't feel much different."

"What *does* feel different?"

"Mentally, nothing. It's all physical. This body is bigger. The legs and arms are longer. Things seem…further away sometimes. My skin feels tight on occasion. Almost like scar tissue. But I'm adapting."

"The worst part may be your teeth," Bryce said.

"My teeth? What the hell is wrong with them?"

"Nothing's wrong with them, I guess. They're just….sharp."

I frowned, ran my tongue over my teeth. They *were* sharp. Now that I paid attention, I could feel it. There'd just been so many new sensations with the Baadon body. That was one I hadn't noticed.

"What do they look like?" I asked, curling back my lips to show him.

Bryce gave a quick little shake of his head. "Don't do that," he said. "You look like a shark."

I started to question him further but the sound of running footsteps brought us pause and we both drew our weapons. Bryce still had the Smith & Wesson .357 I'd given him on Nimeru. I'd left my Colt revolver behind on that moon during the fight with Vessoth, but drew my runeblade. I'd come to prefer the sword to the gun anyway.

Then Chalathar hove into view with Shai at his heels. Bryce and I sheathed our weapons and I jerked my chin in the direction of the body of the Ss'Korra—Tesluc. Chalathar knelt beside it. He ran his hands through the air above the still form, not touching it, and after a moment turned to look at us. His eyes were inscrutable.

"Is this exactly how you found her?"

"Exactly," I said. "We didn't touch anything."

Chalathar nodded, looked back at the corpse. He drew a long-bladed silver knife from his belt and cut the ropes binding the dead. Rigor had set in, though, so the muscles held Tesluc's form in its awkward position. Chalathar sketched a rune in the air over the victim and the body abruptly relaxed. He closed her eyes, rose to his feet.

"I can't read anything from her," he said. "But she was a formidable warrior. Whoever took her must be even more so. They also had surprise on their side, and they still have it."

"We'd better make sure everyone stays in groups of at least three or four," I said. "Our killer won't stop now."

Chalathar nodded. "I already told the others to stay together in the main grotto. We'll keep to groups. It won't help us identify the fhaze but it should save lives."

"Isn't there anything physically different about a shapeshifter that you could use to identify it?" Bryce asked. "I mean, it looks just like whoever it mimics on the outside. But what about the inside?"

Chalathar frowned. "That's a good question. One I don't know the answer to. We can't cut everyone open to see what their internal organs are like. But if there were a way to...."

Without further elaboration on his thoughts, Chalathar turned away toward Tesluc and gathered her up in his arms. So deeply was the neck cut, he had to cradle the head to keep it from coming off. We followed him to the chamber where he'd stored Tuunshin's body, though this time I did not go in with him.

After Chalathar returned to us, however, I brought up another concern that troubled me. "What about your eventual plan to return me to a cloned version of my own body?"

"You needn't fear on that part," the Asadhie sorcerer said. "After the first cloning machine was stolen, I brought the second one here, to Hael. It's safe. I also managed to find a sample of blood from your original body."

"How?"I asked, frowning.

"From the cloths that were used to clean your wounds when you were first brought to Nald. They were drenched with your blood. Fortunately, they'd not yet been burned. The cloning procedure destroys the sample so it would be better to have your old body as a resource. But we can make do with what we have. I'll start the process running as soon as there's a moment. The more important question involves your original form. Where is it and have our invaders on Nald discovered it? With it and his own cloning machine, Vessoth could make an army of Ruenn Maclangs."

"Wouldn't the fhaze make sure they'd find it?" Bryce asked.

"I don't know. When we were gathered in the temple preparing to make the passage to Hael, I noticed one of my people missing. A Nokarran named Zene. I'd been giving your comment about 'circumstantial evidence' some thought, Ruenn. Zene's name kept surfacing. I assumed he was our traitor and was hiding from us to join his friends. It's clear now, though, that the fhaze came with us and murdered Tesluc."

"So," Bryce said. "What does that have to do with my question?"

"I believe the traitor *was* Zene, but that during the confusion of the attack he altered his form to match someone else among my people. Whether he killed *that* person or not is unknown. But, if he was rushed and didn't have time to tell our enemies where Ruenn's body was hidden before he joined us, it might still remain so." He frowned then, as if another thought had occurred to him. "Or…" he added.

"Or what?" I asked.

Chalathar gazed at us. "You saw those ruby panels I was activating just before we left Nald. There's a little surprise there for our invaders. If the fhaze hid Ruenn's body in the wrong place, it might well be vaporized by now. Our fears might be for naught."

"But we can't know for sure," I said.

"Agreed," Chalathar said. "Just one more reason we need to uncover this traitor, and quickly. There is much to demand of him. Or it."

"We need a plan," I said.

"Yes," Chalathar said. "We do."

However, he spoke no more on the subject until after we returned to the others, who gathered around in a babble of questions. The Asadhie held up his hands for silence.

"I know how to identify our traitorous shifter," he said. "I'll need a little while to prepare myself mentally. Then I'll run the test."

Gasps met the sorcerer's words. A few hopeful smiles followed, but suspicion still ran rampant. Everyone seemed to be watching everyone else, but no one wanted to get too far away from their fellows either. Keep your enemies close, a Taleran saying goes, but keep your weapons closer.

I glanced at Bryce, who was still frowning over Chalathar's statement. Clearly, he was wondering why the sorcerer hadn't told us about this test when we were alone with him. I wondered the same, and why he'd chosen to reveal it so publically now. Then the answer occurred to me. All hell was soon to break loose.

CHAPTER ELEVEN

WHO GOES THERE?

Chalathar seated himself with his back to one of the rock walls of our grotto. He closed his eyes and did not move. After a moment, a low hum swelled from his throat. The rest of us began to wait. Some sat. Some paced. Some jabbered to themselves or others. Everyone suspected everyone else, and the tension began to build. I ate passal and kept my hand near my sword.

Valyan and Bryce and Diken stayed close to me. Even they, who had been through so much, were not immune to the pressure. It was worse among the others. I'd never suspected that fear and paranoia had a smell and a taste. They did here, like some combination of sweat, and bile, and rancid butter.

Shai spoke with Rence for a while before coming over to join my group. The pulse in her neck beat fast and hard. She took up a strip of passal and bit off a chunk. She did not appear to taste it.

"Never seen Chalathar enter a trance like that," she said to me after a moment. Her voice was hoarse.

Bryce started to respond, thought better of it and shut his mouth. I merely shrugged.

"Any idea what this test of his is?" she asked. "Rence thinks he's bluffing."

I glanced toward Rence. He was talking with the only Vhichang among Chalathar's people. The Vhichang are avian, but non-winged and humanoid. They have feathers and a small beak. This one was a male warrior named Darmin. He carried a brass-bound, wooden-handled axe resembling a long tomahawk.

"I'm not sure Chalathar is the bluffing type," I finally said in response to Shai's question.

"My thoughts too. Maybe—"

"Semish. Semish!"

We all turned at the sound of a panicky voice. Lyra, the one-time slave, was bent over her friend Semish, the ex-warrior who'd become

Chalathar's gardener. Semish was seated against the cave wall across from Chalathar. I'd thought he was napping. But Lyra was shaking him desperately and he wasn't waking up.

Everyone who was sitting, rose. Shai rushed toward Lyra, whose hysteria was growing. But the woman leaped suddenly to her feet and backed away from both Semish and Shai. I could see her hands as she held them up before her. They were scarlet with blood.

Shai halted. Lyra screamed as she saw her own red hands. Rence slipped up behind her and suddenly grabbed her shoulders, but she tore free of his grip, spun, and raced away down the glass corridor we'd originally followed to this grotto.

People milled about, startled and unsure of what to do. Shai dropped to her knees beside Semish, lifted him up a bit by the shoulders so that we all saw the bloody wall behind him.

"He's been knifed," Shai said.

"Lyra's the shifter!" Rence cried. He grabbed Darmin by the shoulder, pulled the Vhichang after him. "We'll get her!" he shouted as he tore off down the corridor after the woman.

"Wait!" I shouted, but it was too late.

We heard Chalathar's voice then. I turned to see him on his feet. "Ruenn," he said. "Take Diken and Valyan. Go after them. Lyra can't be the shifter. I've got to see about Semish." He ran toward the knifed man.

I didn't understand how Chalathar could know that Lyra wasn't the shifter but at the moment there was no time to ask questions. Shouting for Diken and Valyan to follow, I tore after Rence, Darmin, and Lyra.

In a moment we were racing down the glass tunnel, with our way lit only by the phantom glow of the sea creatures outside. As with all the corridors here, this one curved. We could not see those we were pursuing. But after another few minutes we heard clashing weapons ahead.

Putting on a burst of speed, we came around a curve and out into a wider area. It was the same place where Chalathar's sphere gate had first deposited us on Hael. The sounds of battle had vanished but one victim of the fighting remained for us to find. Rence lay slumped on the floor, blood dribbling thickly from a stab wound in his right leg. He was conscious, but clearly in pain. His twin kahnna blades were sheathed at his sides.

"Wasn't Lyra," he said, groaning. "Darmin is the shapeshifter. He's after Lyra now. Gotta stop him." He tried to rise but slumped back to the floor with a fresh moan.

I bent quickly over Rence, then glanced up at Valyan and Diken. "Go after Darmin and Lyra," I said. "Be careful. I'll help Rence back to the others."

My friends stared hard at me, and only after I nodded did they turn and hurry on. I grasped Rence's right hand and pulled him to his feet. With his right arm over my shoulder, we started back toward the others. He limped and winced but was able to make progress. Already, the bleeding in his leg had slowed.

"How do you know Darmin is the shifter?" I asked him.

His mescal-brown eyes met mine. "Something weird. His form… flickered for a moment when we were fighting. It startled me. That's why he was able to cut me." He added, "You should have gone with your friends. They may need your help. I could have waited."

"No, I'm right where I need to be."

Rence gazed at me, frowning as if puzzled by my words. He went on after a moment. "I expected Chalathar to be with you."

"Of course," I said. "You hoped he would be."

Rence stopped walking. I released his arm and stepped back from him. His lips were curved into a moue of distaste beneath a cold and staring gaze. "You are acting most strangely," he said. "Speak what you mean."

"I'll speak a question," I said. "Is the real Rence dead or alive?"

He stiffened. His hands dropped to the hilts of his blades and he took another step away from me. I noticed that he did not limp and that the blood no longer ran from his wound. For a moment his face looked furious. Then he smiled.

"What gave me away?" he asked.

"Two things," I said. "One. The clashing blades we heard. Steel on steel. But Darmin's axe has a wooden handle bound in brass. The sound was wrong. I imagine you made the sounds we heard by clanging your own kahnnas together."

"And the second thing?"

"The wound in your leg. A stab wound. As with a sword. Not an axe."

The being who was not Rence smiled again. "Unfortunate for you that you figured it out. I'm afraid I'll have to remove that knowledge with these." He drew his blades, the twin kahnnas that Rence had been so adept with.

I did not reach for my own sword but lifted a hand. "Before we fight. I would ask again if the real Rence still lives. He was a friend of mine."

The fhaze shapeshifter shrugged. "I left him bound for the Bull-men to interrogate. They are not kind to prisoners but he may yet live. For a while."

"And the emptied body of Ruenn Maclang that you stole?"

"Ah," he said. "Understandable curiosity, Ruenn. But I'm afraid I just don't want to indulge it."

"Why not?" I asked. "If you're so sure that I'll soon be dead."

When it came this time, his predictable smile seemed more of a smirk. "You know," he said. "the two of us are not so different."

"I can think of quite a few differences."

"Superficials. You needed a new body. You took one. I do much the same. We just use different means. I mimic rather than possess. But all in all, we are much like our masters, the Asadhie."

"Chalathar is not my master," I said, allowing myself to grow angry.

"Of course he is. Inside, you know it."

Now I drew my sword and snarled. "I wonder what you are like... inside."

The being chuckled. "I'll show you," he said. "As a last gift before you die."

CHAPTER TWELVE

THE SHAPE OF THINGS TO COME

The fhaze lunged, the steel of his twin kahnnas flashing. He wanted to end our fight quickly. I wasn't prepared to die yet. I blocked with my rune-blade, stepped back and drew a dagger into my left hand, giving me two blades against his two. The dagger was useless for an attack but it could parry one. My rune-blade was heavier and slower than my enemy's kahnnas, but also much longer. I had to use that advantage of length to keep him from closing with me.

In the momentary pause that followed our first exchange, I spoke: "I don't understand your purpose in killing Tesluc and attacking Semish. I would have thought Chalathar to be your target."

"The sorcerer will die soon enough," the fhaze said. Again he lunged; again I parried and backed away.

"But that will strand us all in this place," I said. "Even if you kill the rest of us, you'll still be stuck here."

His smile became a gloat.

"Unless," I said, "*you* know a way to escape."

He attacked in a blaze, trying to finish me. I backpedaled, parrying and parrying again. My back struck the wall. I blocked one flashing kahnna with my dagger, the other with my sword. For an instant our weapons locked together, and as the fhaze broke away from that impasse I twisted my sword and cut him across the forearm.

He leaped back convulsively, and the smile he'd worn on his face like a mask dissipated into a frown of concentration. He'd not expected that I could touch him with a sword. This being must be incredibly old and experienced. No doubt he had killed hundreds—by stealth *and* face to face. How could someone like me match him, especially in a body that was unfamiliar?

Certainly my level of experience was less than his. But perhaps he'd overlooked something. Weapon masters often say that hand to hand combat is more a matter of mind than body. In truth, it is both. The mind gives the orders, considers the strategies, fights its own fear. But the body knows the dance, the nuances of the movements. And those movements are much the same in any battle. The body of Baadon might be new to me, and that required some adjustments. But it was created as a warrior's body and it recognized the dance.

"Perhaps you killed Tesluc to evoke fear," I said. "That would explain the head. People who are afraid make mistakes. Even Asadhie sorcerers. Even," I added, "fhaze shapeshifters."

"You are a fool if you think I'm afraid of *you*, Ruenn Maclang."

"Then I am indeed a fool."

The fhaze did not respond but began to stalk me, probing with his blades for an opening. I fought on the defensive, keeping him at bay. From the moment when I'd awakened in Chalathar's surrogate room, my old mind and my new body had been learning each other. Finally now, in battle, they began to function as one, with no miscalculations, no missteps. My enemy could not break through my defense.

The fhaze shook his head. "You seek to delay me," he snapped. "You hope your friends will return. Or someone else. It's time for an end."

"Make an end," I said. "If you can."

The being chuckled. I heard a ripping sound, saw that the cloth of his shirt had torn open at the right side, just at the lower level of the ribs. My eyes widened as a hand coated with a pale slime poked free of the cloth, its fingers writhing. A wrist pushed out from behind the shirt next, then a forearm, an elbow, an upper arm and shoulder. From the other side of his body, another arm extruded. Each of the new hands drew a dagger from his belt.

"Four blades," he said. "Against two. And I doubt you can grow more arms to equal my own."

I chuckled myself. "I've fought a being with four arms before. A Syber named Rathgar. I'm still here; he's all gone."

The fhaze laughed, loudly. His form flickered, blurred, disappeared.

CHAPTER THIRTEEN

HOW DO YOU KILL WHAT YOU CANNOT SEE?

Perhaps the fhaze had lived too long and fought too many battles. Perhaps he'd found his victories too easy for too many years. He expected his disappearance to give me pause. He expected me to wonder how I could kill the unseen. I did not wonder.

At the instant the shapeshifter turned invisible, I twisted the hilt of the rune-blade in my hand, brought it to shoulder height and threw it like a spear. I aimed it directly between four objects I *could* see, the glittering steel of the fhaze's weapons, and I hurled it with all the strength of my shoulder and back.

An awful thunking sound came, as of a boot stomping into mud. A howl rose, wavered, broke. The fhaze's kahnnas and daggers seem to fall out of the very air to clatter on the floor. A gagging sound followed, and the shapeshifter reappeared. It did not look like Rence now. Nor like anything in my experience. Imagine a grubworm grown to the size of a man. Imagine it pierced by a sword and spilling strings of silver rheum from its wounds.

The thing writhed on the floor. A dozen short, clawed legs grasped at the sword in an attempt to pull it free. The claws slid on the steel, scraping at it with an awful sound. Bile rose in my mouth; I spat it away.

The thing mewled. Currents of darker matter moved beneath its sickly, pale skin. Small protuberances rose along its cylindrical body and rippled through a series of color changes before subsiding back into its form. It was trying to create shapes. But something, perhaps its wound or the sword itself, interfered.

A voice called my new name. "Baadon!"

Startled, I turned my head. Chalathar stood there but was not gazing at me. His eyes focused on the fhaze. I wondered if the look upon his face was of distaste, or of regret.

"Step back from it," Chalathar ordered. I did so, though the thing seemed incapable at the moment of posing any threat.

Chalathar moved to stand beside me. "Who do you serve?" he demanded of the creature.

A strange voice came whispering, the sound of it like the crawling of spider legs on silk. "Death," it said.

"And so you offer yourself up to your master," Chalathar said.

Again the whispering voice came. "Yes." The thing lifted its carapaced head. I detected no eyes, but it *saw* us. And now it added to its answer, "Though not quite yet." Despite the monster's inhuman qualities, I could hear the gloating in its words.

I frowned at Chalathar. His eyes suddenly widened. "Run," he said.

But in the instant that he spoke, a wave of lily-white light erupted from the fhaze, swirled into a sphere. *A gate!* Somehow the thing was opening a gate. My whole body tingled with the power of it.

Time turned glacial. I strained to turn my head. Could not. Chalathar's mouth was wide but no sound came from it. Out of the corner of my eye, I could see the fhaze and the glass floor upon which it lay. I could see the wall beyond it and the strange denizens of the ghost sea without. Everything other than the fhaze and Chalathar began to fade, began to erode into darkness.

The sphere gate was open; it was dragging us through. But slowly, ever so slowly, as Chalathar fought it with everything he had. I wanted to fight as well but did not know how. I could not even move my eyes in their sockets. The strain grew unendurable.

Shadows began to surround us, filled with firefly lights. We were fully inside the gate now. The grotto and the ghost sea within Hael were gone. But against the shadows, Chalathar began to move. His mouth opened and closed on words I could not hear. One of his hands clawed at the air, scoring lines of lavender light into it. The other reached and took my wrist.

The shadows flamed into brightness. The stillness shattered. Chalathar's hold on my arm tightened. And we were falling, twisting and turning as we did so. I hit hard on one hip. Chalathar's grip broke and I was thrown away from him. Something hard as iron struck me across the back and breath fled me. My skull rang; my skin felt as if I'd been dragged across gravel. I skirted close to blacking out but managed to hold on. The pain helped.

Long moments passed while I struggled to breathe. Finally I was able to lift my head and look around. I'd hit a tree standing at the edge of a copse of trees. These were smooth-trunked and short, no more than fifteen feet tall, with thick foliage at the top. They looked almost like stalks of broccoli, one of many earth plants brought to Talera in the past. A prairie of sere grass stretched away from the woods. In the distance drifted towering dark clouds with a faint greenish shimmer below that might be a reflection of water, either a large lake or a sea.

My main concern was for Chalathar and I called his name while using the tree trunk to pull myself to my feet. The Asadhie sorcerer was laying very still when I saw him, but did not look quite dead. I called for him again as I pushed away from the tree and staggered in his direction. He'd fallen against a thick clump of tree roots that extruded aboveground. A knot swelled over one of his eyes. At least he breathed.

I grasped the sorcerer's shoulders and shook him. His head lolled. I shook him again and this time he groaned. His eyes opened, blurry and confused.

"Do you know me?" I demanded.

He licked at his dried lips, started to nod and thought better of it. "Ruenn," he finally croaked.

I nodded with relief. That probably meant his skull wasn't cracked.

He struggled to sit up and I helped him with an arm under his shoulders. He looked dazedly around, but his thoughts seemed to be clearing.

"Any idea where we might be?" he asked.

"No," I said. "Woods and prairie nearby. Maybe a sea in the distance."

"We're near the equator," he said. "The sun is directly overhead."

"A long way from home," I replied, thinking of Nyshphal and of Rannon, my blue-eyed queen.

Chalathar nodded, started to get up and slumped back with a groan against the rock.

"Better wait a bit," I said.

"Shouldn't wait. Not long. We may have broken free of the sphere gate but whoever the fhaze serves will soon be seeking us."

"How did the *fhaze* open a sphere gate?"

"It didn't. It was implanted with a milkstone. The stone triggered automatically. Probably when the creature came close to death."

"To take it home to its master," I said.

"Yes."

A thought occurred. "We could have found out who it served. And where."

"No," Chalathar said. He tried to rise again, succeeded this time. He stood swaying as he explained. "The gate would have been controlled by the sorcerer at the other end. He could hold us within it until he gathered all the forces he needed to kill or capture us. We had no choice but to break out. As it is, the fhaze's master will be able to track back to the point where we escaped. We must not be here when that happens."

He lifted his hands, began to sketch a spell into the air. I recognized his actions. He was opening a sphere gate. Only, nothing happened. He tried again, and apparently tried several other things. He mouthed words; his hands moved. Nothing other than those movements happened. Finally, Chalathar stood frowning.

"What's wrong?" I asked.

"An unexpected problem. My milkstones. The toir'in-or. They're not…working. I've never had to escape a gate that way. Maybe breaking free drained the stones somehow. Seems they're nothing more than actual rocks now. I've never known such a thing to happen, but I don't know what else could explain it."

I frowned myself. "Can you…live without a working milkstone?"

He nodded. "There's no immediate danger. Eventually, though, things will start to deteriorate. Once that happens, it can go fast."

"Then we better find a more conventional way than sorcery and sphere gates of getting out of this place," I said. "Especially considering the nature of the forces that must already be looking for us."

"Agreed," he said. Abruptly, and unaccountably, he grinned. "You thought I was no more than a human named Chalathar when you first came to know me, Ruenn. Now it seems that is true."

The Asadhie actually seemed to be enjoying the thought of being a mere human. I could not help but grin back at him, but had a few words to add as well. "Well, let's hope the hell that sword you always carry is more than a decoration. We're likely to need it."

"Assuredly," he said. "But let's go before the fhaze's owner comes looking for us."

"It's not the looking that worries me," I said. "It's the finding."

CHAPTER FOURTEEN

A SEA OF SKY

Under the hot green sun of spring, we ran. We set a pace we could maintain for hours without exhausting ourselves. For if pursuit came— and we were sure it would—we'd need to retain enough strength to fight.

We ran toward what I'd taken to be the coast of a large lake or sea. It seemed the most likely place to find civilization, where we could learn both our location and how to escape from it. I'd judged the distance to be no more than two verlangs, about three miles in Earth reckoning. But as we approached our goal I began to doubt that we were approaching water.

A steady breeze blew in our faces, and if there were a sea ahead of us we should have been able to smell the salt air and hear the boom of surf. If it were a fresh water lake we should see verdant plants and smell the living creatures that make such places their home. We detected neither of those things.

Our pace slowed, and slowed some more. "What the hell!" I exclaimed. "It's green. As the sea should be under the spring sun. But that can't be water." Then we both realized what it was and came to a complete stop. "By all the gods," I muttered.

Chalathar seemed as stunned as I, but recovered more swiftly. He strode closer to the green shimmering, stopped on the very edge to study it.

"A sea of sky," I said.

Chalathar nodded.

"Maybe the edge of some vast cliff?" I asked, though not quite believing such a thing myself.

Chalathar looked cautiously over the side, shook his head. "Don't think so."

Moving forward to stand beside him, I looked over the edge as well. The earth felt spongy and my legs wanted to quiver. We stood on a jut of land, with the ground below us slanting gradually inward and under. It was like standing on the chin of some giant statue. I could see thirty or forty feet of mixed soil and an intricately knotted web of roots—with nothing else for many thousands of feet below that to where a mass of dark clouds clotted the air.

I stepped back from the edge. Chalathar joined me. "Could it be a great mesa?" I asked, grasping at straws. "Tall enough, perhaps, to stretch above the clouds?"

"No," Chalathar said. "I should have recognized immediately where we were." He looked up and pointed.

My gaze followed the Asadhie's outstretched finger. Half a verlang above us hovered another mass of dark clouds. I'd noted it when we first arrived here and thought nothing more about it. Now we were close enough to pick up details. Atop the clouds, like a wedding cake rising above its plate, grew a vast tangle of greenery. Atop that we could make out individual trees, and the ruins of a white keep. Chalathar pointed out two more clouds in the distance that were more than clouds, and I saw smudges in the sky beyond those that might mark others.

"The Floating Isles," Chalathar said.

"But I thought…."

"Thought what?"

"Some of the scholars in Nyshphal wrote about these isles. But I think they must never have seen them. They certainly didn't describe *this* reality. I envisioned them to be no more than masses of plants. Not soil. And trees. And," I pointed to the ruined keep on the island above us, "people."

"Hard to imagine if you haven't seen them," Chalathar agreed. "I did once. Long ago. But only…."

He paused and turned away to look back across our own island. Though curious, I did not ask him about something that was clearly private.

"How *does* such a place exist?" I asked instead.

"The floating plants you read of," he said. "They are called Vyn'ishad-or. They begin life drifting on the sea. Their roots are swollen like bladders and filled with air. This keeps them afloat. As they mature, the air in the bladders becomes displaced by a gas called 'ishad,' which the plants themselves manufacture. Ishad is lighter than air.

"Eventually the plant sheds the surface and takes to the sky. They gather in great masses to share nutrients. Together they generate an energy field that draws in dust and any other small particles floating on the winds. The field anchors the islands together. Thus they grow. Year after year. Until there is enough soil to support other plant life, even trees. And people."

"But such a process would take eons," I protested.

"Not so long. The air is more full of detritus than you believe. Much can be gathered in a mere thousand years. And as the various plants die and decay they add more soil. Too, some of the islands originally had help in forming."

"You mean Asadhie help?"

"Yes."

I said something I'd been thinking for a long time. "But not *your* help. Or Vohanna's. Or Vessoth's. Or that of Kamrack, Heshval, Ivrail, or others of your kind."

"What do you mean?" Chalathar demanded.

"I mean that those who call themselves the Asadhie now are not the 'First Gods' who made this world and built its wonders."

I expected Chalathar to be angered by my words. He was a proud being. And I did not doubt that he had great power. But he showed no anger. At first his face seemed empty of all emotion. Then he turned his head, as if he heard some voice on the ether. Finally, he met my gaze again and spoke.

"This is not the time to discuss such matters."

It was my turn to demand. "When *will* be the time?"

He shrugged. "First we must live."

I heard then what Chalathar must have already heard. The air throbbed, not quite with a whine, nor a scream. I glanced back toward the distant copse of trees where we'd first fallen when we escaped the fhaze's sphere gate. An opalescent light played there, an evil light. I recognized it. Another gate was opening. A large one. It remained open longer than normal, and when it closed it left behind...howling.

CHAPTER FIFTEEN

LETTING GO

"That howling," I said tensely. "I've heard it before."

Chalathar frowned. "Where?"

"In the old dungeons beneath Jystral Castle. During Vohanna's siege of Nyshphal (See *Witch of Talera*). Something like hounds, but much larger. Brindle furred, with massive jaws and shoulders. They had six limbs, one pair being human arms and hands. 'Kurshan,' I believe they are called. Not this specific type, but the name for all such Asadhie-manufactured monsters."

"Created hybrids. Yes," Chalathar said. "And vicious. Sounds like they are many. And no doubt they are accompanied by worse."

"The beings with them in the dungeons were big and ugly. Faces like boars, with tusks thrust up over their lower lips. We call such things trolls on Earth."

"Chalathar nodded. "The Drowg," he said. "And their man-hounds."

"Which Asadhie do they serve?"

"Not just Asadhie. Anyone who pays them. They are mercenaries. I imagine they are working at the behest of an Asadhie now, though."

"I thought that Vohanna brought the Minotaurs and the…Drowg to Talera from somewhere else. I'd never read about them in the histories. But apparently they are a lot more common here than I'd thought."

"There is still much about Talera that is unknown to the scribes of Nyshphal who wrote those histories you were reading. But, in a way, they spoke truth. Originally, the Minotaurs and the Drowg, and others like them, were not found on Talera's surface at all. There is a world *inside* this world. Several of them, in fact. Each has its own inhabitants, its own kind of life. Or it had. For a long time now, creatures like Vohanna and Urthrik have been raiding those strange climes for slaves, or recruiting armies from them."

"Well," I said, somewhat nervously, "wherever they're from, if the Drowg's man-hounds can follow a scent like true dogs they'll soon find us here."

"They can follow it but it'll take them a while to work it out. However, these islands are not very large."

"Then we'll have to fight or hide. And soon."

"Whoever sent the Drowg will have sent many. I imagine there are Thye Vessoth or some other sorcerers among them, too. Without my own sorcery, a fight would likely end in defeat. Not only would *we* die, but those we left behind inside the Hael planetoid would soon run out of supplies and starve. I'm the only one who knows how to open a gate into that place."

I thought of my brother Bryce. And of Diken and Valyan. And of Shai. Starvation is not a pleasant death. "That narrows our options to hiding," I replied.

"There are few enough places for such on these isles. The man-hounds can climb trees and dig out burrows."

I looked behind me, toward the edge of the island. "Perhaps there is one place we can hide," I said. "Where we can disappear."

For a moment, Chalathar followed the direction of my gaze. Then he gave me a long stare. Hesitantly, he moved back toward the edge and I went with him. Together, we looked over the side. The thick webbing of roots growing under the island would provide handholds and footholds aplenty. But unless we could find some ledge on the way down, or some way to anchor ourselves, we'd have only the strength of our arms and legs between us and a death-fall. No man's strength lasts forever.

Of more immediate importance was the fear. My legs trembled even while I stood on solid ground. How much more would they shake with me suspended over an abyss? The sweat started on my brow at the thought.

"I do not relish such an adventure," Chalathar said at last, showing that he experienced his own brand of fear.

Somehow that made me feel better. But in the next instant the howling of the man-hounds increased in intensity and I knew our enemies must have found our trail and be coursing along it. I shook my head and sat down.

First I removed my boots, which would only be a hindrance in our endeavor. Stripping them of their lacings, I stuck those in my pocket. The boots went over the side so they wouldn't be found by our pursuers. How far would they have to fall before striking the surface of Talera? Making sure all my weapons were firmly fastened, I finally lay down on my stomach at the very edge of the island.

"Relish or not," I said to Chalathar. "We seem to have little choice. Starting may well be the toughest part. Grip my feet until I secure a solid hold below. Once I'm anchored, I'll give you a hand."

The Asadhie nodded, took off his own boots, stripped their lacings, knelt beside me. His hands grasped my ankles firmly and I shifted forward a bit, leaned over the edge and reached down as far as I could. Small roots grew within my grasp but would never bear my weight. A little further down, a long, wide root seemed promising. It was as thick as the body of a python and stretched out almost like a hammock. Its rough bark should provide a firm grip.

"Hold tight!" I called up to Chalathar, then slid forward until fully half my body hung off the edge of the island with nothing but sky beneath. I could just reach the big root. It's bark felt slicker than expected, perhaps because of the sweat on my hands. Getting a good grip was not assured. I dried my hands on my shirt, yelled up to Chalathar:

"I need a little more but *don't* let go!"

"All right!" Chalathar called back. His grip tightened further around my ankles.

I squirmed forward an inch, and another. My heart pounded; the breath rasped in my throat. My back burned with the strain of reaching toward the root. Baadon was a few inches taller than Ruenn Maclang had been. That was good. I stretched for everything extra that I could, got my wrist over the root. It still wasn't enough.

A terrifying thought occurred then; cold sweat drenched me. Already I belonged too much to the sky. Its ragged fingers tugged at me, urging me toward destruction. Only Chalathar's grip kept me from plummeting to my death. That grip also kept me from reaching a goal that might save us.

Through lips that trembled, I called again to Chalathar. "When I say to, let go!"

"You just told me *not* to let go," he shouted back.

"Now I'm telling you different."

"I dare not."

"You must!"

I heard the sorcerer curse, then heard, "All right. All right."

"Get ready…. Now!" I shouted.

Chalathar released my ankles and at the same instant I made a lunge forward. My legs swung free but my right arm went over the root. I hooked it with an elbow while my left hand shot up to grasp my right wrist. My lower body plunged downward toward the invisible surface of Talera, snapping me taut against my hold.

My arm slid along the root; the green sky wheeled beneath me. For a sickening instant I felt sure I was going to fall. Fear locked my grip tight and I hung there for a long moment while powdered bark sifted down into my face. Finally, I brought my leg up, hooked it solidly over the root. A long breath shuddered my body.

"Ruenn! Ruenn!

"I'm all right! I need…just…a second, a shri."

"Take it," Chalathar replied. "But know the howling is getting closer."

I allowed myself only a few deep breaths before setting to work. Drawing the two tough rawhide boot-laces from my pocket, I first tied them together, then tied one end around the big root. Making a loop at the other end, I tossed this up to Chalathar, who was already lying on his belly near the island's edge. He snugged the thong tight over his arm before reaching down as far as he could toward me.

"Not sure I wouldn't rather die fighting," he said.

I braced myself solidly and reached my hand up to meet Chalathar's. We grasped wrists.

"Let's try not to die either way," I said.

Chalathar nodded and slid forward a little more. As gently as I could, I pulled him free of the Isle's edge and swung him down toward me. The supporting thong helped. Only for an instant did I have to bear his whole weight as he swung past me and clutched tightly to our big anchor root with legs and arms both.

I heard him sigh with relief and called down to him. "Are you happy with that attempt or do you want to climb back up on the island and try again?"

"I believe I'm satisfied," he replied dryly.

The howling of the man-hounds carried clearly to my ears now. We needed to move. If the hounds or their masters happened to glance over the side of the island they'd see us, and if any among them had bows we'd be dead. I turned toward Chalathar to see him already working his way like a monkey farther down the slope of the isle.

Now that we'd succeeded in climbing down under the island I could get a better idea about the overall structure of this bizarre geographical anomaly. It reminded me a bit of a toadstool. The surface was wide and relatively flattened. Then it tapered to a thick stalk that extended a long way beneath us. From the surface, you couldn't even see most of the underside. It consisted of a web of roots and captured soil, thick and impenetrable near the top but thinning out as you made your way down.

About halfway down the stalk, the toadstool comparison began to fall apart. Roots still extended into this area from above, but here, bushes and trees had actually taken root as well. Only, they grew upside down, like a reversed jungle. I wondered for a moment how that could be before realizing that—on a floating island—sunlight would fall on both the surface and the bottom, depending on the time of day. Plants grow toward the sun, wherever it may be in relationship to them.

After we entered the upside down jungle, the travelling became easier and my fears of having to rely purely on the strength of our muscles dissipated. As with any jungle, this one was rich with the smell of both growth and decay—with flowers and fungi and sweet, dripping sap. Chalathar and I clambered through a rich world of ferns and mosses, with arm-thick vines, tree limbs, and some taproots from above to give us plenty of support. We were also hidden from the view of anyone on the surface of the island.

I began to breathe a little easier—until rustling noises started coming from the greenery all around us. Something—or some things—paced us through this shaded underworld. Every second seemed to bring them closer.

CHAPTER SIXTEEN

SCARLET ON THE GREEN

I called Chalathar's attention to the noises in the jungle around us. His only suggestion was to keep moving. I had no idea what would happen when we reached the very bottom of the island and could go no farther. Soon, that moment was upon us.

The last half-dozen trees were big ones, with thick, twisted limbs that grew in every direction, including the perpendicular. On one such limb we found purchase for our feet. Gazing out beyond the forest was like looking through the bars of a great cage, with the cage resting on a dark cloud that churned slowly upon itself. It did not seem like any normal storm front, though flashes of lightning sometimes ripped through it. I thought the island must be creating the cloud in some way, but there was no time to study the phenomenon.

The whole jungle crackled with the sound of movement now, and I turned with Chalathar to make our stand. Many of the leafy limbs around us were nearly as big as the trunks of lesser trees. We put our backs against the thickest bulwarks we could find.

Drawing a dagger, I cut one end of a vine that stretched far into the forest above. I passed this to Chalathar, nodding toward the sky below and saying:"Tie it around your waist. In case we get knocked off our perches and out there."

He nodded, did as he'd been bid. I cut another vine to tie myself off and drew a second dagger into my other hand. Chalathar did as well. The quarters here were too close to ply a sword. The shorter blades would have to serve.

I began to see movement, the quaking of leaves and vines, but could not make out the shapes of our pursuers through the dark denseness of the wood. I glanced at Chalathar and him at me.

"If we survive, I have many questions to ask you," I said.

"If we survive, I will answer," he replied. Then he grinned. "Some of them."

I grinned back, tightened my grip on the daggers. The forest came alive, filled with movement and noise. My heart thundered but I was ready for a fight. Finally, we saw what manner of beast hunted us.

Chalathar laughed. A moment later, I joined him.

A horde of small creatures poured from the deeper jungle to take up watch a few feet in front of us. Dozens of them clung to every branch and vine, and to each other. Perhaps there were a hundred of the little things. Perhaps more. They were about the size of puppies, with big, liquid eyes and long inquisitive snouts that appeared to be prehensile. A motley assortment of colors ran through their lush fur. Even their scent was pleasant, like cinnamon and honeysuckle. They reminded me of lemurs on Earth, though the nose was certainly different.

"We seem to have been fleeing from some children's toys," I said.

Chalathar nodded, but followed that with a frown. For the first time we heard the creatures voices, a chorus of small chirrups that sounded almost like those of baby birds. One of the beings, somewhat larger than the others, pushed itself closer to us along a vine. It chirruped loudly and its companions fell silent. It stood up on its hind legs, its nose quivering, its front paws slowly raking the air with climbing motions. It vented a long sequence of chattering notes, followed with a chirrup that sounded almost like a question.

I glanced at Chalathar.

"I think it's trying to communicate," the Asadhie said. "I have no idea what."

I looked back at the small beings gathered before us. Were they truly sentient, I wondered? There were many intelligent races on Talera, though none I'd ever heard of so small as these. Even the Toibel were quite a bit bigger, about the size of large foxes. And as far as I could tell the Toibel were only marginally sentient, although they were sweet and loving creatures.

Before my thoughts could explore the issue any further, the "leader" of the lemur-like beings chattered at us again. It chattered louder this time, and a faint emotional shock flashed through my mind. Next, a chilling shadow of fear raced across my shoulders.

"Almost seems like it's warning us," I murmured.

"But of what?" Chalathar asked.

When neither Chalathar nor I responded as the leader of the small creatures seemed to wish, it turned to look at the others of its clan. In the next instant the horde of them scattered swiftly away through the trees. I heard something else then, a sound like a rushing wind.

"Get ready for *What*!" I shouted, and heard Chalathar's words echoing mine.

Only the leader of the creatures remained, and now it gave a loud shriek and leaped with a terrific bound into the massed jungle growth above us. In the next instant, a tapered green head the size of an ale keg battered through a wall of leaves and vines and thrust its way into the more open area in front of us.

Snake! A huge one.

I should have known. Vessoth was the Snake God. We'd fought his monstrous serpents on Nimeru. This was not the same kind but no doubt it served the same evil master. And what better place than a jungle for it to hunt.

Chalathar cried out in rage. This time I echoed *him*. We lunged forward together, stabbing, stabbing with our daggers. I tried for the emerald blaze of the eyes but could not reach them. Our blades cut flesh, though, and the thing reared back and away, spraying scarlet blood across the jungle.

The respite was momentary. The thing struck at us again and there was very little chance of dodging. Its mouth opened; a wave of foul breath struck me; a purple tongue lashed my face. I slashed at the tongue, cut a wedge in it that flapped.

The thing's head wove back and forth. It hammered into me, knocking me sideways. I fell to my knees on my precarious perch. The beast struck at Chalathar. The Asadhie dropped his daggers, grabbed desperately at the snake's upper and lower jaws to keep them away. He caught them, held them, the muscles in his arms bulging like snakes themselves. It couldn't last. The thing had no fangs, only coarse ridges of raw bone in its mouth. But it was a constrictor, immensely powerful. No man could hold it long.

I thrust my daggers into my belt, drew my rune-sword as I lunged to my feet. A snarl sizzled between my lips as I threw myself forward. There was no room to swing the blade. I grasped the hilt with both hands, dropped again to my knees beneath the thing's upper body. With all my strength, I slammed the three foot blade straight up from below, slammed it up and through both jaws of the snake. It erupted out through the top of the thing's skull in a shower of flesh and blood.

The monster had moved powerfully before. Now it raged. It thrashed its head back and forth, tearing the rune-sword free of my grip. Chalathar tried to maintain his hold on the thing's jaws but was hurled aside like a doll for his troubles. I saw him slam into a massive branch, slide down it into a huddle on one of the cross-limbs.

I drew a dagger again, tried to slash the thing's throat. It twisted aside. A coil of its body struck me but it seemed to have lost any urge to attack. I fell backward as the thing turned to escape, the sword still lodged like a giant nail through its mouth, pinning its jaws closed. As the fleeing beast cut a fresh and bloody hole in the jungle, I grabbed for something to break my fall. I missed, and in the next instant plunged downward into open sky.

CHAPTER SEVENTEEN

ARRIVAL OF THE RAPTORS

I fell free of the island, with nothing below but cloud and distance, and somewhere the hard surface of Talera. There was only one chance. I dropped the dagger, grabbed for the vine I'd tied off around my waist for just such an emergency. My fingers brushed it, missed a hold. In the next instant I hit the end of that tether. It snatched me up brutally, nearly jarring me free of air. But it stopped my fall.

I hung upside down, struggling to breathe. Tendrils of the island's base-cloud swirled around but weren't thick enough to keep me from seeing the deadly drop below. My fingers grasped for the vine lariat that cinched my waist like a vice. Finally, I was able to clutch on to it. Pulling myself upright, I looked up at the jungle half a dozen feet over my head. A powerful sense of relief swept me. The thrashings of the great snake might well have torn the vine loose from its moorings. Thankfully, that didn't seem to be the case.

Relief fled and terror rushed in. A snapping sound erupted from within the dark of the island, followed by a whole series of them. For just an instant, I saw the vine that held my life whipping back and forth as it came loose from its anchors. I plunged downward, crying out.

Three feet, I fell. Five feet. Six. Thoughts of dying filled me. Abruptly my fall was arrested again—a hard, agonizing stop. It felt like the vine had cut me in two. I hung there shuddering, gasping. Eventually I was able to look up. Eddies of cloud alternately obscured and revealed the jungle above me. But I was able to see what had saved me.

The vine had completely broken its moorings. But Chalathar, with what must have been a desperate lunge, had caught my lifeline and snugged it tight around a thick branch. Gradually, he rose to his feet and put fists to the vine. By main strength, he began to haul me upward. I felt as helpless as a full water bucket at the end of a well-rope, but was very glad to be alive.

A high pitched sound punctured the sky behind me, like the cry of a hunting eagle—if such an eagle had grown to monstrous proportions. I tried to turn my head but could not control my movements there on the end of my tether. The sound was forgotten a moment later as Chalathar pulled me within reach of the lowest of the forest branches. I reached out, seized them tight. Rough though they were, they felt wonderful.

Now I was able to give my benefactor some aid, and before long stood once again firmly within the sky island's jungle. Chalathar stood beside me, his feet braced wide on massive limbs. His breathing came harsh and a sheen of sweat coated him from his efforts.

"Thanks," I said.

He shook his head. "If you hadn't stabbed that snake from beneath... I'd be halfway down its gullet."

I nodded. "Thanks to us both, I guess. Hate to lose that rune-sword, though."

He grinned. "Guess I owe you a good blade."

"I think," I started to say, then heard again that eagle-like cry.

It was closer, and there was more than one. We both looked for the source, and saw it. A flock of forty or so birds winged their way toward us. These were no ordinary birds. They were huge, as big and sleek as prehistoric tigers, with wings to match. I knew them as kryll. The kryll is a raptor. It hunts live prey, hooking it with spurred claws and tearing it apart with its scythe-like beak. Most are green-eyed and sulfur-yellow in color. They will kill and eat a man.

These kryll were not hunting us, though. They were not wild. On their backs sat riders. I could not yet see those beings clearly but the wink of green sunlight on armor and weapons told me they were warriors. Their direction of flight, which aimed straight toward us, told me that they knew we were here.

"I'm starting to miss my sword even more," I said to Chalathar.

The Asadhie shook his head. "I don't think we'll need blades for these visitors."

"Such has not been our luck of late," I cautioned.

"Look at our little friend who has returned," Chalathar said, nodding toward an upside down oak tree growing to my left. Sitting on a limb of that tree was the small, lemur-like creature that had tried to warn us of the snake. It was chattering again, but not to us this time. It peered out toward the approaching flock of kryll, and the sounds it made definitely seemed happy.

"It seems to like whoever is riding those birds," he continued, "and I'm inclined to trust its judgment."

"Doesn't seem we have much choice," I agreed. "If we climb deeper into this jungle to hide, we run the risk of stumbling on another of those snakes. And with fewer weapons this time. Besides, I'm getting a little tired of running."

Chalathar nodded, and so we stood and watched as the kryll and their riders approached. Soon, I recognized those riders, even though I'd only read about them in books and seen them in illustrations. They were Indigo Llurns.

Llurns are human. Or nearly so. My friend Valyan was a Llurn, of the type commonly called "Green," or sometimes "Emerald." But there are other types, the Black or Ebon, the Gold, and the Indigo. All of them, at some distant past age, had been biologically modified by the Asadhie. No one knows the reason. Or perhaps there was no reason, just the mere urge of sorcerers to tamper with nature.

For the most part, the differences between Human and Llurn are cosmetic. The Llurns differ from standard Humans in the colors of their skins, and hair, and eyes. The Ebon Llurns, for example, have jet black skin that is far more uniform than the myriad shades of dark brown seen on Earth. And their eyes and hair are like burnished silver. There must be some internal differences between Humans and Llurns, though. While children are sometimes born of unions between the two, and between the primary types of Llurns, these offspring themselves are always sterile.

While I considered these thoughts, the flight of kryll winged past us and one of the riders performed quite the daring feat. He kicked his boots free from the saddle bird's stirrups, stood upon the bird's back, and leaped from there into the jungle above us. I watched in amazement as he shimmied down a tree and came to stand before us. He was young, just entering manhood, and before acknowledging us he turned toward our lemur-like observer and bowed deeply.

That creature chattered swiftly and the youth answered back in the same tongue. For a moment or two they conversed like that, and then the small creature emitted a last chittering burst of sound and raced away through the jungle foliage.

The young Indigo Llurn turned toward Chalathar and me. A sheathed rapier hung at his back, but his hands were empty. He offered us a quick bow and straightened just as quickly, grinning broadly, as if immensely pleased with himself.

"The Evrisanie will watch for us, warn us if one of the great ophid-ians, or some equally loathsome beast approaches. Such monsters are thick in the jungles beneath the Isles. Apparently the small ones tried to warn you, but you did not understand."

"They tried indeed," Chalathar said. "We understood too late."

The youth nodded. "Evrisanie are sendahts. Some of my people pos-sess enough of that mental skill to pick up the gist of their messages. I am one such. It is how we were able to locate you here at the bottom of the island. But," he shrugged, "if you lack the ability, their language seems no more than noise."

As the young man spoke, I had a moment to study him. Indigo Llurns are sometimes referred to as "The Beautiful People." I began to see why. The lad was tall and lean, though well muscled. He wore leather armor of black and gold, but his arms and head were bare. His skin gleamed a dark purple, though lighter on the palms of his hands and around his lips. His irises were wine-red. His long hair was a very light, silvery-purple, and braided at the back with silver wire.

"Welcome to the Sky Islands," the youth said. "I am Jubyl Versath Miesh Vokule."

"I'm Chalathar. And this is my friend, Baadon."

Jubyl bowed again, somewhat more deeply. "Chalathar!" he said. "We've heard of you."

Chalathar looked surprised. "You have?"

"Yes. Your fight against the evil of the First Gods is known to us. We support it. Much welcome. And to your companion."

"If you know of my struggle, know as well that followers of the Snake God, Vessoth, have invaded the very island upon which we stand."

"Yes, in pursuit of the two of you apparently. A guard at one of our watchtowers observed the events. He signaled my warriors and me." Jubyl waved a casual hand toward the troop of kryll riders who circled in the green sky a few hundred yards away. "We arrived to deal violently with the issue. I'm sorry we were not here sooner. We had to come from quite some distance."

"Understandable," Chalathar said. "Are our mutual enemies still on the island?"

"They are encamped on the surface and sending out search parties for you. They do not appear to be aware that you inventively climbed beneath them. We intend to," he smiled, "uproot them from their comforts. Since the Evrisanie approve of you, and we are aware of who you are, perhaps you would care to join us?"

Chalathar smiled, and I joined him.

"We would," I said. "I'll just need to borrow a sword. Or something a bit more substantial than this." I patted the last remaining dagger at my belt.

He laughed. "I believe we can accommodate you."

"I should also warn you that they are likely to have Thye Vessoth sorcerers with them," Chalathar said.

Jubyl chuckled. "Not sorcerers. Just priests now. And probably not many. The Thye Vessoth already know that their magic will not work here and they cannot escape through a gate if they are challenged. If any are among our foes, they'll have to fight with swords for a change."

"Their magic won't work here?" Chalathar exclaimed. He looked astonished and I'm sure my own expression echoed his.

Jubyl shook his head. "No toir'in-or sorcery will work in proximity to the Evrisanie. Their mind power. Their talent for sendahtia. It seems to block the function of the milkstones whenever a sorcerer tries to project power outside of himself. Somewhat like a…wet blanket smothers flames." He looked at Chalathar. "But are you not yourself a sorcerer? Surely you have noticed the effect as well?"

Chalathar nodded. "Yes. I have. I just did not know the reason." He seemed relieved to have an explanation for why his own toir'in-or milkstones had malfunctioned.

"Unless you have someone elsewhere who can open a sphere gate for you at a distance," Jubyl said, "there are only two ways off one of the Floating Islands. You fly. Or you fall!"

CHAPTER EIGHTEEN

A WAR OF FEATHERS, FUR, AND STEEL

From the back of a predatory kryll in flight, I gazed down at the encampment of our enemies. Only one of the beings in that camp was a Thye Vessoth sorcerer, and according to Jubyl he would be without any power at the moment. The rest, more than seventy warriors, were a motley assortment of Human, Ss'Korra, and Klar, along with a dozen of the Drowg, those troll-like monsters who controlled the man-hounds. As for the hounds themselves, at least twenty of the vicious brutes howled up at us as we passed over.

The nearly eighty killers and twenty hounds in that encampment had been sent after two men—Chalathar and me. Quite an honor to be considered such a threat. It was unclear if it was Kamrack the Bull, or Vessoth, or some other who had sent this enemy against us. I had my suspicions but they did not matter at the moment. I cared only that we were about to go into battle; my blood pulsed hot.

The kryll are large raptors, capable of carrying double. On the bird in front of mine, Chalathar rode behind Jubyl the Indigo Llurn. I rode behind one of Jubyl's warriors, and my hand clutched a twelve-foot lance with a head of gleaming steel. There'd been no spare swords among Jubyl's followers, but each had a dozen spears sheathed below their saddles. Such weapons are as lethal as any sword, and I had trained in their use.

We came down to land some one hundred tahng beyond the enemy encampment. That was just over a hundred yards and gave us time and space to dismount and form a line of skirmishers. Extra weapons were taken from the saddles of the kryll. I borrowed a second lance before the birds were shooed into the air. They began to circle above us, venting their harsh calls of their hunting natures.

I stood beside the Llurn who'd given me a ride. She was female, as were nearly a third of Jubyl's warriors. Her name was Lann something, something, something. I'd caught only the first name. Lann was lean and tall, as are most women of her race. She almost reversed the coloration that Jubyl exhibited, with skin of a light purple and hair almost as dark as indigo. Like with many of her compatriots, a sword hung over her shoulder, a rapier in design, and she wore a small buckler belted to the leather armor covering her left arm. But she had also taken a bow from her saddle, strung it, and seated an arrow.

Jubyl strode a few steps out from the rest of us, called in a loud voice to our foes: "Surrender yourselves and only the Thye Vessoth will be executed."

I heard the Thye Vessoth priest cursing at the young Llurn's threat, and grinned to myself. I was quickly becoming fond of the youth's enthusiasm. But the answer to Jubyl's words came from another being, the leader of the enemy's warriors, who were far more to be feared at present than any sorcerer. This being, too, stepped out from the others around him. He was broad as a barrel, muscled like a god. *A Minotaur*! This one had not removed his horns, as had most of those I'd seen before. They were black and gleaming and curved down beside his bullish face. Their tips winked like dark ice.

"Give us the two criminals among you," the Bull-man called back to Jubyl, "and we'll thank you for bringing them to us by allowing the Indigo Llurns to go in peace."

Jubyl laughed. "I do not think you understand," he shouted. "Your lives are already forfeit. We have only to choose and we can take them."

For a moment, a memory washed over me. I recalled another island—very far from here—where a warrior named Jedik had faced off with a Klar commander in a disagreement over my life and the lives of friends of mine. Their exchange had been much like this one (See *Swords of Talera*). That time, Jedik had won the exchange; I'd lived and kept my freedom. I wondered if history would repeat itself here.

"You speak as a child," the Minotaur continued. "We outnumber you better than two to one. And you have women among you."

Again Jubyl laughed. He seemed in great good humor. He turned toward Chalathar and me and winked. "I don't believe the fool can count," he said. He turned back toward our enemy and called out loudly. "Our men are worth two of yours! Our women are worth three!"

The Minotaur shook his head.

He was a professional, a blooded soldier. His scars attested to that, as did his armor, which was well cared for though it bore the marks of long use. But I wondered if he had often commanded troops, and I thought that Jubyl was right. He was a fool.

"Line up," the Bull-man shouted to his soldiers. "Arbalests to the front."

Despite their multiple nationalities and races, our foes were disciplined. They aligned themselves smoothly to face us, with those who carried arbalests front and center. An arbalest is a type of crossbow, slower than a long bow but powerful and deadly. Against their bolts, the small shields that the Indigo Llurns wore would provide no protection.

On the flanks of our enemy's skirmish line stood the Drowg. Each held a series of gleaming chains attached to the necks of man-hounds. Those hyena-like beasts snarled and snapped to get at us, and even the powerful Drowg were hard pressed to hold them. I had fought man-hounds before. They were not sentient, though each had a pair of perfectly formed human arms sprouting from its shoulders, the fingers of which were sheathed in metal claws.

"Release the hounds!" the Minotaur roared. "And fire!"

"Down," Jubyl yelled in response.

The Drowg dropped the chains they held and the man-hounds came charging. At the same instant, the enemy's crossbowmen fired. But Jubyl's command sent every Llurn diving to the ground, Chalathar and I with them. I heard the arbalest bolts thrum past over my head. Someone cried out as they were struck. Then we came back to our feet.

Beside me, Lann drew back the string on her bow, let her arrow fly. Other Llurns did the same. I'd expected them to fire at the hounds, which were closing on us swiftly, but they sent their arrows instead into the massed ranks of the enemy. I saw a few of the mercenaries fall, but most had shields and heavy armor and the arrows did little damage.

I had brought two spears so I could throw one. I lifted that one, preparing to hurl it at the racing man-hounds. Before I could do so, Jubyl released a fresh shout, this one directed at the kryll circling over our heads. That shout was in the form of a command, "Korash," which is a signal for the kryll to attack.

A tremendous screeching filled the sky and the kryll folded their wings and fell upon the running hounds with hot fury. The beasts were not expecting it. They had no defense against it. Several of the monstrous creatures were carried into the air. They flailed with their human hands at the talons holding them, but were torn apart by beak and claw. A red mist full of gobbets of flesh rained down.

Again the enemy arbalests fired—at the kryll this time. A few birds were struck. One crashed to earth a dozen feet in front of me. But most only screeched their anger in reply and turned their attention toward their new enemy. Another flight of arrows scorched from our own ranks as well, and this time did more damage against an enemy disconcerted by the gory deaths of their man-hounds.

"Charge!" Jubyl shouted. The whole group of us exploded forward from where we stood.

"Attack!" the Minotaur war-leader roared. And our foes came

Enemy crossbowmen and Llurn archers threw down their bows— there was no time to reload. Steel sang from sheathes. Shouts filled the air from both sides. I ran in silence. My breaths came easily. My bare feet hammered the grass. I knew that Chalathar and Lann ran beside me. But my focus was all on the enemy. A badly injured man-hound lunged at my legs. I crushed his skull with the butt of my lance and ran on.

A Klar raced to meet me, a snarl on his reptilian face, an axe in his scaled hands. Some of the Klar have honor. I did not know if this one did. Nor did I care. I whipped up my right arm, with the spear gripped tight. I hurled it.

The Klar tried to counter my throw. He imposed his shield of lacquered wood reinforced with iron. But the Baadon body was immensely strong. The spear struck the Klar's shield, burst through and buried itself in his chest. He staggered and went to his knees, and I cut his throat with a slash of my other spear as I passed him.

And so we all came together beneath the hot green sun. The world smelled of blood to come. A Drowg challenged me. He carried two swords, wove them back and forth in an intricate dance meant to confuse. I was not confused. At the right moment I lunged. My lance was far longer than his swords, with a leaf-shaped head that shone in the sun. The shining part went into his throat, beneath his troll-like jaw with its upthrust tusks. He tried to scream and choked instead on blood. I smashed him aside, leaped forward to face my next foe.

The Minotaur stood before me, the leader of our enemies. His massive chest was dappled with crimson. He wore a shield on his left arm, carried a three chained flail in his right. Gore dripped from the flail's spiked metal balls. He'd killed with it already.

He snapped the flail toward me, trying to end our fight quickly. I dodged, though blood from the weapon's chains spattered my face. I slashed at him with my lance. He blocked with his shield. We started to circle.

With a war-cry shrieking from her lips, the women warrior, Lann, attacked from the Minotaur's left side. That beast was blazingly fast. His shield licked out, smashed the Llurn aside. Lann fell, her jaw broken, but for an instant our enemy had left himself open.

I lunged, thrusting for his chest. He tried to snap his shield back into position to block my lance. Yes, he was fast. But not quite fast enough against me. The broad head of my spear took him beneath the breastbone, cut its way through sinew and flesh to rupture free from his back. Purplish blood sprayed from both entrance and exit wounds. The Bullman grunted.

For a moment, the being's eyes locked with mine. His were dark brown, with whites that were rust-red from broken blood vessels. He snorted through his thick nostrils, swung his flail at me. I was out of reach at the other end of the spear.

The Minotaur snarled, shook his left arm free of his shield. It clunked heavily to earth. He reached down with his free hand and grasped the shaft of my lance. That shaft was of polished ash, wrapped thickly in gold and silver wire to provide both strength and grip. It quivered as the Bull-man grasped it firmly. He pushed forward on his feet, forcing the lance further through his body as he sought to close with me and crush my skull with his flail.

It was an act of courage and hate. Some men might have been daunted. But it was not enough. I smiled at him, and with another lunge thrust the spear almost completely through his body. He swung his flail but I was close enough to catch his wrist in my hand. He tried to hook me with a horn but I caught that with my other hand as I released the spear.

We stood toe to toe. He towered nearly half a foot over me, but his great strength was waning. His free hand slapped at me, struck me on the back, but the blow did no more than sting. I pulled down on his weapon arm, twisting as I did so. His wrist snapped and this time he cried out. He started to fall and I took the flail from his hand as he toppled. But there was no reason to use his own weapon against him. Death had staked its claim.

Turning, I looked for more foes. There were none. Chalathar stood nearby, his chest heaving, his sword coated with multicolored blood. He nodded at me. I saw that some of our enemies had surrendered. But not many. The Thye Vessoth wizard had already been butchered, primarily by the beaks of the kryll. There were Indigo Llurns dead as well, though, and I mourned their loss.

Jubyl came toward me, and he was not now in a happy mood. He knelt beside Lann, offered her comforting words that I did not clearly hear. I smiled at her over his shoulder. She grimaced back. She would live, though solid food would not be passing through her jaws anytime soon.

Chalathar came up to me. He sniffed, made a face. "That Minotaur's blood smells rancid," he said.

I shook my head. "I hadn't noticed." Meeting his gaze, I added: "We survived. It seems you have some questions to answer."

He nodded wearily. "Let us accompany the Llurns to their base. I believe we've found some potential allies against Vessoth, and we need to cement that alliance. Once that's done and we can get away from the influence of the Evrisanie so that my toir'in-or regain their functions, I'll take us back to Hael. I'll answer your questions there, but I believe Shai should be present as well. And Bryce if you wish it."

I nodded, suddenly too weary to speak. I looked down at the bloody flail in my hand. My fingers opened. The weapon dropped to lie beside the master it had failed to save. For just a moment, its fall disturbed the flies that had already gathered around the dead. They did not seem to mind the Minotaur's rancid blood, or any other. Except for their buzzing, the world grew quiet in the aftermath of slaughter.

CHAPTER NINETEEN

THE BEAUTIFUL PEOPLE

I flicked the up-rein, and the kryll took the sky in an explosion of bright wings. The wind streamed past like a river. Exhilaration swept me. It had been a while since I'd ridden a saddle bird, but one does not forget the experience, nor dare to forget the skills. This bird was well trained, too. Without prompting, it emitted the high pitched call that signals a flock to assemble. We circled, waiting for the remainder of the saddle birds to join us.

The Indigo Llurns had lost seven warriors in our recent battle. Others were injured. We'd taken a dozen prisoners. Some of Jubyl's men stayed behind with the dead and wounded, and with the prisoners, to await extraction by airship. These were not standard Taleran airships, of course, which rely on the toir'in-or for lift, but lighter than air vessels that make use of the Vyn'ishad-or gas in much the same way zeppelins on Earth use hydrogen. The rest of us winged our way toward the island above ours, where—we had been told—lay the current home base of the Llurns.

Riding a saddle bird is not all that different from riding a horse, although you move through three dimensions instead of two. And the results of getting thrown off one's mount can be quite a bit more serious. A bird-saddle sits just forward of the wings and is usually made of extremely light-weight leather. It looks like a stripped down version of a horse's saddle, with no cantle or horn. It does have stirrups, and attached metal rings through which piggin strings are passed for riders to tie themselves on.

The bird's movements are guided by four reins: left, right, up, down. These are attached to a hackamore encircling the bird's beak, and run through a metal collar around the mount's neck. The left and down reins are held in the left hand. Right and up reins are for the right hand. You pull back on all reins to slow and hover, loosen them to speed up. Directional movement just involves working the proper rein. There is also a wing-stick, a two-and-a-half foot prod with a metal tip. This can be used to control the bird if the reins break or are lost, but its primary purpose is to beat the saddle bird around the head if it decides to eat its rider.

Our current flight did not last long, although I might have wished to joy in it further. We climbed above the base-cloud that marked the island above ours, and passed over a white keep built of bleached wood rather than stone. It was the same keep that Chalathar had pointed out to me earlier from the island below. It had been key to my understanding that we were actually aboard a floating island and that some such places had inhabitants. I had believed it to be a ruin at the time, but it was a watchtower that allowed Llurn guards to keep an eye out for approaching danger.

The keep was not our destination, however. We flew past it, and over a forest where the trees grew right-side up. The sky island spread out before us, shaped like a wide, shallow bowl. At bowl's center stood the city of the Indigo Llurns, although "encampment" might have been a more accurate term.

Only one structure of any great size could be seen. This was a large, tower composed of living trees and roots that were intricately intertwined and had clearly been groomed that way in their growth. In concentric circles around the central tower stood the rest of the Llurn town. It consisted almost entirely of tents, particularly a type called a yurt. I had seen examples in the Far East. Herds of taverels and goats wandered among the tents, but I had little time to study the overall layout of the town. The population of the whole place could be no more than a few thousand.

We landed in an open space before the great tower and men rushed to take the reins of our kryll mounts. Jubyl waved Chalathar and me over to him. With a few more of his men around us, the youth led the way toward the entrance into the tower. No door barred our passage and we strode directly into a hall filled with the play of light and shadow.

The floor beneath us lay thick with a springy moss that cushioned our boots like the richest of carpets. The walls were made from the curved boles of ahmbr trees, whose already polished bark had been inlaid with thin veins of silver. Here and there, through carefully sculpted "windows" in the growth of the trees, sprays of emerald sunlight fell upon us, refracting back from the silver in the walls so that we were drenched in ethereal light.

As we passed along the hallway, small rooms opened to our left and right. Men and woman worked in many of these rooms, going about various duties that were unfamiliar to me. Then the hall fell away from us and we stepped out into the central chamber of the tower. A type of tall, wide tree known as carbaxus formed the walls here. Some thirty feet above our heads, the trees' leaves and needle-rich branches wove together into a natural roof pierced through in places by great shafts of sun.

Since Jubyl had mentioned taking us to see his "Queen," I'd expected some sort of throne room. This was like no such room I'd ever seen. It felt more like entering a cathedral. In front of us lay an aisle with rows of wooden pews to either side that had grown from the floor. At aisle's end, where a throne might be expected to rest, stood another triad of pews, these strewn with wool pillows dyed in bright colors.

Only the center pew was occupied. A woman lounged there, but straightened as we approached. Jubyl paused at the end of the aisle and went to one knee, bowed deeply. We followed his lead, then rose again as he did. He motioned us to wait for a moment and strode forward, leaning down to kiss the queen on the top of her head before murmuring softly into her ear for several moments. I heard our names mentioned, and the word, "Mother." Perhaps I should have guessed at that relationship, given Jubyl's easy familiarity with command at such a young age.

Jubyl's mother, the ruler of this land, rose from her seat and walked with quiet steps toward us. I have heard it said that the Indigo Llurns, the Beautiful People, seldom show much sign of aging until they are extremely old. This certainly seemed true of the queen, who could have been anywhere between thirty and sixty.

She would have been tall for a female Human, though was not overly so in comparison to other Indigo Llurn women. Unlike the others of her people whom I'd seen so far, she was not dressed in leathers but was clad in a sumptuous gown of ivory silk. The gown flattered her, though the flattery was scarcely needed. She was indeed a beautiful woman. Her hair and skin were lavender, with the hair slightly darker. Her eyes were a striking violet. She held out her hand to Chalathar, and after he had taken it and bowed over it, she offered it to me and I did the same. Our gazes met. She smiled.

"Welcome," she said, her voice throaty and melodic. "My son champions you both quite highly."

"It is he who should be championed," Chalathar said. "He led his warriors with aplomb. And fought like a ghyre."

A ghyre is a Taleran predator, much respected for its strength and cunning. Imagine a panther-wolf hybrid with a tiger's size and habits. To call someone a ghyre is to honor them.

The queen glanced back at her son with a mother's fondness. He seemed embarrassed at the attention, but perhaps it is the role of good parents to embarrass their children with pride in their accomplishments. When she turned once more toward us, her gaze brushed again over mine. Then she moved her focus to Chalathar.

"I am Lavisa Mersath Tanishmora Vokule," she continued. "And pleased I am to meet the great Chalathar and his companion."

"As I mentioned to your son," Chalathar responded, "I am...surprised to be so recognized."

Lavisa chuckled, and it was no dainty thing. Clearly, she was a woman of passions.

"The fame of he who defeated the Witch-Queen Vohanna and freed the Northern land of Nyshphal from her tyranny has spread far across the world," she said. "That tale has been told and retold, and passed on like a coin of great value." She smiled impishly. "I am only surprised that you are not truly twelve-feet tall and made of iron."

Chalathar blushed. I had never seen such from him before.

"I had much help in that war," he muttered after a moment. "In truth, others bore a much greater burden than I. And deserve more of the credit for Vohanna's defeat."

Lavisa nodded. "Of course. Tales are also told of the great Warlord, Ruenn Maclang. And of his ravishing battle Queen—Rannon. And of the Knights of Fire—Valyan the Emerald Wolf, Heril Gold Mane, Diken of the Blade, Rajan Dark, Kreeg the Shield, and Rhandh the Lorn."

"Great heroes all," Chalathar agreed.

"The ones named Heril, Kreeg, and Rhandh gave their lives in that war," I added.

Lavisa nodded, and her face was somber. "Many have died over the ages in battle against the predations of the First-Gods. Never has such a battle been victorious. Never has such a God been defeated. Until now."

"There is another who must be defeated," Chalathar said. "If you know the legends of the First-Gods, then know that Vessoth is real and has escaped his prison. It was he, or some minion of his, that sent the hunters after us on the island below. By aiding us, you have made yourselves his enemy."

"He was already our enemy. He has just become aware of it. Such as he are ever and always the enemies of those who wish only to live, and love, and leave a better world for our children."

"You have the right of it," I said.

She gazed at me, seemed to reach some decision. "There is much we need to speak of," she said. "I believe it is time for my people to once more take an active hand in this war for the khi of Talera. But I need time to reflect on what has happened. We need to interrogate the prisoners that were taken. And you two," she nodded toward Chalathar and me, "need to rest and recover. We have a place where you can eat, bathe, and sleep. We will speak again later."

"Forgive me, Queen Lavisa," Chalathar said. "Before we can rest, there is one more thing we must do. We came to the Floating Isles because of sorcery. And we left friends behind who must be desperate with fear for our fates. We need to return to them. But perhaps we can bring them back here. To continue our discussion." He smiled. "Some are the heroes whose names you mentioned a few moments ago."

"Ah," Lavisa said. "You need to get to a place where there are no Evrisanie. So that you can once again access your own magic."

"Yes."

The Queen considered swiftly: "I have a slightly modified proposal," she said. "My son, Jubyl, can take you, Chalathar, to a very small floating isle not far from here. It has no population of Evrisanie so you should be able to work your spells. You can gather your people and return to that same isle. We will make one of our own brand of airships available to bring you back here." She glanced at me. "In the meantime, your charming companion, Baadon, can stay with us and we can begin the sharing of information that is necessary when an alliance is formed."

Chalathar glanced toward me; one eyebrow arched slightly. I shrugged in response. He nodded a few times to himself before turning back to the Queen.

"An excellent idea," he said. He glanced toward me again. His eyes spoke far more than the words that came from his lips. "I will return with the others as soon as I can. It may take some little time to finish what we started there."

I knew what he meant, a warning to me that he was not quite ready to trust Queen Lavisa with all our secrets. Well, Lavisa seemed likable, but I was not a particularly trusting sort.

"I'll be here," I told him.

Queen Lavisa smiled.

CHAPTER TWENTY

A SECRET REVEALED

Candlelight gleamed on a table of polished wood, and on the face and hair and bare shoulders of Queen Lavisa, who sat across from me. I'd bathed. A servant had treated my scratches with burn-root and given me a new pair of boots and a fresh shirt of black chamois to replace the torn one I'd climbed through a jungle and fought a battle in. Then the man had brought me to the Queen in a quiet corner of her great tower. I'd thought the gown she'd worn earlier had been flattering. I had been mistaken, as the gown she wore now clearly revealed.

She'd invited me to join her at a table already set with silver platters piled with foods—diced chevon from the local goats, spiced with carsoli and whitethorn, purple she-ashin grapes, a honey-grain cake threaded with walnuts, and rich yellow bread baked from cymer, a Taleran equivalent to wheat. For drink there was spice-mead, also made from honey-grain, and verhlis tea. A basket of crimson hysis hung above the table on a small silver chain, and the scent of the flowers mixed with that of the candle wax and washed over us like a soft, cool breeze. The Queen's perfume added a warmer undercurrent to that breeze.

I was extremely uncomfortable.

"I have never seen a being such as you, Baadon," the Queen said. "Of what race are you, might I ask?"

"Kurshan," I said, giving her the first term to come to mind. It was not really a lie.

The Kurshan are manufactured beings made by sorcerers like Vohanna and Vessoth. Chalathar had indicated to me that the Baadon body had belonged to Vessoth and was unique. Kurshan seemed an appropriate term for it, and I did not imagine that Queen Lavisa understood the word.

"I do not know any Kurshan," she said. "But Talera is a big world. Many races inhabit it that I have not yet met."

She took a sip of her spice-mead. It seemed to add a glow to her cheeks, a twinkle to her eye—though perhaps it was the candlelight.

"I find meeting new beings fascinating," Lavisa continued. "Don't you?"

"Yes."

"And you are most intriguing."

"Thank you."

She picked up her loaf of bread, tore free a piece, dipped it in mutton gravy and ate it delicately.

"Do you, Sir Baadon, find me...equally intriguing?"

I coughed. "Most certainly, your Highness."

I quickly tried to follow the Queen's lead with a piece of bread, but managed somehow to get a tiny smear of gravy on my new shirt. Even in Ruenn Maclang's body, I had not been the most graceful of diners. Now, in the Baadon body, it seemed I'd forgotten all the motor control I'd learned over the past few days. My fingers were clumsy, my hands like fists in gauntlets.

Have I mentioned that I was uncomfortable?

"What do you call your city here?" I asked, striving to turn the conversation away from personal matters and toward something else, anything else.

Lavisa smiled faintly. "We do not call it a city. We knew a city once, and will not live in another until we can return to that one. We call the settlement around us "Yteril."

"That is a term meaning 'exile,' is it not?"

Lavisa inclined her head. "It is."

"I do not wish to intrude," I said. "But the city you spoke of? Does it still stand?"

Lavisa's voice grew distant, and cold. "Nakish-amora was taken from us. The Indigo Llurns were once a populous people. The flower of our race was decimated in defending our city. Those of us who live today remain...in motion. The tower here," she nodded around at our surroundings, "is permanent. And there are other such towers on other islands. They recall to us Nakish-amora. But all else is temporary. At all times we must be ready to depart."

"I am very sorry for that," I said.

Warmth returned to her voice. "And we appreciate your kind thoughts."

"May I ask? Where lies Nakish-amora? Is it in the Floating Isles?"

"The first and largest of the Sky Islands is Priminiphal. Ages ago, long before the coming of people to these lands, Priminiphal was struck from above by a rain of great iron rocks. The resulting wounds have never healed. One can still see the craters, for most plants do not grow well in the metallic soil left behind there.

"Priminiphal was already heavy with a great accumulation of dirt, and with the remnants of generations of living things. The additional stone and iron of the rocks proved too much for the Vyn'ishad-or to support. With the plants unable to bear up the added weight, the island began to sink. Eventually, it settled on the surface of the ocean where, to this day, it travels with the great equatorial currents.

"When my people first came to this area, for reasons that are lost to history, we did not come in airships or on the backs of saddle birds. We arrived on rafts made from chelaquin logs. The tales say that we were few in number in those days, and near to death from thirst and starvation. Priminiphal was a sending to us from the true gods. We disembarked there, and have never returned to the sea.

"In the largest crater of that island, we found the slagged remains of some ancient city. We excavated the slag, used it in the building of our own city. At the heart of the crater, we grew a great tower from carbaxus tree seeds we had carried with us on the rafts. We called the place Nakish-amora—love from death. In other craters on the island, we built other settlements and grew other towers, but none as grand as Nakish-amora. Those were glorious times. The Indigo Llurns bloomed as a race. We grew in numbers and wisdom and strength. And we lived in peace with all."

"You have the wisdom and strength yet," I said. "Your son is evidence of that."

Lavisa nodded. "Yes," she said, though her thoughts were clearly still distant.

I did not wish to disturb the Queen's heart further, but curiosity has always been a powerful goad to me. Too, I'd begun to think that—perhaps—the story of the Indigo Llurns might provide insight into the many questions I had about Talera.

"And those who took your city from you?" I asked.

"They came in great fleets of warships, some as big as temples. They had with them some saddle birds, and a few airboats. They did not even try to negotiate with us for land, but fell upon us like ravening demons. We fought them. We burned their fleets. In individual combat we were their match. But they had numbers far beyond ours, and they used their saddle birds and airboats to bombard us from above with fiery pitch.

"When we realized that we could no longer save our land, many claimed it was fate and that we should die in battle with our feet anchored in our home soil. But others among us said we should look to the saving of our race. A group of the latter stole saddle birds from our enemies and fled to other of the Floating Isles. Thus we became exiles and nomads.

"Our foes did not give up easily. They still raid us when they can. But the presence of the Evrisanie on all of the bigger Isles prevents them from using sorcery to locate or attack us. By necessity, our people became expert saddle bird riders. Now we breed them. And we have survived."

"Were there no Evrisanie on Priminiphal?"

"No. For reasons that are unclear, the Evrisanie live only in the forests *under* the islands. And there is no under for Priminiphal. Only water."

I nodded. "And these enemies? What manner of beings were they?"

"They *are* Bull-men. Those you name as Minotaurs. And the reptilian Klar. In the years since the conquest, other beings have joined them. Outlaws and pirates mostly. And many Drowg. But the Minotaurs and the Klar are the backbone."

The Queen fell silent. I let that quiet linger while my soul hurt for her and her people. They had suffered much. Many had suffered at the hands of the First gods. Finally, I managed to ask a question I was almost afraid to receive an answer to.

"Minotaurs and Klar. And you mentioned sorcery. The Minotaurs are known as servants of Kamrack the Bull. And he is an Asadhie. Many Klar worship Heshval. He, too, is Asadhie. Both are sorcerers who claim to be among the First Gods. Was it...these Asadhie and their servants who took your city?"

"Kamrack the Bull led them personally. It is believed he still leads them. And fattens himself in our city. Though he has not been seen by people of my race for many hundreds of years. Of Heshval...." She shrugged. "We know nothing of him other than rumors. But is not one Asadhie monster enough?"

"One is more than enough," I agreed.

"So, you see, we have reason to hate the Asadhie, reason to join you and Chalathar in the battle against them. Since the taking of Nakish-amora, my people have had no true hope of victory. Now we can have such hope."

I felt some of that hope myself. Many varied pieces had just fit themselves together. Chalathar was sure that Kamrack the Bull had allied himself with Vessoth. And, it seemed likely the fhaze shapeshifter had served Vessoth, or possibly Kamrack. As the shifter lay dying, a milk-stone implanted by some Asadhie had been activated, opening a sphere gate to take it back to its master, and that gate had sucked Chalathar and me along. We'd ended up here, in a place where Kamrack had carved himself an empire far in the past. So, when Vessoth escaped us on Nimeru, was it not likely that he'd fled to an ally's base? Fled here?

Chalathar had already suggested to the queen that it was Vessoth's forces we'd just fought—with the help of her son and his warriors. I repeated this again for Lavisa, and explained my theory that Vessoth might have joined Kamrack in Nakish-amora. It was clear she believed it.

"It would seem indeed that we have a common enemy," she said.

"Yes. And we must make common cause against them."

"That is all well and good. But to beard Kamrack in his lair would require an army that the Indigo Llurns cannot muster. We have less than fifteen hundred fighters, while we believe that Kamrack has over seventy thousand warriors on Priminiphal. And there are also many hundreds of pirates who scout for him and help protect against any sea-borne attack."

"A very large army indeed," I said.

"What of Chalathar?" Lavisa asked. "What resources does he claim?"

"No army. He has a dozen men."

She sighed. "What of Ruenn Maclang. He is ally to Chalathar, and is he not King of the nation of Nyshphal?"

"He is," I said, and it felt strange to speak this way of myself. "But Nyshphal has recently borne the brunt of bloody wars on all fronts. They have not the resources for such a battle either."

Lavisa sighed. Her shoulders slumped a bit, but she shook off that mood and once more focused her gaze on me. A greater warmth entered her voice as she murmured: "Let us not deal with such worries this night." She placed her hand upon mine. "Let us instead seek solace in each other's company."

I reached out and very gently disengaged my hand from hers. "I would be forever your friend, your highness. But...."

"But what?" Her voice was flat.

"But I am pledged to another."

She did not respond for a long moment. Then: "And nothing would tempt you from her?"

I met her gaze, my own unwavering. "Nothing!"

She nodded, a little wistfully it seemed, and rose from her seat. A few steps away were all she took, but she turned her back to me. Her shoulders began to shake. Stricken at what I took to be a sign of pain, I rose from my own chair. But Lavisa heard me and looked back at me. She was smiling. It was not tears that caused her to shake, but something more akin to joy. I frowned.

"Rannon Jystral is a lucky woman," Lavisa said. "To have such a great love. I had to be sure of it before I committed the last of the Indigo Llurns to a cause that—just as it might be—could well end us as a race."

My heart pounded. "I do not understand."

The Queen smiled. "Though you wear a different body at the moment, I know who you are—Ruenn Maclang."

CHAPTER TWENTY-ONE

GIFT OF STEEL

Queen Lavisa's words shocked me. My mouth opened to deny her assertion, then snapped shut. I could see in her face that no lie would dissuade her from what she knew to be true.

"How did you figure it out?" I asked.

"I know much more about the Asadhie and their habits than you suppose. I know they can change their bodies, have suspected they could change others. I know also that Chalathar is Asadhie. Though he seems at odds with most of his own kind."

"He is indeed."

"You like him, do you not?"

"We are friends."

"So I believe. And I know that Chalathar and Ruenn Maclang are friends. I know they have often fought together. It is not only rumor that tells me this. Ever since the fall of the Witch Vohanna, I have sought out information on you both."

"It still seems guesswork," I said.

"But there is more. When I saw your current form—Baadon—I did not recognize it as being of any known race on Talera. And you claimed to be 'Kurshan.' You thought I would not know that word. I do. The Kurshan are created beings. Created by the Asadhie. You told me the truth, even when you sought to dissemble. I have heard that Ruenn Maclang does not lie."

"Whoever you heard that from, lied," I said.

She smiled. "But there is still more. My son, Jubyl, mentioned to you that some Indigo Llurns possess a small grasp of sendahtia, that ability to communicate mind to mind. Jubyl has a bit of it; he can converse in a simple way with the Evrisanie. But his powers do not approach my level. Nor," she gazed very directly at me, "do yours. Though you too possess some ability."

I shook my head. "Not enough to be of any use. I have tried."

"Your rational mind blocks it. Too, you are much stronger in receiving than in sending. But from the first moment I met you, clear impressions have come through. Enough to convince me completely that you are Ruenn Maclang."

"What kind of impressions?"

"Mostly those having to do with strong emotions. Your concern for the friends you left behind. Those who Chalathar has gone to fetch. Your great anger at Vessoth. Your dismay and despair when I told you of my people's tragic history. And most strongly, in the last few minutes, the absolute love you hold for a woman named Rannon."

I let out a breath I hadn't known I was holding. "I miss her."

She moved toward me, rested a hand on my shoulder.

"Since the day we met," I continued, "it seems there has been one battle after another to keep us apart. I would give nearly anything for peace."

"Therein lays the difference between people like us and beings such as Vessoth and Kamrack. We would give *nearly* anything for peace. But we will not give up those we love. Beings such as the Asadhie do not love. They give up nothing, and strive for only one thing—absolute power."

"Yet," I said. "Chalathar is Asadhie and I believe he is capable of love. At least he is capable of honor and loyalty and trust."

"And in that, perhaps, lies hope for Talera."

I nodded.

"Let's finish our meal," Lavisa said. "Before it grows cold."

I returned with her to the table, and did not worry now if I spilled a drop of gravy on my new shirt. It was good to laugh and relax. Finally, when the last grape was gone and the Verhlis tea nearly dregs, Lavisa told me one more thing.

"I have a gift for you," she said.

"Your friendship is gift enough, Milady."

She chuckled. "What gallantry," she said. "But I am sure you behave such with all the Queens with whom you dine."

"Other than my wife, I'm not much in the habit of dining with Queens," I said.

This time she laughed out loud. Then she picked up a long, vellum wrapped package that leaned against the wall next to her. I'd noticed it but paid it little mind. She handed the parcel across the table to me. Its nature was clear before I unwrapped it.

"A sword," I said, drawing the weapon from its sheath by an ornate basket hilt of black steel.

The blade itself was some thirty-five inches long, and beneath the candlelight it shimmered like oil on water. I knew that moiré pattern. It indicated steel that had been folded and refolded during the forging process. On earth, such blades were sometimes called Damascus steel. They were flexible and very strong, and would hold an edge long after standard blades had become too dull to cut a rotten apple.

In make, this sword was neither a rapier nor a saber, but some hybrid of the two. It was straight like a rapier, but double-edged as with many sabers. The blade was wider than that of a typical rapier, but because of the fine quality of the steel it was scarcely heavier. One could wield such a sword deftly, and cut or thrust at need.

I sheathed the blade, stared across the table at Lavisa. "I have held Tyzinn swords," I said. "But none of finer workmanship than this one."

"I told you of the great iron rocks that fell in ancient times upon Priminiphal. When the Indigo Llurns dwelt on that island, in the city of Nakish-amora, the ore from those rocks was often used in the fashioning of swords. The weapons so forged were stronger and sharper than anything save Tyzinn steel."

"And is this weapon from that time?"

"It is. When our ancestors fled Nakish-amora, they took with them as many of the blades as they could. This one we have carried with us since that time."

"Then it should go to one of your own people," I said. "To Jubyl perhaps. Or to another son you may bear some day. Not to a stranger such as myself."

"You are no stranger, Ruenn Maclang, though you and I have just met. Your khi is of kindred make to my own."

I inclined my head. "Thank you. I pray for a chance to use it on Vessoth."

"I pray so as well. Such a sword is well suited to slaying a god."

CHAPTER TWENTY-TWO

A PLAN OF ACTION

"It's suicide," Bryce said.

"I don't intend it to be," I replied. "But by all means, give me a better alternative."

Bryce sighed. Other sighs echoed his.

Two days had passed since my dinner with Queen Lavisa. Chalathar had returned from Hael with our friends. It was very good to see my brother, Bryce, as well as Valyan, and Diken, and Shai—and the others of Chalathar's followers, even though I hardly knew most of them. All of us sat around a big table in the tower of Yteril, the settlement of the Indigo Llurns. Queen Lavisa sat with us, along with her son Jubyl. Other advisors to her court had also joined us.

"We interrogated the prisoners we took after our recent battle," I continued. "Common soldiers and mercenaries. They knew little but admitted serving Kamrack. They bragged of it. They knew nothing specifically of Vessoth but were aware that some powerful sorcerer had recently joined their master. All signs point to that being Vessoth.

"We also know Kamrack has a huge army that we have no chance of overcoming. And while Kamrack might have been resting quietly for a long time, Vessoth won't let him remain idle much longer. They'll use that army on someone. Certainly on the Indigo Llurns. Maybe on Nyshphal, or on someone innocent of any knowledge of them at all. Or maybe for something worse."

I didn't recount the legend about Vessoth, that he wanted to break the atmospheric barrier protecting Talera and let the outside poisons wash the planet clean of life. I didn't have to. Everyone here knew that story.

"We need to hit them as soon as we can," I continued, "but we have to be judicious in how we use our small number of warriors. We can't match them man for man but we might be able to cut off the head that rules them. That requires knowledge. We need to know exactly where Kamrack and Vessoth are so we can make sure we outnumber them at the point of attack. Someone has to go in and get the information we need, and I'm the only one of us here with any hope at all of doing so."

"We've not established that as fact just yet," Chalathar said.

"Who else could do it?" I asked. "Any Indigo Llurn who showed up anywhere near their base on Priminiphal would be instantly killed. Or taken and tortured. Diken, Valyan, and Shai can't go. Vessoth knows them. He's marked them. He'll have his men watching for them. He knows you, Chalathar. Better than any."

"Do you forget that I am Asadhie? I can take another form."

"You know that an Asadhie can't hide from another Asadhie for long" I replied. "Their sorcery would know your sorcery. I have the best hope of passing unnoticed."

"But the body you wear once *belonged* to Vessoth," Chalathar protested. "As soon as he sees it, he'll know immediately that something is wrong."

"*If* he sees it. I don't plan to walk up and slap his face. Besides, you told me when I first awoke in this body that Vessoth couldn't see what he wasn't looking for. And, you said there might be a way to use this body to trace Vessoth. If that's true, I'm especially suited for the task at hand. Maybe you can tell me everything you know about that."

He shook his head. "I've had no time to consider it. I only know there's potential. In some fashion, you two are connected."

"Maybe I can discover how, and use it."

"There's also the matter of the fhaze," Chalathar said. "If it survived returning to its master, it has no doubt told both Kamrack and Vessoth about you. They may be especially watching for you."

"There is that chance," I agreed. "But the fhaze is one being. Possibly dead. That still makes my odds better than anyone else's here."

In apparent frustration, Chalathar threw up his hands. No one else spoke for a long time. Finally, Jubyl asked a question.

"So what exactly is your plan for finding out where Kamrack and Vessoth are? No one can land a kryll anywhere on the island of Priminiphal without our enemy knowing. We used to raid them, for food, or just to harass them. But they developed some kind of warning system to detect encroachment from the air. We can fly over the island as long as we stay up high. But anyone coming in low enough to land is instantly detected. You'd never make it through."

"All right," I said. "But there's been a lot of talk of the pirates that both shelter under Kamrack's protection and provide him with far reaching eyes and ears. Men come and go among pirate crews all the time. There's my way in."

"You'd become a pirate?" Bryce asked.

"I'd start at the edge of Kamrack's sphere of influence and work my way in."

Many around the table were nodding.

"It'll take time," Bryce said.

"Time that the rest of you can use recruiting every possible ally and training for the actual attack. Nyshphal may not be able to send a lot of troops but she can send some. There are also our friends on Korosphal, on Jedik's Isle, on Talen. There's Shai's homeland. Call in every favor you're owed."

Everyone quietened as Queen Lavisa spoke: "Much as I dread the risk to our colleague here, I think Baadon's plan is something we have to pursue. We won't limit ourselves just to that. But it seems like the best chance we have."

"I've got an idea, too," I said, "about how to send up a signal once I locate Kamrack and Vessoth. That is, if I can't escape myself. I'll need a few items—sulfur, charcoal, niter. I'll need a mortar and pestle to grind them. And something like papyrus to wrap them in."

Lavisa nodded, gestured toward one of her people. "Find Bekleen. She should have those materials." The Indigo turned and left, and Lavisa looked around at the rest of us. "Bekleen is our phoros, and something of an alchemist as well," she explained.

Once again silence descended, and lingered. I broke it.

"All right. Let's start hammering out the details. The next thing I'll need is every bit of information possible on these pirates. Including maps if they're available. And plenty of coin. Also," I looked up, "I'd like to learn more about the Evrisanie. I've got a feeling they're going to be important allies in this venture. Not quite sure how yet, but we need to figure it out before I leave."

CHAPTER TWENTY-THREE

THE COST OF PASSAGE

In the first full moments of the night, Jubyl of the Indigo Llurns brought our kryll mount in for a landing on a wild and rocky coast. I slid from the saddle bird's back. Jubyl dismounted and joined me a moment later, holding onto the bird's reins while it preened and pecked at its own feathers.

"We're on a big island here called Karphal," Jubyl said. He pointed off toward the east. "Kamrack's base on Priminiphal is somewhere out there. A long way out." He pointed again, this time down the coast from where we stood. "And there's Drin's Landing."

"I can see a little light coming from there," I said. "Not much."

"Must be burning something or you wouldn't see that. Drin's Landing is mostly a big sod house that serves as a combination tavern and inn. There are a few outbuildings. Family huts mostly. Probably no more than twenty or thirty people live there. All related somehow to Drin. He's a big fellow, by the way. You won't have trouble recognizing him."

"And you say pirate ships visit him?"

"Most every night. There's a stream for fresh water and Drin keeps goats and pigs and wurstids. He's got a garden, though I don't even want to think about how he fertilizes it in that rocky soil. He brings in tipit fruit from the forest north of his place. A lot of ships stop there for food and water. Pirate ships especially. Drin doesn't much care whether the gold and goods he takes in are stolen or not."

The wurstids that Jubyl mentioned are varmints, like a raccoon-sized cross between a rabbit and a possum. The wealthy never eat them; the poor often do. I also knew of the tipit, a bright orange fruit that isn't particularly palatable either, but which stores well for sea voyages and helps prevent scurvy.

"Only the pirates know where their main base is," Jubyl continued. "But if you really insist on meeting some of them, here's the place. I wish you'd rethink your plan, though. They're more likely to kill you than take you in."

"I've run afoul of pirates before," I said, thinking of a battle with Klar slavers I'd fought in not long after first arriving on Talera. "You just have to give them what they need."

"And that is?"

I smiled. "Generally a knee to the face."

"Hope you have enough knees."

"Me too."

He shook his head, but said: "I'll check back here around the same time every night for a tenday. After that, I'll assume you've either found a ship. Or that you never will."

I nodded. A tenday is the Taleran equivalent of a week. He was giving me plenty of time to do what I hoped to do.

"Be...careful, Baadon," Jubyl added. "I like you. And so does my mother."

"I appreciate that. I'll be as careful as I can be."

He nodded, remounted his kryll without another word and took off into the sky. I watched him for a moment, then turned my feet in the direction of Drin's Landing. Nimeru was rising, painting my pathway in pale blue light. But that light was dimmer than it had once been. I glanced up at the moon many Talerans call the "Little Dreamer." The great crack that had torn that orb open and freed Vessoth from his prison was clearly visible as a green-black rift.

The memories of my time on Nimeru were not pleasant and I forced my mind to return to the world of the now. The path was visible enough to follow, and the night here *was* pleasant. At my right hand lay the sea, calm beneath a fish-scale sky. I scented salt and seaweed. Scrub brush grew to my left, with a dark forest rising further back from the coast. Frogs and night birds called. A few lightning bugs winked on and off in the trees. They weren't quite the same insect I'd known from Earth, but close enough to bear the name.

Nearly a dhaur passed before I strode into the Landing. There was no street, only a big rectangle of packed dirt with half a dozen mud huts around it, and one long sod house that I took to be the tavern-inn that Jubyl had mentioned. Under the moonlight, I could see a smallish, two-masted sloop riding at anchor in the bay. A ship's boat was tied up at the dock. Gentle waves rocked it, banging it occasionally against the timbers. Someone was visiting Drin; I had no idea if they were pirates or not. Some national flag that I couldn't make out flew from the mast, but that didn't mean much. Most pirate ships sailed under some flag or other.

Pushing back the tavern door, I stepped into a low, wide room floored with rush-covered planks. The air smelled of burnt meat and spilled and spoiled liquor. Smoke drifted, from lit torches and a cook fire at one end, and from the rolled jitter grass bangers that some of the room's denizens puffed on. Jitter grass is a mild stimulant, used on Talera much as tobacco is on Earth; a 'banger' is a slang term that essentially means cigarette.

A long wooden bar ran along the back of the room, with tables scattered in front of it. A half dozen rough looking customers sat at two tables near the cook fire. Behind the bar, another man stood. He was a virtual giant, a Human nearly seven feet tall, and with girth to match. I began to see how this Drin had been able to avoid the potential pitfalls of dealing with pirates.

Two women were also in the room. Though not quite as large as Drin, they looked enough like him to make me feel sure they were his daughters. One cooked; the other fetched drinks and food to the customers.

I crossed to the bar under the watching eyes of everyone in the room. The bar was old and scarred and black with years of grime and grease, but it was solidly built. I leaned on it and let my gaze find Drin. I smiled, just with my lips and without looking at all at the others in the room. The big proprietor came down my way, stopped in front of me.

"I'd like mead, if you have it," I said, laying three copperns on the bar and pushing the coins toward him.

Drin didn't move. "Not many strangers make their way alone into these parts," he said. "And I ain't never seen any quite as strange looking as you."

"That's the exact same thing my daddy told my momma when I was born," I said.

Drin stared at me for a moment, then slapped the bar and guffawed wildly. After a moment, he calmed down and wiped his eyes.

"Mead, you say?"

"If you've got it. Been walking a while and I'm a might dry."

Leaning down, Drin pulled a stoppered brown jug out from under the bar, uncorked it, and poured a healthy amount of dark liquid into a mug that had seen much use and might not necessarily have been cleaned lately. He took two of the copperns, let the other one lay.

The mead didn't look like much, but it smelled strong and sweet. I took a sip and it tasted as good as it smelled. I'd had better but this was better than expected.

"Not much place to walk *from* around here either," Drin remarked as I drank.

"I wasn't walking when I started out. Left Karish a couple of days ago aboard a saddle bird. Unfortunately, the bird was…uhm…wounded by an arrow during my somewhat hasty departure from that fine city. The bird made it for a while, but finally left me stranded a couple of verlangs up the coast."

"Seems like the Karishians didn't like your appearance any more than your daddy did," one of the men at the tables called out. I turned toward the group of them, lifted my cup in a toast. They were laughing and I chuckled along.

"Just so," I agreed.

And now I had a chance to study them. They were six, of various races and sizes. Pirates, for sure, though apparently not very successful examples of the breed. Their faces were dirty. Their clothes were mismatched odds and ends, with very little in the way of armor among them. One being was missing an eye. Another lacked a left hand. The latter was a common penalty for petty thieves on Talera.

"Anyway," I looked back at Drin and continued with my tale. "as I was walking along the coast after my bird died, I saw the light of this place and thought I'd drop in. I'm a sociable sort, after all. And as luck would have it," I glanced back at the pirates, "I discover a fine ship at anchor in your harbor. Surely I can obtain passage away from this... rather lonely frontier."

The leader of the pirate group was a Nokarran, of that race who look much like tailless, upright-walking snow leopards. I doubted he was captain of the ship anchored in the bay. Maybe First Mate. A half dozen mead cups stood empty on the table in front of him, but he didn't appear intoxicated. He laughed at my words, with a smirking, sidelong glance at his companions. They joined in his humor, but it seemed a little forced. I did not think this being was particularly popular with those under his command. That could be of use to me.

"Passage on such a fine ship as *The Painted Maid* can be costly, stranger," the Nokarran called to me. "I'm not sure you can afford it."

I straightened and turned sideways at the bar, letting my right hand fall naturally to the hilt of the sword that Queen Lavisa had recently gifted me. The sheathed blade swung slightly on the scabbard hooks of my belt. Even the dim light of the room would set that hilt agleam. It was a fine weapon, an expensive weapon, but a warrior's weapon. And they could see that my leathers and boots were of better quality than their own. They could also see my face, and it was not a pretty one. I let my eyes go cold.

"I believe I can afford it," I said. "Whether it's to be paid in coin. Or blood."

The laughter stopped. The Nokarran's slanted eyes narrowed further. Like many of his race, he had gold irises, the irises of a tiger. His fur was tinged with red as he pushed back in his chair and rose to his feet. His hand dropped to his own weapon, a broadsword with a hide-wrapped hilt. Clearly it had seen much use.

"That sounds very much like a threat," he said.

"Let me clarify then. What I meant was that I'd be happy to kill you if need be."

The Nokarran's eyes lit with anger. "Krutt-lover!" he snarled.

He drew his sword, stalked toward me. I sighed elaborately for the crowd, drained my mug of mead and sat it down. Stepping away from the bar, I drew my own sword. It winked with light from the torches.

The Nokarran was as tall as I, and heavier. But a layer of fat padded his muscles. I thought he'd not been truly challenged in a long time. I lifted my sword, assumed a fencing stance.

The Nokarran paused for a moment, shook his head. "If you think this is gonna be some pretty duel, boy, you've got a lesson coming your way."

"And how much will that cost?" I asked.

The remaining pirates laughed again, but this time the humor wasn't directed at me.

At that laughter, the Nokarran snarled again. "Everything," he said in answer to my question, and lunged.

He was fast; his steel blazed. I parried easily and stepped aside. As his attack carried him past me, I whapped him on the ass with the flat of my blade. He spun around, his face contorted with rage.

With a yowl, he leaped at me, his sword weaving back and forth as he sought to hack away the gap between us. I backed up, parrying only when necessary. He pressed me hard, but his wind wasn't good. After another moment his attack faltered. At that instant I riposted, cut his cheek to the bone before stepping back again.

He lifted his free hand to his wound, gazed for a moment at the blood slicking his fingers before flicking it at me. It fell short. He didn't seem to realize that he could have lost an eye if I'd cared to take it.

"I'm going to enjoy carving you open," he growled.

"You aren't very smart are you?" I asked.

Again he attacked. This time I met him squarely. I blocked one blow in a clang of steel, riposted to cut him on the left shoulder. He swung at me again. I blocked again, riposted and cut him on the right. He screamed, threw himself upon me. I could have killed him but I caught his wrist, twisted his arm down using his own strength against him. I drew my sword very lightly across his throat, leaving a thin line of red behind, then pushed him away.

"Drop your sword and walk away and I'll let you live," I said.

His hand darted to his throat. He stared at me. This time he knew I could have finished him. He looked over at his fellows. "Kill him!" he screamed at them. "All of you! Kill this rucker."

I glanced at the others and shook my head at them. They did not seem eager to "kill" me. None of them moved. Looking back at the Nokarran, I tried one more time to spare his life.

"Lose the sword. Walk away. Catch a ride on another ship. *The Painted Maid* has no place for you anymore."

The tip of his blade dipped groundward. His shoulders slumped. I thought maybe he was going to listen. Then he kicked a chair at me and put everything he had into one last lunge with his sword.

I slapped the chair out of the air with my free hand, slid to one side to avoid his strike. My sword darted out as with a life and anger of its own. The tip took him in the throat, opened it in a gush of crimson. I stepped past him as he stumbled and went down. His blade clattered on the plank floor. His arm lifted, dropped again.

I walked over to the bar, sat my sword down on the scarred wood. "Another mead, if you have it, friend," I said to Drin.

He nodded his head, poured me a fresh mug. I placed another coppern down to go with the one still lying there.

"By Venghi's withered paps," he said. "You carved him like a roast."

"A roast might have had more sense," I replied. "He could have walked away."

"Sometimes all a man has is pride," he said.

I nodded.

Another of the pirates approached me, making sure to keep his hands far from his weapons. He was Vhichang, an avian race, and missing an eye. His beak was badly scarred. He reached out and placed four copperns on the bar.

"His next two are on us," he said, jerking his chin in my direction.

I glanced his way. "Thanks. I have worked up a thirst."

"Come sit with us," he said. "We can talk about passage aboard *The Painted Maid*." He chuckled. "The cost has gone way down."

CHAPTER TWENTY-FOUR

THE PAINTED MAID

Beneath the broken moon of Nimeru, we rowed out to *The Painted Maid*, the five remaining pirates from Drin's Tavern, and me. The pirates were singing. I was not. They'd had more mead. The Nokarran's body, we left behind. I'd paid Drin good coin to bury it, burn it, or whatever. Besides us, the boat carried supplies and a large, clanking sack that I'd also paid for.

As our boat nestled up to *The Painted Maid* like a nursing calf, a net was thrown over the side of the vessel. Supplies were handed up to willing hands on the ship. Then we started up the net ourselves. I climbed last over the rail and put my boots down on the plankings of the deck. It had been a good while since I'd travelled on a sea-going vessel, but the sensations were familiar. My legs quickly remembered how to compensate for the swaying motion.

Torches burned against the dark. Besides the salt air, I smelled pitch and smoke and the sweat of unwashed bodies. Rigging creaked; the tips of furled sails flapped languidly in the faint breeze. The ship itself groaned as it pulled against the anchor that chained it.

Someone must have noticed a change in the roster between those who had gone ashore, and those who returned. Most of the *Maid*'s complement of crew members seemed to be on hand and watching curiously as I climbed aboard. The crew was more numerous than one might expect on a sloop this size, but that was standard procedure for pirates. To forcefully board another vessel means you need more men on the attack than the other ship has on defense.

Jelvin, the one-eyed Vhichang who'd first made friendly overtures toward me, started to introduce me to the crew but was interrupted by a bellowing Nokarran who thrust his way through the crowd.

"Where is Dharus?" the Nokarran demanded. Dharus, I'd learned, was the name of the Nokarran I'd killed on shore.

Jelvin glanced at me. A warning flickered in his rosary bead eye before he looked back at the being who stood in front of him.

"I'm afraid, Khene, that Dharus chose to accost the wrong fellow." He nodded toward me. "It didn't work out w—"

"Ahh, get out of my way," the one named Khene bellowed. He shoved the much smaller Vhichang aside and turned on me. He stalked his way into my face and wrapped his big fists into the front of my shirt, shoving me back against the rail.

"Who by all the hells are you?" he demanded, spittle flying from his mouth. "Dharus was my friend."

I reached up and gripped Khene's wrists with my hands, began to exert pressure. For a moment, surprise rushed over the Nokarran's face. This one was as big as Dharus had been, and with no fat on him. I doubted he'd met many beings as strong as he. He redoubled his hold on my shirt, but I twisted his wrists and broke his grip. His look of surprise turned to one of incredulity as I pushed him slowly away from me.

"You're wrinkling the shirt, friend," I said. "And it's probably worth more than you are."

With a sudden, explosive oath, Khene jerked free of my grip and swung a brick-sized fist at my face. I slid the blow, grabbed him by the back of his head and slammed his forehead into the deck rail. He vented a half-hearted bellow. While he stood stunned, I grasped him by the back of his shirt and by the seat of his pants. He was heavy but I didn't let the strain show as I picked him up and threw him over the side into the drink. He made a very big splash.

I turned to gaze at the other crewmen. A few faces showed anger, but most looked either neutral or actually cheerful. It seemed that Khene the Nokarran wasn't any more popular aboard *The Painted Maid* than Dharus the Nokarran had been.

"Now," I said, brushing my hands together as if knocking off dust. "I felt badly for all you good fellows out here while some of us were ashore guzzling grog. So..." I reached down and hefted up the big sack I'd paid for, shaking it so that it clanked again. Untying the string holding it closed, I drew out one of many corked jugs of mead. "Drinks are on me."

Cheers met my words and in a moment the crowd pushed in close to take the jugs as fast as they could be handed out.

"Jelvin," a voice called.

The Vhichang stood not far from me and I followed his gaze as he looked up. *The Painted Maid* was a two masted vessel, lateen-rigged. Such ships had often been called war-sloops on Earth. The Captain's cabin on a ship like this stood at the stern, beneath what was called the poop deck. Jelvin was looking toward that deck, at a man who must be the *Maid*'s captain.

The Vhichang strode to the steps leading up to the poop deck and climbed them. He and the other man fell into conversation and I watched with half my mind while the crew continued to gather around and slap me on the back in appreciation of the gift of mead. After a bit, Jelvin beckoned and I managed to duck away from my new 'friends' to meet the man who would decide my immediate future.

The fellow nodded as I approached. I returned the gesture. He was not what I'd imagined. He stood of middling height and was slender. A neat beard framed his chin. His long, curly hair had once been blond but was graying. He wore no hat, but had on a brass-buttoned blue coat over a shirt of purple velvet. A rapier hung at his belt. It was not the fact that he was Human which surprised me. He looked almost "bookish," and certainly too mild mannered for this sort of crew.

"Captain Stefan," Jelvin said, introducing him to me. "And this is Baadon," he added, with a gesture in my direction.

I nodded again.

"Baadon," Stefan said by way of greeting.

"Captain."

Stefan looked at Jelvin. "You're my new first mate," he said. "Try to keep everyone from killing each other over that mead."

Jelvin nodded, left us.

"Join me," Stefan said.

I followed as the man led me to his cabin beneath the poop deck. He lit a lantern hanging by the door, took it with him as he entered the room. I had to stoop to join him. The cabin was bigger than expected. A table sat bolted to the floor roughly in the center of the room and Captain Stefan moved over to a chair next to it and sat down. He placed the lantern on the table to one side, and I sat across from him.

"So, Dharus challenged and you killed him," he said

"I offered to let him walk away. He wasn't capable of doing that."

"So Jelvin says. He was my First Mate, you know. Dharus that is."

"Not a terribly good one, I wager."

He studied me for a moment. "Indeed," he finally said. "It would not have been long before he and his bravos found a way to rid themselves of me. And for him to become Captain."

"Bravos? Such as the other Nokarran, Khene?"

"Yes. You'd best watch that one."

"Are there others I should watch as well?"

Dharus had a few friends aboard. Though perhaps cronies is a better term for them. I don't believe they shared any particularly positive feelings among themselves. Emig is an Ss'Korra. There's a human named Timbun. The few others don't matter much."

"And what happens if these few challenge me? What would the Captain of the ship say?"

"This Captain makes a point of not getting involved in the personal quarrels of his men. Unless it interferes with a raid, or with the safety of the ship."

I nodded, and understood. Captain Stefan didn't trust or like the men he'd named to me. He'd expected a mutiny from them soon. Now, he'd essentially given me permission to take care of them for him. I didn't mind being thusly used; I needed to ingratiate myself with this man. Of course, Captain Stefan didn't know me well either. I might turn out to be worse than what he was already dealing with. At the moment, though, making a deal with me probably seemed the best option available to him.

"So…Baadon. Jelvin says you fled the city of Karish just ahead of a rope."

"Not quite the complete story," I said. "I liberated a certain item and, as a result, some soldiers tried to poke holes in me with arrows. They succeeded only in poking holes in my saddle bird."

"And that's how you ended up at Drin's Landing. Conveniently, at the same time as we were visiting there."

I shrugged. "Looks to me like quite a few ships of your sort stop at Drin's Landing. Sheer coincidence that it happened to be yours on this particular night."

He nodded. "And now you want to become a member of my crew?"

"Actually, I was merely hoping to book passage to a more civilized clime. Drin's Landing lacks certain amenities I've become accustomed to."

"*The Painted Maid* is not a passenger ship," Stefan said.

"So I had surmised. And if becoming a member of your crew helps me eventually find a place to light, I'm quite willing to lend my services to you for the nonce."

"It's not quite that easy."

"Nothing ever is," I said. "But I take your words to mean that it's not just your decision."

"No."

I grinned. "Now you understand the free grog for your crew. You never know when you might need friends."

"I've got a fine crew. But it's not their decision either."

I had my opinions on his 'fine' crew but did not share them. "Who *does* make the decision?" I asked.

"There is a Council of Captains. A council of which I'm not a member. You are welcome to remain aboard the *Maid* for now. But when we return to base, your case will be looked into by the Council. They will give the yea or the nay."

"And what if it's nay?"

"You'll never leave the base again. Except perhaps as food for the sharks."

"A rather rigid system for what I've always heard referred to as the 'free' brotherhood."

"The only true freedom in this world comes in death," he said. "But I expect you know that."

"So I've been told. Can't say that I plan to test that theory anytime soon."

CHAPTER TWENTY-FIVE

A STRANGE INTERLUDE

We stepped out of his cabin, Captain Stefan and I. Across the deck, the Nokarran I'd thrown overboard had been fished out of the drink. Khene, his name was. He stood dripping, with several men around him. His gaze found mine and I felt fortunate not to burst into flames from his glare.

I'd half expected the fellow to attack again the moment he saw me; he didn't seem the patient type. But one of the men who'd watched me duel with Dharus in Drin's Tavern stood near Khene and appeared to be warning him about me. Reluctantly, it seemed, the Nokarran turned to disappear below decks into the crew's quarters, leaving a huge wet spot behind on the planks.

Near where Khene had stood, an Ss'Korra watched me closely. I imagined it to be Khene's crony, Emig. I studied him for a moment, immediately marking him as far more dangerous than the Nokarran. He was tall for his race, nearly six feet. His fur was long and almost black. He wore a rapier at his hip and carried himself like a swordsman. I finally acknowledged his stare with a faint smile. He returned it, though his was far more mocking.

Stefan, who had noticed our clashing gazes, spoke quietly from beside me. "Emig is very good with a blade. Don't underestimate him."

I glanced toward the captain. "I won't."

When I looked back, Emig was gone. If he'd meant to leave an impression, he'd succeeded. Stefan strode to the end of the poop deck, called down to Jelvin, his new First mate.

"If the supplies are stored, Mr. Jelvin. Get us underway. Up the coast at our best speed."

Jelvin raised a hand in acknowledgement before snapping out orders: "Up anchor. Man the sails. Prepare to hoist them."

Stefan nodded once to me and turned to reenter his cabin. I strode down the stairs to the main deck and paused beside Jelvin. Two men worked at the hand-cranked winch that was supposed to raise the anchor. It wasn't budging.

"We're hung up on something," one of the men called.

"Well unhang it!" Jelvin ordered.

Seeing where help was needed, I went over to add my strength on the crank. The thing still wouldn't budge. Jelvin came over himself to lend a hand.

"Throw your backs into it," he ordered, and we did.

Sweat popped out on my brow as the muscles corded along my back and arms. The wooden housing for the winch groaned with the pressure; the chain sang. But the crank began to move.

One turn. Two.

Trails of bubbles streamed up from the bottom, burst on the surface with a stench that made me think of swamps.

"The anchor's moving," one man crowed.

"But we're bringing something up with it," I added.

"Something dead or alive?" Jelvin asked.

"We'll find out soon enough," I said.

Jelvin called for archers to stand by just in case. I didn't blame him. I'd heard of laiths getting caught in an anchor chain. One of those monstrous sea-lizards could do serious damage to a ship this size. Especially if it were hurt and angry.

A blizzard of huge bubbles suddenly ruptured the surface. It sounded like a drowning giant. But the anchor crank began to turn more easily. The cross-shaped top of the anchor popped through the surface of the water, black and wet beneath the moonlight. Something hung on one of the great hooks. Mud streaked the thing, but in places it gleamed as if it had been painted. It had, I realized, as soon as I recognized it.

"What by the hells is it?" one man asked. "Looks like metal."

"Must be a piece of a sunken ship," Jelvin said.

A piece of a ship indeed, I thought. But not the kind these men suspected it of being.

Those who had been born to Talera would have no idea what they were seeing. I knew because I was from Earth and had been back to a modern Earth where such ships were common. What we were looking at was the wing of an airplane. Our anchor must have hooked on the plane where it lay half buried in sea-bottom muck. Our efforts at the crank had finally broken the wing free of the rest of the machine and dragged it up from its resting place.

An image could be seen painted on the wing—a white star against a dark background, with rectangular stripes on either side. It was the emblem of the United States air force. Someone other than me and my brother Bryce had come through a sphere gate from Earth. And it had been recently. I couldn't recognize the model of the plane from just this wing, but I didn't believe the thing had been in its grave long. There was very little rust on it.

The wing snapped in two as the anchor broached the surface. It sank back down into darkness; I watched it disappear. What of the pilot, I wondered? Had there been a crew? Had anyone made it out of the plane before it crashed? Were there other Earthmen alive here on Talera now? Or did they lie dead and sunken on the bottom of the sea just beneath the keel of our vessel?

It seemed unlikely that I'd ever find the answers to my questions.

CHAPTER TWENTY-SIX

VENOM AND STEEL

The bunk that once belonged to Dharus the Nokarran had become mine by right of victory in battle. Someone pointed it out to me in *The Painted Maid*'s crew quarters and I dropped a few items on top of it but decided not to sleep there. I wasn't that trusting.

Taking a blanket, I returned to the deck and made a pallet beneath the ship's boat. Such boats are always suspended a little bit above the deck to allow for drying. There was space enough for me to slip under, and for any little breeze that happened by to find me.

Though it was spring on Talera, it was quite a warm night this far south and no covers were needed. Certainly, this was not the most comfortable bed I'd ever slept in. It also wasn't the worst. I remembered, for example, the Lava Mines of Andertalen where, not long after first arriving on Talera, I'd served a stint as slave. I'd slept on stone for many weeks in that place while coated in my own sweat and grime as I toiled for the Klar.

At dawn, I arose and stretched and gazed around at the sea. Having studied the maps provided by the Indigo Llurns helped me know roughly where we were. We were sailing north toward the equator, though still a good ways south of it. The coast of the island of Karphal, where Drin's Landing lay, stood off to our starboard. Far to port, too far to see, would be the continent of Kotheriuhm.

Heading down to the crew quarters, I visited my bunk. My seemingly haphazard arrangement of things on the bunk had not been haphazard at all. Clearly, someone had messed with the bed but tried to hide their actions. I did not let my knowledge of that fact show as I pulled back the top blanket, but I was ready for anything. Good that I was. A coiled serpent struck viciously at me. I caught it behind the head with my left hand.

The night crew of the *Maid* was coming down to sleep. The day crew was up and moving about. By the light of lanterns burning along the center aisle of the quarters, many saw me catch the snake. Gasps of shock came. In an instant that emotion spread and the room fell quiet and still. Only the serpent moved, writhing and twisting to escape my grip. I didn't let it, and after another moment it coiled its glistening body around my arm and went still as well.

I did not recognize the snake's species—something like an Earth mamba perhaps. Its head was bright purple, its body a purplish black. As I squeezed the back of its head, its mouth opened, showing a sulfur-yellow on the inside. Two ivory fangs became visible, each dotted with a pinprick of venom.

"Well, well," I said, loudly. "Looks like someone picked out a pet for me."

A few ripples of nervous laughter greeted my words. I looked around and the ripples fell silent. Neither Khene nor Emig were in sight, but Timbun, the Human who was said to run with them, stood near the back of the room. His face looked bland and innocent, too bland when compared with the shock that still molded the faces of everyone else.

Remembering a recent bluff that Chalathar had run when he claimed to know a test for identifying shapeshifters, I decided to put on a little show for my new comrades. Lifting my left arm toward my face, I took a long, slow sniff along the snake's body. All I could smell was snake, but I wasn't going to let that stop me. Since no one in this crew had ever seen a being quite like me, they couldn't know what sensory feats I was capable of.

"Ah," I said. "Seems that I smell your previous owner on you."

A stir swept through the crew, all of whom were held rapt at the moment. I started down the center aisle between the bunks, stalking slowly while swinging my head from side to side, my nose up in the air as if questing for a betraying scent. Men shrank away from me. Fear and curiosity and disgust mingled on their faces.

I came to Timbun and stopped. That fellow had moved to stand behind his bunk. His pinched face was no longer bland and innocent. He looked terrified. I turned toward him, took a step forward. He blanched and pushed back against the bed behind him. He clearly wanted to run but still hoped somehow to bluff his way past this.

I leaned toward him and sniffed, then smiled broadly so that he could see my teeth. I'd had a chance by now to have a good look at the teeth that had so discomfited my brother, Bryce, when I'd smiled at him. They were large and white, triangular shaped with serrated edges. As Bryce had said, they made me look like a shark. They certainly didn't seem to comfort Timbun.

"There you are," I said to him. I nodded my head toward the snake that was still wrapped around my forearm. "I believe this is yours. You want him back?"

"I...I...I don't know what you're talking about," he stuttered. "I've never seen that thing before in my life."

"That's not what the smell says."

"The smell lies!"

I stopped smiling and let my eyes go cold. I reached out with my free hand and placed it on Timbun's shoulder. He flinched as if my touch burned him. From the corners of my eyes, I could see that others were looking speculatively at Timbun. I don't think any of them believed him. I didn't believe him.

"Leave him alone," a voice snapped.

I released Timbun and turned slowly. Emig, the Ss'Korra swordsman, stood staring at me. His hand rested lightly on the ornate hilt of his rapier. I took a sudden step toward him. His hand tightened convulsively on his weapon and his eyes narrowed. But he did not back up.

"You always interrupt conversations?" I asked.

He spat on the planks near my feet. "You come in here. You murder our First Mate. You shove people around. The Captain may tolerate it, but I won't. I think it's time you learned who your betters are."

I spread my arms wide, still holding the snake in my left hand. "Ready anytime you are."

"Up on deck," he said. "Now!" He spun on his heels and stalked out.

I followed the Ss'Korra up the stairs. Everyone else followed me and spread out along the rails so as to leave the central area of the deck open. Such would be our battle circle. Emig drew his sword, then unhooked his sheath from the scabbard hooks on his belt and tossed it aside. Again I followed suite, and our blades glimmered under the green sun.

"What goes here?" a voice called, and Jelvin the Vhichang stepped into the space between Emig and me.

"A private matter," Emig snapped at Jelvin. "In accordance to the Brotherhood's rules. You can't interfere."

Jelvin glanced toward me. I nodded at him. He shook his head but stepped aside. I looked around at the crowd. Neither Timbun nor the Nokarran named Khene were visible to me. But they were not my immediate concern. The warrior who stood in front of me was my concern. I lifted my sword, gave him a brief salute. He did not return it.

I waited. The sun was bright overhead, though it was early yet. The sea breeze filled the sails with salt air and *The Painted Maid* glided swiftly through the waves. Only a gentle rocking troubled my balance. I didn't mind; I'd fought on the decks of moving ships before.

Still, I waited. After a moment, Emig began to frown. Finally, he spoke:

"Well, throw the snake over the side so we can begin."

I smiled at him with a great showing of teeth. "I've taken a liking to it. I think I'll keep it."

"Don't be foolish. You can't fight a duel while holding a snake in one hand."

"I don't believe the rules of sword fights address that issue," I said.

"Curse you!" he said.

He looked toward Jelvin and received only a shrug of feathered shoulders.

"A private matter," Jelvin said. "As you proclaimed."

Emig snarled but came stalking forward. I'd marked a line where one deck plank met another. At the instant Emig crossed that line, he lunged forward with his sword out. I parried. Sparks flew as our steel clashed and rebounded.

Emig straightened, stalked around me in a circle. I turned slowly to keep my face toward his. He launched a fresh attack, feinting with a lunge, then spinning right with his sword sweeping around in a tight arc. I ignored the feint, parried the real attack. He spun back to the left. His sword flashed; I parried it again.

He didn't pause, as many swordsmen would have done, but drove in hard, his sword high and beating down against my blade. Our swords were very closely matched, almost exactly the same length, with his a touch thinner and lighter. But I was taller than he was and a high line attack would not work against me. He must have realized this at the same instant, for he dropped his point of attack and came at me with a fresh flurry of blows. I backed up, parrying. He was good; twice his sword tip nearly nicked me—but did not.

The inevitable pause came—on his part. I did not pause. I thrust my left arm toward him, as if about to hurl the snake in his face. He shied violently, as I expected, more afraid of venom than of steel. In the next instant, I lunged with my sword out, the blade a silver blur.

Emig was very good. He twisted wildly to one side. It saved his life but not his blood. The tip of my sword razored into his left side, cutting all the way to his ribs. He cried out and leaped convulsively backward. My sword came free of his wound. A spurt of crimson followed.

I paused. Emig clapped his left hand over his wound, then brought it up to see his palm all red. I lifted the tip of my sword to my nostrils and let the Ss'Korra watch me take a long, heady whiff of his blood. I didn't like the smell of blood, but he didn't know that. I showed him my teeth again.

"Vhish!" he cursed me. "Stugah dung! Krutt!"

"In a dhorrin or so," I said in a calm voice, "you'll bleed to weakness. If you plan to show me how to respect my betters, you best do it quickly."

He snarled, launched a blazing attack far swifter than anything he'd shown before. This time I did not back up. This time we met toe to toe. Our blades rang a discordant symphony. Sparks sleeted. Sunlight splintered from our steel.

I heard his breath rasping in his throat. His whole side was sodden with blood. Splatters rained the deck. But he did not slow, did not step back. I knew then what was coming. I didn't need to see the momentary flash of his eyes as he glanced beyond my shoulder. Nor did I need to hear the footsteps that suddenly battered the deck behind me.

I flung myself into a crouch to my left. Someone shouted "Watch out!" Emig's sword sang through the air above me. A war-axe smashed downward from behind me into the deck where I'd stood an instant before.

Khene held the axe; he was bent over with the force of his blow. And before the Nokarran could jerk the axe-head free of the deck, I stabbed upward and back with my sword and put six inches of steel through this throat.

The force of Emig's swing had carried him a step too far beyond me. He tried to turn back in my direction, and I reached up and stuck the head of the snake right into the bloody wound in his side and let go.

Emig dropped his sword and screamed. His hands suddenly scrabbled at his side, grabbing for the snake. He grasped it around the body, still screaming as he pulled it out of the wound. But he didn't have control over the front half of it. It whipped its wedge-shaped head backward, then struck him squarely in the chest just over the heart. I saw the gleam of fangs sink deep.

Almost instantly, the Ss'Korra's face tightened into a rictus. His whole body went rigid. He swayed, toppled backward with a thud. The snake tore its way free of his dying clasp and coiled into a venomous threat on his chest. The threat wasn't necessary. No one was getting close to the creature after seeing how swiftly its poison worked.

Still hunched in a crouch, I glanced away from Emig's staring eyes and toward my other attacker, Khene. After swinging his axe down at me, he'd been leaning over when my sword pierced his throat. Only seconds had passed and the blade remained imbedded in his neck. A trickle of blood wicked out around the steel, but Khene himself had not moved. His eyes were glazed with the coming of death.

As I watched, a fist-thick mass of blood pushed the Nokarran's lips apart and drooled out. I felt Khene's weight pressing against my blade and rose quickly to my feet, my sword coming free of flesh with a tiny snicking sound. Khene fell face forward, booming the deck when he hit.

It was so quiet aboard *The Painted Maid* that I could hear the slow drip, drip of blood from the tip of my sword onto the deck planking. I glanced around at the crowd. Shock twisted every face. These were hardened men, pirates all. They'd expected death but nothing quite like what they'd seen.

Now, I glimpsed Timbun in the crowd, that ally of Khene and Emig. Fear tore away the shock on his face when he saw me looking at him. He tried to dodge backward through the crew but several men caught him and hurled him out into the open space with me and the bodies of the slain. He shied away from the corpses, fell to his knees.

"Please, please," he begged. "It was them. Not me. They made me do it. Made me put the snake in your bed. I didn't want to. Please don't kill me!"

I walked toward him. He gave a little bleat of terror but did not try to run. There was nowhere for him to go. He lowered his head. His whole body shook.

"Look at me," I demanded.

His shaking intensified but he looked up. Tears and snot stained his face. I lifted my sword very slowly, wiped the blood of his former friends off onto his shoulders, first the left, then the right.

"I won't kill you," I said. "But I won't have you on this ship with me. You'll have to swim for it."

He glanced toward the railing. The shore of Karphal made a distant gray-green haze to starboard.

"But. But the water," he said. "There's…things in it. Laiths. Other things."

"You'll have to take your chances with the water, or with my sword."

He nodded, wiped his eyes and mouth. Climbing slowly to his feet, he moved toward the railing, his feet clopping on the deck. Once, he looked back at me, as if seeking for pity. I didn't offer him any. He wiped his face again, kicked off his boots and dove cleanly over the side of the ship. I watched him go under and surface quickly again. He came up swimming strongly and it seemed likely he'd make it to shore.

"Oh, Timbun!" a voice called.

It was Jelvin who spoke. And in the water, Timbun paused and looked back toward the *Maid*. A fragment of hope spread its way across his face.

"Better swim a little faster," Jelvin yelled at the fellow. "I think your pet wants to return to your bosom."

Jelvin reached out with an oar, scooped the snake off Emig's chest and flung it over the ship's railing into the sea. The reptile immediately began carving s's through the water in the direction of the shore. I didn't think it had any interest in Timbun, who was between it and a safe haven, but Timbun didn't know that. He gave a strangled shriek, turned and began to flail madly against the waves as he tried to escape.

Jelvin laughed, as did some of the others. I only turned away, toward the steps leading down to the crew's quarters. Captain Stefan stood there. I could tell by his face that he'd seen the whole thing. Other crewmen realized it too and again quiet swept the ship. Everyone watched the captain.

Stefan focused his gaze first on me, then looked beyond me at the others. "Throw these bodies overboard," he said. "And get this deck swabbed clean. I want this ship ready for action when we have to fight someone other than our own. There's gold yet to be made on this voyage."

He turned and stalked off.

CHAPTER TWENTY-SEVEN

WHITE SAILS ON THE GLIMMERING SEA

Despite Captain Stefan's promise that there was gold to make on our voyage, no chance of making any appeared to us over the next week. By day we crossed a gentle sea with scarcely a cloud in the sky. The wind was steady but weak. It moved us at no great speed. No sails other than our own showed on any horizon. At night the four moons of Talera paraded overhead, and no lights appeared on shore or over the water. We sailed on, up the coast of Karphal and across the Narrow Sea to the continent of Kotheriuhm, and down the coast there.

At noon on the sixth day after boarding *The Painted Maid*, I leaned on the railing next to Jelvin, the first mate. With Khene and Emig dead, and Timbun gone, all had been peaceful. I'd slept well in my new bunk, and though I was the newest member of a crew of pirates, no one wanted to hassle me. I suppose killing an enemy with a venomous reptile on your first day cements one's reputation as someone to leave alone.

"I take it, there *are* ships that sail this sea?" I asked Jelvin dryly as we looked out over the empty waves.

"There are," he replied. "But not many. These aren't prime hunting grounds for such as we."

I frowned. "Then why are we hunting here?"

He gazed at me with his one eye, and answered my question with another question. "What do you think of Captain Stefan?"

I shrugged. "He seems a decent sort."

He nodded. "Exactly. And therein lies the problem."

I also nodded. "I see."

"Six captains run the Red Brotherhood. There's another twenty-five or so who sail under the Skull Flag. The Six and their cronies take the best hunting for themselves. The captains and the crews who aren't tight with the Six get the leavings."

"How does one get 'tight' with the Six?" I asked.

"You sell them your services. You pledge to fight under *their* flag. That means you give them a share of everything you take. It's made all of them rich. But they make sure you get assigned to prime waters so you have a chance to get rich too."

"And if you hunt where you're not assigned…."

Jelvin's small beak opened, his tongue showing scarlet behind it. It was a Vhichang smile. He also ran a finger across his throat, a universal sign that everyone recognizes.

"So Stefan won't pledge his services," I said. "Any idea why?"

Jelvin shrugged his feathered shoulders. "There's three other captains like him. All too stubborn, I guess, to want to take orders. I think, too, that Captain Stefan doesn't much care for the way the Six handle their affairs. Or at least how most of them do."

"What do you mean?"

Jelvin glanced up toward the poop deck, where Stefan leaned against the rail and gazed off across the sea through a spyglass.

"The Captain knows that piracy is bloody work. Sometimes you have to kill. But he doesn't kill unless he has to. He ransoms prisoners. Or just lets 'em go. He won't abide no rape or torture. He don't hurt young ones. Or allow 'em to be hurt."

"So the Six think he's soft."

Jelvin bobbed his head. "I imagine that's why they made sure Dharus and Khene were on Stefan's crew. I figure they were planning to get rid of Stefan and put one of their bully boys in command of the *Maid*. You did the Captain a favor getting rid of that bunch. By all the hells, you did every one of us a favor."

"And has no one ever lifted a hand to break the Six's monopoly on the Brotherhood?"

Jelvin's one yellow eye focused hard on me. "I wouldn't advise you to get any ideas. The Six have got the numbers, sure. But that ain't all they've got on their side."

"What else?"

He spat. "Well, you see, the Six ain't exactly unfettered themselves. I don't know what kind of deal they have set up, but they're allies with some powerful folks on an island called Priminiphal, which is east of here. Rumor is, one of those allies is an Asadhie sorcerer. And I've seen enough weird things to believe it."

I tried to maintain an outward calm. Here was my first independent verification that what the Indigo Llurns suspected about the pirates was true. They served an Asadhie, indirectly at least. Maybe I could find out which one, although it required caution. Jelvin seemed friendly enough but I wasn't willing to bet my life on that friendliness.

"Asadhie!" I exclaimed. "Always figured that for a myth."

"No myth," Jelvin replied in his raspy voice. He shrugged. "At least there's sorcery involved. I've seen it. There's at least one powerful wizard on Priminiphal. Maybe more. I couldn't tell you if that one is really an ancient Asadhie, or if he's just masquerading. But he's dangerous and he backs the Six. He's got an army with him, too."

"What kind of sorcery have you seen?" I tried to sound skeptical.

Jelvin glanced at me sharply, then rubbed his scarred beak. "I've seen beings appear out of nowhere. Seen 'em disappear again. First there's nothing. Then a mist forms. Beings step out of it—or things that no one can name. I've seen a gray powder that burns hotter than any lamp oil or candle. And if you coop it up, it gets angry and explodes."

What hair I had stood erect. I couldn't hide it from Jelvin and didn't try. I only hoped he'd take it as a normal and healthy fear of the uncanny. The mist he'd described, the beings appearing and disappearing, had to mark sphere gates opening and closing. That definitely meant an Asadhie presence. But more frightening to me than the gates was the 'gray powder.' Jelvin had to be talking about gunpowder.

Vohanna had stolen the secret of gunpowder from men of Earth, from people I'd known. She'd tortured and murdered those men, and I'd hoped she'd died before passing the secret on to any other Asadhie. But now? Did Jelvin's words mean that Vohanna had handed the knowledge of gunpowder to others? Perhaps to her husband, Vessoth? If so, Talera was in even greater danger than I'd feared.

"Dahh!" I cursed. "Glad not to have seen that. So does this…sorcerer have a name?"

Jelvin shook his head. "Not really. Not that I've heard. Well, sometimes members of the Six call him 'The Bull.'"

Kamrack the Bull, I thought, and elation swept me. I *was* on the right track. The elation crashed. If Kamrack had been joined on Priminiphal by Vessoth, and if together they'd gained the knowledge of gunpowder, I had to move more swiftly than had been possible so far.

"Sails, ho!" a voice called excitedly.

I glanced up, startled. Our lookout in the crow's nest was pointing off to our southeast. I gazed in that direction but could see nothing yet.

"Finally," Jelvin said. He seemed happy at the prospect of action.

We both turned to look toward Captain Stefan as he called up to the lookout: "One ship or more?"

"One," the pirate called back. "A three-masted vessel. Square-hulled. Five degrees to port. Can't see the flag yet."

"Square-hulled!" Jelvin exclaimed. "Almost certainly a merchant vessel."

Captain Stefan was busy trying to locate the vessel with his spyglass. His own excitement was clear.

"I see the flag now," the lookout called. "White on green." The fellow lowered his own spyglass. "Fueire's Hold," he finished.

"Krutt!" Jelvin exclaimed.

"What?" I asked.

"Fueire's Hold. It's a city well south of here on Kotheriuhm. We don't see many of their ships this far north."

"So? Are they not merchants?"

"They can be. They've probably got plenty of goods aboard for the likes of us. But Fueire's Hold is a theocracy. Most of their sailors are priests of their religion."

"Priests? And that's a concern? Most priests I know aren't exactly warriors."

"You don't know these priests. Fueire is a war-god. His worshippers are fanatics. They won't give up without a fight. We'll probably have to kill most of them."

"Ah." I glanced again toward Captain Stefan. "What do you think the Captain will do?"

"We've been a long time without taking a prize," Jelvin said. "I'm not sure the Captain has any choice about trying for this one."

Stefan lowered his glass, called out so that all of us could hear. "Helmsman! Make a turn to port. I want to cross that ship's bow. The rest of you! Raise the flag. And make ready for war!"

I heard men cheering at the prospect of battle. I heard a snapping sound at the main mast and looked up to see the Skull Flag unfurl. It was black as midnight, black as Rannon's hair. And like the Jolly Roger of Earth's pirates, it was marked in the center with a white skull, although no crossed bones lay beneath it.

The skull itself was not human.

CHAPTER TWENTY-EIGHT

BENEATH THE SKULL FLAG

Jelvin had claimed that the ship from the city of Fueire's Hold would be carrying warrior priests who worshipped a warrior god. Despite that, as soon as they saw our black flag emblazoned with a Bane's skull, they tried to run. I could understand the urge. The Bane is a horrific monster, the offspring of a demon and a ghost. Its skull is gorilla shaped, though flattened on top. Four sharply pointed horns arise at the four corners of the skull, and tusks extend from its lower jaw to the level of the eye sockets.

Such would not be a comforting image to see coming at you across the waves, especially when one knows that it means pirates. So, our intended victims fled. We followed after, and steadily closed the gap.

Their ship was bigger than ours but nowhere near as swift or maneuverable. Nor were they as well armed. *The Painted Maid* carried two ballista on the poop deck and two more on the foredeck. These were much like giant crossbows and were mounted on swivels. Each fired four arrows at a time; these were sheathed with iron, with heads of serrated steel and weighing some twelve pounds each.

We weren't in range to use the ballistas yet. We crowded on sail until *The Painted Maid* swept after the other ship like a race horse closing on the finish line. Soon, I could read the name of our prey inked in black letters across their stern—*Fueire's Whisper*. There would be no whispering when our ships came together.

Men in white robes stood at the stern of *Fueire's Whisper*. They were Human men, tall men. Their heads were shaved and they wore bamboo hats against the sun. They certainly looked like monks, but swords and axes were belted around their waists and many carried crossbows. Some of the crossbowmen assayed a shot. The bolts fell short, though it would not be long before we were in range.

Captain Stefan had abandoned his habitual post on the poop deck and moved to the foredeck where he could more easily measure the distance between us and the prize he hoped to seize. Now, he called out an order.

"Issue shields!"

Jelvin touched my arm, then motioned several others to follow him. We rushed below decks. Behind the crew quarters, a door opened on the *Maid's* armory. Bales of arrows were piled there, along with war-axes and swords by the dozens. Shields hung in stacks on the walls. We seized these, dragged them down. I grabbed a lance as well and we returned to the deck with our goods.

Pirates gathered around as I handed out shields left and right. These were not the heavy, oval-shaped iron shields of the north, but smaller and rounded and made of thickly interwoven wicker. An axe or a sword could hack through them with half a dozen bold strokes, but they'd serve to block crossbow bolts. And so they did as we came within range of the *Whisper* and enemy bolts began to fall upon us like a hard rain.

Even under that barrage, we closed upon our prey. Where the enemy ship passed, salt droplets sprayed back upon us. I tasted them, licked them from my lips. We were running straight up behind the Fueirean vessel and I did not understand our Captain's intent in doing so. It meant that we had to fight their wake. That slowed us down. And, we could never board at the stern, which was the highest portion of their ship. Then it all become clear.

"Forward ballistas fire!" Stefan shouted.

The *Fueire's Whisper* was guided by a massive steering oar that extended down the left side of the ship's stern. When our ballista fired, the big arrows shredded that oar and the enemy ship immediately lost its ability to maneuver.

"Hard to starboard!" Stefan shouted, and our helmsmen yanked the wheel to the right. We crossed out of the *Whisper's* wake and pulled up beside her.

Stefan called out another command: "Aft ballistas fire!"

I could see more of the Fueire monks standing at the starboard railing of their ship. Crossbow bolts thudded into the deck all around me. I heard one pirate yelp in pain. Then our aft ballistas released and their arrows shattered the railing of the *Whisper* into kindling, mowing down the men standing behind it.

"Hard to port," Stefan screamed. "Prepare the nets! Brace for impact!"

All around me, pirates had been running to and fro about unfamiliar tasks. I'd just tried to stay out of the way. But now men grabbed at railings and masts for holds, and I suddenly saw the well-practiced plan behind the apparent chaos.

The Painted Maid ploughed into the side of *Fueire's Whisper*. The ships ground together, planks shrieking like the damned. Water sprayed high. I hadn't heard the ballistas being reloaded but they fired again. This time they shot grappling hooks with nets attached.

The hooks arched up and over the *Whisper's* rail; the nets unfurled behind them. The hooks struck deck and grabbed hold. The nets stretched taut, and there lay our road into the heart of the enemy.

"Drop shields!" Stefan screamed. "Follow me!"

I saw the Captain whip free his sword and leap onto the nets as our two ships butted against each other. A wild, roiling cry surged up from the throats of the pirates all around me. They charged after their captain. I hurled my own war-shout at the sky, threw the shield off my arm, rushed the net.

We swarmed up and over the *Whisper's* destroyed railing. My boots found the deck and I drew my sword left handed. My right hand still held the lance taken from the *Maid's* armory. The planks at my feet were littered with bodies clad in robes of stained white wool. Blood and gore splashed the scene. But the *Whisper's* crew wasn't finished. They came howling upon us. We met them with our own violence.

My heart pounded; blood sang in my ears. Fear and courage thickened the air. I smelled sweat and blood, salt and iron. Every color was intense, every sensation magnified, every cell alive. By the gods, I joyed in it.

A big man with a black axe charged toward me. I speared him through the chest, yanked the lance free again as he screamed and fell. To my left, Jelvin fought hard to keep from being forced back over the railing by two men. I spun toward him, lanced one fellow through the side. Crimson gouted from the wound.

The injured man twisted wildly, tearing the lance free of my grip as he pitched over the rail into the sea. I switched my sword from left hand to right, blocked a blow from another fellow's blade and riposted. Steel shrieked against steel before my sword daggered into him. He fell away, crying out; I knew not if he lived.

Stefan was working his way forward along the deck toward a thick cluster of warrior monks. The Captain of the *Whisper* fought there. He was a whirlwind, a dervish. His rapier glittered and gleamed as it leaped and struck. I shouted for Jelvin to follow me, began carving my way toward Stefan. Foes got in my way; I hacked them down.

The *Whisper's* captain was a grizzly of a man. He'd stripped off his robe, fought naked save for a loincloth. His guard tried to close around him as he engaged a pirate. He killed the pirate, shouted his guards away. His eyes were wild, rolling. I could see the berserk coming upon him. He lifted the axe in his hands, screamed something at the sky that must have been an exhortation to his god. He charged directly at Stefan.

Stefan met him, and in that first instant of wild battle had his hands more than full. And now more of the defending monks came rushing in to try and overwhelm Stefan with sheer numbers. He was swarmed, surrounded. For a moment I couldn't see him. Then I reached his side. Jelvin arrived as well. We hammered those monks back, tore them open.

More foes fell upon us. The quarters became too close to ply our blades. One man sought to grapple with me. I twisted his arm and broke it, smashed in his teeth with my sword hilt. He went reeling back. A fist struck my shoulder, another blasted into my jaw, wearing a ring that gouged flesh. In the burning present, I could barely feel it. But the act of it angered me. I snarled, lashed out in a fury with fists and boots. Men fell away beneath those blows.

We could not be moved. Jelvin, Stefan, and me. We held against all odds—if only long enough for more pirates to surge around us. Those reinforcements ended the battle. For another moment, I cast wildly about for fresh foes. Finally, I realized there were none, and all the sounds of combat had stilled.

I turned to look for Stefan. He stood wearily in the midst of corpses. One of them had been the commander of the ship we'd just captured. Stefan's face and clothes were sluiced with crimson. I took a quick step toward him before realizing that almost none of the gore belonged to him. One shoulder of his coat was torn, and scarlet seeped through his shirt there. A cut on his left cheek still wept. Other than that, he appeared unharmed. The rest of the blood came from his foes.

Jelvin crowed happily and slapped his captain on the back. Stefan looked around, seemingly surprised to find our short war over. He grinned, a bigger grin than I'd ever seen him wear. His teeth glistened white against the battle grime that coated his face.

Other pirates gathered around as well to congratulate their captain. With the removal of the treasonous elements from his crew, and after the brilliant victory he'd just won, Stefan seemed to have cemented his leadership of this band of rowdies. In doing so, he'd cemented my own position aboard *The Painted Maid*.

Jelvin drifted over to me.

"Mild mannered!" I said to him, nodding toward Captain Stefan and echoing the way the First Mate had spoken of the man only a short while earlier.

Jelvin shrugged, flashed me a Vhichang smile. He turned toward Stefan and called out. "By the gods, Captain, we're going to have to nickname you, 'The Bloody.'"

Stefan's gaze found mine before settling on Jelvin. "I was inspired by Saar Baadon's use of a snake for a weapon," he said.

Laughter followed his words

Then Captain Stefan put his smile away. "All right," he said. "We've got a lot to do. Someone cut the ships apart. Let's get the sails down here until we can replace the steering oar. I want any prisoners searched and ready to be interrogated. We'll also need this deck cleared before we sail our prize back home.

"And let's just see," he added, raising his voice, "if there's any treasure to be had."

Cheers cracked against the sky.

CHAPTER TWENTY-NINE

TREASURES

While his crew prepared *Fueire's Whisper* for sailing and searched the decks and below for treasure, Stefan sought out the quarters of the *Whisper's* captain. Jelvin and I accompanied him. If there were any significant wealth aboard this ship, that seemed the most likely place to find it.

The dead Captain's quarters were much bigger than Stefan's cubbyhole aboard *The Painted Maid*, but still smaller than expected. The bed was an ascetic's cot with a straw mattress and no pillows or blankets. On a wooden table at the foot of the bed, an acrid incense still burned in a small clay censer. Next to it lay a map of Karphal Isle with the city of Karish marked with an X—no doubt, this ship's destination.

The table also held an alembic, which seemed to contain only water. A few brass sailing instruments lay scattered about. The only thing in the room that could be called a decoration was a wooden replica of a temple mounted against the wall behind the cot. I assumed it represented some major worship site for the god Fueire.

Jelvin leaned down to look under the cot, the last place in the room that we couldn't already see. With an eager, "Ha," he pulled out a typical sailor's chest ensconced there. When he threw it open, it held only papyrus scrolls tied with yellow cord.

"Dahh!" Stefan said. "Nothing!"

Jelvin sighed. He picked up a few of the scrolls, stood holding them with a look of distaste on his face. "Maybe some of these are worth something," he said. "To the right people, anyway."

"They're yours," Stefan replied, and turned to go.

"Wait," I said. "There's something wrong here."

Stefan looked back toward me. "Wrong? Wrong with what?"

"Wrong with the cabin," I said.

Both Jelvin and Stefan stared at me. Frowns marked their faces. I ignored them, strode over to the wall where the temple replica hung. Someone had gone to a lot of trouble to create this model. It was made of wood but scored and painted to resemble the stone that the original was probably built from. It showed a building that was almost square but with rounded corners. Windows had been represented with black lacquer. The peaked roof had been painted jade green.

Just in front of the temple doors stood an obelisk, also painted green and surrounded by a reflecting pool done in blue lacquer. The obelisk was slightly off kilter. That imbalance didn't match the care taken with the rest of the model. I drew my sword, stepped back, used the tip of the blade to press down on the obelisk. A snick occurred. Just to the left of the cot, a straight, thin crack appeared in the wood-plank wall.

I glanced at Jelvin and Stefan. Jelvin's one orange-yellow eye lit with eagerness. Stefan continued to frown.

"Be careful," he said.

I nodded. Keeping my distance, I inserted the tip of my sword into the crack and applied pressure. Just as I became afraid that my blade would break, something gave. A hidden door popped open in the wall. From holes all around that door, spears clashed together, then slid back apart. Their tips were coated with a clear grease that no doubt indicated some kind of venom. Anyone forcing that door open with their body would have gotten stabbed in the face and chest, and been poisoned for the privilege.

"Trapped," Stefan said.

"That means something inside worth protecting," Jelvin added.

I nodded to both their comments.

"What made you guess it was here?" Jelvin asked.

"Looking at the cabin from outside," I said, "it should have been bigger. Plus, the obelisk on the model. The model was so perfect but the obelisk wasn't straight. I figured it must move."

I stepped forward to peer into the opening behind the door. Stefan joined me, with Jelvin alongside. We saw a small, irregularly shaped room that mostly followed the contours of the ship's bow. Lipped shelves lined both sides of the room and were packed with small jeweled casks, candlesticks of silver, strings of pearls, and cloth of gold.

In the center of the cramped space sat another kind of treasure. She was a Human girl of perhaps ten or eleven years, with the baby fat still in her cheeks. Her eyes were dark, her hair curly and even darker. She wore a shift of white linen but hanging behind her was a child-sized wedding gown of silk, lace, and pearls. Anger clenched my fists; my lips curled back from my teeth. The girl saw those teeth and shrank away from me.

Cursing my mistake, I stepped back from the door and let Stefan go in front of me. He squatted facing the girl, tried at least two different languages without success. She just kept shaking her head.

"Fetch Korhd down here," the Captain told Jelvin. "The people of Fueire's Hold speak Fensai. Korhd knows that tongue. Or enough to get by anyway."

Jelvin nodded, went quickly to carry out his order.

"An arranged marriage?" I asked Stefan. "Or slavery?"

A humorless smile quirked the corner of his lips. "Much the same thing in this case, I imagine."

I nodded. "Good thing for the Fueire Captain that you already killed him."

He gazed hard at me. "Fueire's Hold is not only a theocracy but a patriarchy as well. Women might as well be slaves there. Of course, there are plenty of other places where that is also true. And some where it is the reverse."

"I do not like slavers of any stripe," I said. "But when they traffic in children…." I could not finish and changed the focus of our conversation. "What will you do with this child? With the prisoners? The ship?"

Stefan chuckled. "Well, I'm not going to sell her. I wouldn't want you for an enemy after what you did to Emig.

I smiled thinly at his jape.

Stefan continued. "Once we can talk to her, I'll find out what she thinks of all this. And what she wants to do."

"She'll probably want to return home," I protested. "She doesn't know there's anything else."

Stefan shrugged. "*Is* there anything else? A pirate ship is certainly no place for a girl child. We can't just drop her off along the coast either. She'd be enslaved again within a day. And if we take her to Karish, whoever was at the other end of this bargain," he gestured toward the wedding dress, "will not have changed his mind."

I gave a long sigh.

"As for the prisoners," he said. "I might normally try to ransom them, but that's a risky proposition. And with the treasure in this room, I don't think the men will care too much about a few more handfuls of gold. There's likely a decent cargo in the hold below as well. That'll add more coin. We'll probably drop the crew survivors along the coast of Kotheriuhm. They'll find their way home from there, though it'll take time. We'll keep the ship."

"You plan to turn it into a pirate vessel?"

Stefan shook his head. "It's no good for that. Too big and slow. We'll sell it on Priminiphal. The Lords there like ships such as this. Good for carrying cargo and troops."

My heart skipped as excitement grabbed me. Priminiphal was my target. It was where Kamrack the Bull had established his empire, and probably where Vessoth now laired. Jelvin had already confirmed for me that a relationship existed between the pirates and the 'Lords' of Priminiphal. Now, Stefan had suggested a possible plan for how I might legitimately visit that island. If we were to sell *Fueire's Whisper* on Priminiphal, maybe I could be aboard the ship when we did.

Striving to control an excitement that could give me away, I pretended to ignorance. "The Lords of Priminiphal? What or where is Priminiphal?"

"It's an island a good way east of here. A rather unusual island. It moves. Though, the sailing masters there make sure to put out navigation markers for ships coming in."

"The pirates do a lot of trade with Priminiphal?"

Stefan nodded. "They buy from us, and we don't raid them. It would be pretty stupid to raid them anyway. They have a huge army and most of their ruling class seems to consist of sorcerers."

I snapped my fingers as if I'd suddenly remembered something. "Jelvin told me about that," I said. "I'd forgotten. He said the Six captains who run the pirate Brotherhood were allied with Priminiphal. He also said the ruler of that place was rumored to be an Asadhie."

Stefan arched an eyebrow. "Surely you don't believe that! Their ruler is a god?"

I shrugged. "Maybe not a god. Maybe just a very powerful sorcerer. How would you tell the difference if you met one?"

The Maid's captain nodded. "I see your point."

"I'd like to see this Priminiphal," I said. "A drifting island full of sorcerers. How about when we take this ship there to sell, you let me be in the crew?"

Stefan studied me for a moment. "Most of my men don't much like going there. I'd be happy to have you. But, ultimately, it's not just my decision."

"Who else's?"

"The Six have to approve you as a member of the Brotherhood first. I'll vouch for you. I'm sure Jelvin will. But there's a test you have to pass? To prove yourself."

"What kind of test?"

"I'm not allowed to tell."

CHAPTER THIRTY

LOVE AND HATE

When the pirate named Korhd entered the secret treasure room and began to speak to the girl in her native Fensai, she started to chatter wildly and kept pointing at me. I left the room rather than upset her further, and went out onto the deck. Jelvin soon joined me. His presence seemed to have troubled her as well.

Jelvin went away after a moment to see about getting the *Whisper* ready to sail. As First Mate, he'd be placed in charge of the Fueirean prize. I had no such duties so simply leaned on the rail while waiting for Stefan.

It was a quiet moment. The bloody battle we'd fought for this ship only a short while before seemed very distant. The sea moved gently beneath us. The rigging creaked and the planks groaned softly. A school of silver fish raced past us through the waves. The sun shone warmly, and though it was still green, a weak golden cast had begun to tint it. Summer was coming to Talera. I took a deep breath of the salt air, willed myself to calmness. It wasn't easy, despite the peacefulness of my current surroundings.

The cabin door banged open and Stefan came out to lean on the rail beside me.

"You were able to communicate with her?" I asked.

He looked up at me. "Yes."

"And?"

"Once she realized we weren't going to hurt her or sell her, she made her wishes clear. She wanted…. No," he shook his head, "she *demanded* that we return her home. Apparently the marriage that was arranged for her is with one of her people's ambassadors to Karish. I knew the Fueireans had an enclave there."

I sighed. "She doesn't even know what freedom means. We should give her a chance to learn it."

"Aye, perhaps. But if we decide her future for her, how are we better than those who have done it for her already? Besides, we have no safe place for her."

"She won't be truly safe in the bosom of her people either," I said. "She's a commodity to them. She could be taught a better way."

Stefan glanced at me again, then away. His voice was soft when it came. "It would take a lot of teaching. What she was chattering about when you left. Korhd translated it for me. She was ordering us to remove you and Jelvin. She said that you were both vile, that you were contaminating the air she breathed. Fueire's Hold is a Human only city. They don't allow other races. They hate anyone who is not like them, and from speaking with this child, it seems that hate is acquired early."

He straightened, nodded at me and strode off. I remained leaning on the rail a bit longer. My thoughts were of Rannon as I remembered our rooms in Jystral Castle, in the rose-stuccoed city of Timmuzz, the capital of Nyshphal. I remembered how Rannon had first shown me those rooms, and how one had clearly been decorated for the children she hoped we would have.

I thought of how children are taught—not so much by words as by deeds. My parents had never *told* me to judge others on the basis of actions rather than appearance. It was just something they did themselves.

I thought of the little girl on this ship, who hated and feared me for not looking like her. And yet, my original form had been as Human as hers. I dwelt now in a different body and it had changed some of the things I could do, but—I hoped—none of the things that I was. The Fueirean girl had been taught differently, had learned differently. To teach her another way would be almost impossible.

The thoughts went black within me. A sudden rage swelled. My hands clenched savagely upon the ship's rail so that the wood began to creak under the pressure. My teeth ground together. A wish came upon me that an enemy would cross my path. I wanted to smash, to destroy. Something. Everything. In the next instant, it was as if a dash of chilling seawater had been thrown in my face.

What was wrong with me?

No one had ever called me a particularly calm man. But the black and blinding rage I'd just experienced was novel to me. Or was it? Had there not been other odd things of late, since the transference of my khi into the body of Baadon? Was I truly as unchanged by that experience as I hoped?

Always, for example, my sense of pleasure in battle had been tempered with a healthy fear and with the knowledge that I was killing other intelligent beings. The fear and knowledge seemed to have fled me of late, leaving only an awful, fearless joy.

I had also taunted enemies—the original First Mate of *The Painted Maid* and his cronies aboard the ship: Dharus, Khene, Timbun. I'd taunted them, not out of any rational strategy needed for victory, but because I liked it. Were these the actions of Ruenn Maclang, or of someone else? They were certainly not behaviors that I wanted to exhibit.

But where did such things come from? Had I only been fooling myself for years about what truly lived inside of me? Or had I put on such behaviors and thoughts when I'd sheathed myself in the flesh of Baadon? Was I still fully myself—Ruenn Maclang—or was I becoming someone else? The potential answers terrified me. In trying to stop Vessoth, I could not lose myself.

A different kind of fierceness swept over me then, an emotion that could not be named but which combined fear, loneliness, happiness, melancholia and love. I wanted so intensely in that instant to see Rannon and tell her I loved her, tell her that I could not wait to know the children we would have together. A daughter perhaps. And a son. I wanted to show them a better way than the Fueirean girl had been shown. Whatever strengths I had, let them have them too. Let them avoid my weaknesses.

Something stung my eyes. I thought for a moment that I was crying. I reached up, brushed at the stinging. Dampness greeted my fingers, but it was not a warm wet, only the cold wet of the salt sea spray bursting over the rail. Baadon's eyes were dry. I doubted he was capable of tears.

CHAPTER THIRTY-ONE

BONEASH ISLE

We soon had *Fueire's Whisper* ready to sail and turned the prows of our two ships toward the pirates' home base, where the spoils of our raid would be divided and I would have my chance to be inducted fully into the Brotherhood of the Skull Flag. Our path lay to the east, with a fair wind. The Fueirean girl did not accompany us. We'd dropped her and the other survivors of her ship along the coast of the continent known as Kotheriuhm, near a trade route they could follow to their home.

On the fifth day of our voyage, our ships passed Drin's Landing to the north. I had to admit to feeling a touch of apprehension growing within me. Captain Stefan had mentioned again the test I would be required to pass to join the Brotherhood. Once we reached the pirate base, there'd be no avoiding that test. Stefan had offered to drop me at the Landing, where I'd first joined his crew. I'd declined. To get to Primini-phal and find out where Vessoth was hiding, I needed to be accepted by the Brotherhood. That was my mission. It was all that mattered.

The morning of the eighth day dawned with a haze to the east. As the sun rose, I saw that the haze came from a thick plume of smoke rising above a brutally rocky isle on which almost nothing grew. I'd become part of Jelvin's skeleton crew aboard *Fueire's Whisper*, and it had been a busy time. It felt exhilarating to get my hands and my back into the work of sailing again, but at the moment I was standing next to Jelvin at the *Whisper's* helm.

"Home," he said, pointing toward the smoke.

I looked at him with surprise and asked: "An active volcano?"

He laughed. "It would seem so, wouldn't it?"

"That means it isn't?"

He gazed at me a moment. "There's no turning back now," he said. "No reason I shouldn't tell you. That's Boneash Isle, home base for the Brotherhood. They send up the smoke at times to make people think it's a volcano. Whatever it takes to discourage visitors."

"Ah."

"Best get to the rigging," Jelvin continued. "We'll be coming into the harbor in half a dhaur. The entrance is hidden so we'll need to drop sail at just the right moment."

I nodded again, returned to my post near the mainsail. Excitement colored the faces of the other crewmembers. They were happy to be coming home. My own excitement had a different source.

We passed huge outcroppings of black basalt worn smooth by centuries of waves. And beyond those lay rippled fields of lava as jagged as if they had poured free of the earth only yesterday. A few wind-shredded trees made a precarious life for themselves in those wicked fields, and here and there rested sea birds whose raucous cries grated on the ears.

We came under the shadow of the volcanic cone, the top of which seemed to have blown away in some titanic eruption. The walls that still remained towered many hundreds of feet into the air and were nearly sheer. No one was likely to be climbing to the top of this island.

As we passed a headland of extruded lava we came into an area where the ocean currents quieted. Ahead of us, the crew of *The Painted Maid* quickly reefed their sails. Jelvin called for us to do the same an instant later, and for a bit I was too busy to pay much attention to what was going on away from the ship.

When a chance came to gaze around again, I found myself struck with amazement. The shoreline of Boneash Isle appeared to have folded open and a long dark channel of water stretched into the interior. Rowboats coming from that interior had already attached woven iron cables to the prow of *The Painted Maid*, and those cables stretched taut and rose dripping and creaking from the sea as some great mechanism within the Isle began to turn.

As I watched, the *Maid* was drawn into the channel and disappeared, as if it were being slowly swallowed down the island's enormous gullet. Not caring much for that image, I tried to visualize another as more rowboats came and attached cables to our ship. Again the cables snapped taut and, with a jerk, *Fueire's Whisper* began to move. I could not shake the vision of being swallowed, and it did not help to feel the much warmer air that came flowing out of the mysterious channel.

"The moist breath of a monster," I murmured to myself, and was only half joking. Or less.

"Ready the poles!" Jelvin shouted.

Sets of long oaken poles had been brought aboard the *Whisper* from the *Maid*. I'd paid them little heed, assuming they were for pushing a ship off if it went aground, or for reaching out to a man who fell overboard. Now their primary purpose became clear. Men took them up and lined the rails as we disappeared into the throat of Boneash Isle. They used them as we warped along the channel to fend the ship away from the walls.

My amazement grew.

The channel was easily wide enough for two ships. The walls were smooth and curved together in the shadows high overhead. The reflected light from outside cut off suddenly and I turned to see that a huge, painted canvas screen had been pulled down to hide the opening. It didn't matter as the dark was immediately punctured by the familiar blue-white shine of light globes placed in the ceiling.

The great cables drew us onward through damp air that smelled of salt and seaweed. Water plashed; the ships creaked. Echoes built upon echoes down the long tunnel. Even a whisper went storming through that air, and bounced back and back until one heard a thousand whispers.

After a bit, a more natural light began growing ahead of us. Soon we came out of the tunnel and under the open green sky. Once more, my amazement grew. Here lay the caldera of some long extinct volcano. A wide and placid salt water lake extended before me. It was several verlangs across and shaped like a crescent moon. The curve of the crescent bordered on a sand beach, and behind the beach stood a pocket-sized city built on terraces up the eastern wall of the volcano.

I could hardly imagine a more perfect abode for a pirate base. They had a large, protected harbor, and there was much more arable soil here than on the island outside. Date and fig trees grew lushly, along with small groves of tipit and the ubiquitous verhlis bushes, from which a sweet Taleran tea is brewed.

No army could scale the outer walls to reach this place. And if any enemy fleet happened to find the hidden opening, they'd never be able to force their way through that long tunnel in the face of opposition. The only avenue of attack would be from the sky, and from what I'd seen airships were far less common in the south than in the north.

I saw, also, the mechanisms that had been drawing our ships along. Two large stone pylons stood to either side of the opening of the great tunnel. They were wide, although not tall, and on the flattened top of each rested a device much like a water wheel. As these wheels turned, the cables attached to our ships shortened, pulling us forward. Although I'd not noticed them, there must be something similar at the other end of the channel to draw ships back out again when they wanted to leave. Perhaps they'd been mounted on the tunnel walls themselves.

The most curious thing to me was how the wheels were powered in the first place. I'd seen such wheels use the flow of water or wind to drive them. Neither of those forces seemed sufficient here. I'd also seen simple engines like this turned by people, or by horses or cattle. A man did stand on one of the pylons but he couldn't have moved the wheels by himself, and there were no domesticated beasts with him.

Pointing at the wheels, I questioned a pirate who stood near me at the mainsail. "How do those work?"

His answer was enlightening.

"Magic," he said. "Near as I kin figure. There be a crystal oar in each o' those li'l buildin's. The man on top," he jerked his chin toward the fellow standing by one of the wheels, "pushes a li'l handle and those oars start blinkin' out light. He pushes it agin and they stop. Long as they be blinkin' the wheels be turnin'."

Magic? I thought. *No. Asadhie-based science.*

I'd seen similar devices in my home country of Nyshphal, albeit not on such a large scale. The smaller flyers of the Nyshphalian air fleet used toir'in-or charged wands to power their propellers. I would have loved to have a look at the "crystal oars" in these pylons, but that didn't seem likely at the moment.

As our two ships approached the pylons, men went to the bows with pole hooks to free the cables that were pulling us. Momentum carried us farther into the harbor and orders were given to hoist a few scraps of sail. A wind did blow here, though not much. It was enough to let us maneuver in among the dozens of other vessels already riding at anchor in front of the beach.

After we'd dropped our own anchor, Jelvin came over to me. "Won't be long now," he said. "Best fetch anything you want to take with you to shore. The Six will already know we're here. They'll send a boat soon to pick up Captain Stefan, and you and I will go with him."

Something dark twisted inside of me but did not reach the surface. I let it subside before speaking. "I guess that means it's almost time for my test."

Jelvin nodded. "Aye. Your test."

CHAPTER THIRTY-TWO

THE BAD PENNY

As predicted, a boat soon pushed off from shore and rowed out to *The Painted Maid* to pick up Captain Stefan. The Captain pointed us out aboard *Fueire's Whisper*, and soon Jelvin and I were clambering down a net into the boat ourselves. We sat on the center bench next to Stefan while four burly Kaldi rowed us across water so clear you could see the bottom some twenty or thirty feet below.

Humans sometimes call the Kaldi the "Bear-Folk." That name is apt as far as general physical appearance goes, though the Kaldi are fully bi-pedal and have five-fingered hands much like any Human. It might have been a surprise to many to see Kaldi pirates, for they are often thought of as a gentle people. I'd seen them fight, though, and not always on the side of right. Every race has its good and bad.

The beach where the Kaldi unloaded us formed the first level of a five tiered pirate city. The sand of the beach was much coarser than it had appeared from the ship, full of ground-down pebbles of pink and gray and black. It made a nice packed surface for walking, however, and a good foundation for a row of huts and warehouses that backed right up against the wall of the caldera. These appeared to be the shops of carpenters, blacksmiths, and shipwrights, as well as storage facilities for looted goods.

A combination road and stairway began at beach's edge and ran up through the city, dividing it into even halves on either side. The second level consisted of huts that housed the bulk of the pirate crewmen. There were women as well, of many races, ages, and dispositions. Most of them were armed. Some stood hip-shot, watching us with calculating eyes. Some were slovenly, their eyes blurred from hard years and hard drink. Still others carried babes in their arms, or shooed along some of the many children who played half naked among the litter of bottles, discarded clothing and general trash.

The third level seemed given over to taverns mostly. These were doing a grand business, despite the earliness of the day. The women here were less varied, at least in attitude. All of them seemed to have that calculating stare. We passed, as well, a few merchant stalls selling a variety of goods, from blankets, rugs, pots and skillets, to fish, figs, dates, tipit fruit and iskit berries.

Larger and nicer huts sat on the fourth level. Some of these might better be called homes. Most of the buildings on the lower levels had been made of wood and palm leave thatch. Some of the houses here incorporated stone quarried from the local lava fields. I was told the pirate captains lived in this section. No debris cluttered the area between the houses here. There were no women or children to be seen. Perhaps they were inside the dwellings, or had gone to one of the other levels for drink, food, or companionship.

At last we came to the fifth level. Only one building stood here, where the six captains who ruled the Brotherhood of the Skull Flag held court. It was completely unlike anything we'd seen below. Built all of polished black lava, it was. It had two square sections, each two stories high, and a long, one story hallway connecting them. Although in far finer condition than any of the buildings below it in this settlement, it gave off a feeling of great age. The pirates had not built this structure. I had no doubt on that subject.

Stefan seemed to know where he was going. He led us up lava steps and through wide open doors into the left half of the building. We stopped there for a moment. No windows showed, and no torches, lanterns, or light globes. It should have been dark as night but the walls themselves glowed. Or, rather, engravings of some blue stone threaded their way through the walls and it was these which glowed. The engravings had no meaning my Human mind could decipher.

To our right stood a wide opening into the long hallway we'd seen from outside. The interior of the building waited in front of us, arranged much like a church. There was a large square area, the nave, where pews might rest, although none were to be seen now. At the far end of the room lay a raised area that might be called a chancel. No altar stood there, but six stone chairs were aligned across it. Three of the chairs were filled, three were empty.

The beings in the chairs were a Human, an Ebon Llurn, and a Vhichang. The Human looked like the pirate every twelve-year-old imagines being. He had black hair and a waxed black mustache under a tri-cornered hat with a scarlet tull feather standing tall from it. His topcoat was crimson with brass buttons. Ivory-colored breeks with black boots encased his legs and feet. A rapier with an ornate hilt hung by his side.

The Ebon Llurn, like so many of his race, was thin, elegant, and arrogant. His hair and eyes were silver. As I have mentioned, the Llurns are largely Human. In contrast to the Llurn, the Vhichang was an anomaly among his people. He was grossly fat, and I had never seen a fat Vhichang before. Half his beak was missing, and big patches of his feathers. He held a large leather jack from which he imbibed frequently.

I started to take a step forward and Captain Stefan grasped my arm to stop me.

"We do not approach until all of the Six have arrived," he said. "Or their representatives."

"Who are these three?" I asked back.

"The Human is Owin Degan. Quite the wealthy fellow, but something of a fop. The Llurn. He's one to watch. A real cutthroat. His name is Shadrack Teltshirn."

"And the Vhichang," Jelvin added. "He is Corlus. A rucker of the first order. I'm ashamed to say he is of my people."

I nodded, started to ask about the remaining members of the Six, but two more arrived even as I opened my mouth. The first was Klar, of that reptilian race who seem often to gravitate toward piracy. An unusual characteristic of this Klar pirate, at least to me, was that it appeared to be a she. Klar females are generally much smaller and less aggressive than the males, although I had heard of rare exceptions. This particular individual had the frill crest of elongated scales at the back of her neck that signaled a female, but she certainly looked as big and dangerous as the majority of Klar males I'd met.

The second new arrival was another Human; his appearance also surprised me. His clothing and weaponry were typically Taleran, but his hair was cut in a fashion I'd only seen on Earth. Unless they are bald, most Human males on Talera either wear their hair long or cropped almost to the skull. This man had a crew cut.

"The Klar is Sobrus," Stefan told me. "Actually a decent sort. Though she doesn't look it. The Human is Wulfe. He also seems to be a decent fellow, although not much is known about him. The last Captain is Tregren, a Nokarran—though a rather unusual looking one. He's vicious and tricky as a reeth. But I know he's off Boneash Isle at the moment. I see his chief flunky coming in to sit in his chair."

I looked where Stefan was looking, saw a slender human striding into the room dressed in black leathers and a blousy shirt of white silk. Silver winked at his throat, and in one ear. A fancy sword hung in a fancy scabbard at his belt.

"That one's name is Duramos," Stefan said. "Slippery as a pig and twice as deadly as a laith if you turn your back on him."

I started. I knew this man. His name was *not* Duramos. It was Durhain Koremos. He was one of the first two Humans I'd ever seen on Talera. The other had been Rannon Jystral, who was now my wife. Koremos had been a Nyshphalian noble. He'd betrayed his people and kidnapped Rannon, wanting her for himself. I'd had a hand in putting a stop to his plans (see *Swords of Talera*). Rannon had exiled him and I'd given him no thought since. But here he was, like a bad penny, as they say on Earth.

Koremos—or Duramos as he styled himself now—had every reason to hate Ruenn Maclang. At the moment, fortunately, Ruenn was gone and I was Baadon. But Duramos wasn't stupid. I couldn't imagine him figuring out who I really was, but if I said the wrong thing, if I gave any hint of a connection with Nyshphal and Rannon, he would surely catch it.

Unfortunately, the mere sight of this "Duramos" threatened to ignite the violent undercurrents that had begun to seethe in me of late. My fist clenched on my sword hilt. Black wings of rage took flight in my thoughts. I fought desperately to keep my outward composure, for any misstep now would be fatal to my plans and to the hopes of my friends.

And still, there was the test to come—of which I had no conception.

CHAPTER THIRTY-THREE

COUNCIL OF SIX

As Duramos seated himself, I finally mastered my inner turmoil. The rage receded to a manageable level and breath started to flow into my lungs again. As I began once more to study the situation I'd stepped foot into, six youths came from somewhere in the wings of the building to stand behind the six captains like squires waiting upon knights—soiled knights to be sure. It seemed curious that the squires were all Human. But perhaps there was some reason for that.

Stefan started across the nave toward the Six. Jelvin and I followed. We stopped again before a short set of stairs that led up to the chancel where sat the powerful leaders of the Brotherhood of the Skull Flag.

"Greetings, Captains!" Stefan said, nodding to them.

Owin Degan, the Human that Stefan had referred to as "something of a fop," returned the greeting. He was seated at the far right of the dais.

"Captain Stefan. Back with a prize, I see. Dare we hope you have more than just a pile of wood and sail to show us?"

Stefan drew a folded sheet of brown parchment from his shirt pocket. He held it out. Degan's squire, a blond lad of fifteen or sixteen years, came to fetch it and return it to his master. Degan unfolded the sheet, scanned it briefly, passed it to the next captain in line.

"Promising," Degan said. "As is our want in the Brotherhood, we will have the treasure independently verified before we divvy up the spoils. I should say, though, that if your cargo manifest is correct, your share will prove quite a comfort to you and your crew."

"It will be verified," Stefan remarked.

"And so," Degan said. "Shall we move on to the issue of the company you've brought with you today?" He waved a hand in the general direction of Jelvin and me.

"Beg pardon, my Lords," a voice said.

I turned my head to see that it was Duramos who had spoken, then quickly looked away again, not wanting him to detect the loathing in my face. Save for Corlus, the grotesque Vhichang, the remaining four captains did not bother to hide the irritation on their own faces as they looked at Duramos.

"What is it?" demanded Shadrack, the Ebon Llurn. "And how many times must we remind you that we are no 'Lords?' Captains is how you address us!"

Duramos inclined his head toward Shadrack. "Forgive me, Good Captains. But my own Captain, Tregren, would think me remiss if I did not inquire about the prize ship's crew. Are we not to expect any ransom to bulge our coffers? Or at least any potential slaves to sell?"

I wondered if anyone else in the room detected the oiliness in Duramos's voice as well as I did. Perhaps so, for none of them seemed to want to hear more from him.

Shadrack shook his head in apparent disgust but finally did look back at Stefan and ask: "Well, Captain. What of the crew? Were there survivors of your raid?"

"There were," Stefan admitted. "However, the ship came from Fueire's Hold. Fueireans are generally too fanatical to make good slaves. And all of you know that the priests of that city do not readily pay ransom. I calculated the inevitable delay in our return here if I requested such ransom. And the almost certain denial of it. I judged that the Brotherhood would be better served by bringing back gold in hand rather than waiting for possible gold that might never arrive."

Stefan gazed at Duramos, and smiled.

"And what did you do with the prisoners?" Duramos demanded. "Let them go with no profit in it for any of us?"

"I let them off along the coast where it would take them many days to return home."

Duramos's mouth snapped open as if he would say something else, but another voice interrupted, shutting up the man I knew as a traitor to my homeland.

"I for one am satisfied with Captain Stefan's judgment of the situation," the Human named Wulfe said. "Let's move on. Like Captain Degan, I'm curious about the nature of the company that has joined us in the Council chamber today." His words were directed at Stefan but his gazed rested on mine.

Stefan nodded his head at Wulfe's comments, then gestured toward me. "This is Baadon. He joined my crew at Drin's Landing. He fought with us when we took the Fueirean ship. His bravery and skill were noted by many in that fight. He is also the one who discovered the secret compartment where the bulk of the treasure was located. He wishes to become a member of the Brotherhood. I stand for him."

"And I am Jelvin," Jelvin said. "First Mate aboard *The Painted Maid*. Many of you know me. I too observed Baadon when we took the ship. He is strong and fearless. His skill with a sword is rare. He also served under me aboard the prize ship when we returned here. I commend him, and stand for him."

Wulfe's gaze had never left mine. Now he smiled. "Indeed," he said. "And so, Saar Baadon. Are these things said of you true? Are you fearless?"

The next few moments were going to be incredibly important for me, and quite possibly for Talera. Any concerns that I had could not be allowed to show. I had to put on a front, play the role I'd taken on from the moment the decision had been made to join the pirate brotherhood.

"Not entirely, Captain Wulfe," I said. "Not…entirely."

Wulfe's smile broadened. Owin and Shadrack chuckled.

"And do you wish to join the Brotherhood?" Wulfe asked.

"Entirely, Captain Wulfe. Entirely."

Next, Shadrack spoke. "And are you as good with a blade as Jelvin claims you to be?"

I took a deep breath before replying. "I've remained alive through many battles such as that we fought aboard the Fueirean ship. Perhaps that means I have some small knack with the sword."

"Or that you are lucky," Shadrack said.

I nodded. "Or that."

Everyone except Duramos and Corlus seemed to approve of my answers. But Corlus might almost have been dead given his lack of response to anything anyone said. It seemed that I'd broken through the first barrier to membership in the Brotherhood.

"Are you aware," Owin Degan said, "that to join us you must pass a test?"

Thus I began to hear of the second barrier.

"I have heard. Although I don't know what manner of test it is. Must I make love to your most beauteous maiden, perhaps? Say, one who at least has most of her teeth? Or," I smiled to show my own sharp teeth, "do you need me to kill a wayward taverner whose swill is more poison than pleasure?"

This time, open laughter came from Wulfe, Owin and Shadrack. Even Sobrus smiled, though the Klar do not often show Human-type emotion. The Vhichang, Corlus, actually came alive enough to take a huge swallow from his leather jack.

"I see you've met my wife," Owin said, still chuckling.

"And my taverner," Wulfe added.

Owin finally regained full control of himself and went on. "Nothing actually so dull as either of those. I imagine you'll find the task… interesting."

"Then I'm ready," I said.

"Follow us," Owin announced.

The Six Captains rose, came down from their dais and turned toward the corridor that connected this building with the next. Their squires followed them, and Stefan, Jelvin, and I followed the squires. The corridor ended at another large, square room. This room also consisted of one big open area, but there was no dais, only a strange glowing artifact sitting in the center.

As a kid I'd seen a painting of Cinderella's carriage, the one magicked up from a pumpkin by the Fairy Godmother. This artifact reminded me of that image. It was about the size of a carriage, and primarily spherical but with a slight flattening on top. That old painting had shown the carriage as glowing with fairy light. This artifact did as well. And that glow made me very uncomfortable. It looked like toir'in-or light, milkstone light, the light of sorcery.

Everyone stopped about ten feet from the artifact. Captain Wulfe gestured toward it as he looked directly at me.

"You step through the sphere's wall. The test begins once you're inside."

I arched an eyebrow. "And what, might I ask, is likely to be my experience on the other side of that wall?"

Wulfe shrugged. "It's different for everyone."

"And how will all of you out here know if I pass the test?"

"If you come out alive," Wulfe said. "And reasonably sane."

CHAPTER THIRTY-FOUR

TESTED

I studied the artifact. My heart pounded. I didn't want to go in there. But there was no choice if I wanted to complete my mission. Approaching the sphere, I reached out and touched the shining wall. It wasn't a wall. My hand slid through with only the faintest of frictions and I immediately jerked back in surprise. I needn't have. There was no pain; nothing grabbed me.

I shook my head. But the decision was made. Taking a deep breath, I stepped forward through the outer envelope of the sphere. The artifact closed over me like water and a pleasant tingling coursed through my body before gradually dissipating. Stopping to look around, I could just make out gradations in the brightness of the light surrounding me. Faint currents of it flowed past, some warm, some cool.

Looking back toward Stefan and the others showed me only their blurred outlines. I took another step forward. The light darkened. A low humming assaulted my ears. A scent struck my nostrils, like the air during a thunderstorm. One more step and everything changed. The light went opaque, deepening to a dark gold. The hum and scent intensified.

Something else forced its way into my awareness. My chest burned. The center of that feeling was just to the right of the breastbone. I slapped a hand over the spot, and even through the cotton shirt my skin felt warm. A vibration erupted under my fingers, from beneath the skin. I jerked my hand away, the fear of the unknown threatening to overwhelm me.

The humming intensified further. It came from four different points in the sphere. At each of those points, a small marble-sized stone floated in the air, with skeins of eldritch light spilling from them.

Milkstones!

They vibrated; Heat poured off them. In sudden understanding, I jerked open my shirt, gazed down at the right side of my chest. A small knot had formed under the skin there, where seconds before I'd felt heat and vibration. The knot fluttered, like a hummingbird's heartbeat.

I'd been implanted with a milkstone! Or, Baadon's body had been so implanted.

Fear drenched me. I'd seen milkstones rupture, seen them explode with a power greater than dynamite, seen them tear bodies apart. I forced myself to take a few deep breaths, tried to refocus my mind. I knew others who'd been implanted. Bryce had been. The stones didn't just blow up, unless they were damaged. And mine wasn't really hurting; it mostly just felt strange. I shouldn't be in any immediate danger. But where had this stone come from?

My first thought was Chalathar. I rejected it. According to Chalathar, he'd never inhabited the Baadon surrogate. It had belonged to Vessoth before his imprisonment. That meant Vessoth must have placed the toir'in-or in Baadon's chest. For whatever reason.

In the next instant, a new phenomena impinged on my awareness. Voices filtered through the layers of liquid light surrounding me. They were distant, tinny, and not voices I recognized. An image flickered into sudden existence in front of my eyes, with each corner of it anchored by one of the four milkstones. It was almost like watching a movie screen.

Two beings were talking, though I could only see one. It was a Bull-man, a Minotaur. He was huge, standing almost eight feet. His features—broad blunt nose, bovine eyes and ears—were exaggerated even for his species. His horns were massive, curling around his head and down to the height of his shoulders. They were tipped with obsidian spear points.

"Our army *might* be sufficient," the Bull-man was saying. "But we lack the ships to move them."

"We can tear out all the crew quarters in the ships we've got," a second voice said. "We can fill the holds with men. We've got enough ships. We need to act."

The Bull-man shook his shaggy head. "That's risky. Then every ship that is sunk takes too much of our army with it. To minimize potential losses, we need to spread our forces over many vessels. Fortunately, we obtain more transports all the time through our alliance with the pirate brotherhood. I've already urged them to redouble their efforts and it shouldn't be long before we've assembled the biggest fleet ever seen on Talera."

I realized suddenly why I couldn't see the owner of the second voice; I was looking out through his eyes. I also began to get a inkling of who the Minotaur was, and in the next instant my suspicion was confirmed.

"You are too cautious, Kamrack. Chalathar is on the run; his base belongs to us. Those fools in Nyshphal are next, and with your abilities you can open sphere gates right off their coast for our fleet to pass through. We'll hit them with overwhelming force while they're still reeling from

Vohanna's attacks. They took the thunder weapons and the new engines from Vohanna's ships (see *Wings Over Talera* and *Witch of Talera*) but they've scarcely had time to understand them or build more. We must destroy them before they can."

Another suspicion filled my mind, crystallized into certainty. The second voice, the being whose eyes I was seeing through, was Vessoth. Chalathar had said that it might be possible to track the Snake God while inhabiting the Baadon body. Was this what he'd been thinking of?

"If you had gotten those secrets from Vohanna before she was lost, we would not need now to act so rashly," Kamrack protested.

"I could not help that she was destroyed before she could free me from my prison," Vessoth said. "She did give me the knowledge of 'gun powder,' and of how to magnify it using the energy of the toir'in-or. Once we have the engines and the thunder weapons from the Nyshphalians, we will have power that has not been seen on Talera since days of yore. All the world will bow to us. And perhaps others worlds as well."

Kamrack scoffed. "To make a single explosion big enough to level a city! I will believe it when I see it."

"The power to level *more* than a city, my ally. And you will see it. If we move quickly!"

To level more than a city! By intensifying the power of gunpowder with a milkstone? I had no idea how such could be accomplished. But it did not bode well for Talera.

Kamrack sighed, sounding very Human. "I just sent word to the pirates that we need more ships. Those should be coming soon. And, against Nyshphal we'll need airships to cover our fleet. Mine are still sacking Chalathar's base. Some of the traitor's traps have destroyed a *few* things, but they've made a rich haul so far and claim there's more."

I hoped that one of the things destroyed by Chalathar's booby-traps had been Ruenn Maclang's old body. The fact that Kamrack hadn't mentioned the body specifically was promising.

"They're also searching for the bolt hole that Chalathar and his deluded followers fled to," Kamrack continued. "I can bring them back when we're ready to attack but I'd like to keep them doing what they're doing until everything else is ready."

"And how long will that take?"

"Two weeks maybe. That'll give us time to get a few more troop ships and to strip the ships we have so they can carry more men. I'll start those arrangements immediately. It would be better to have more time, though."

My heart stuttered in my chest. Panic surged up. Perhaps no more than two weeks remained before an attack was launched against Nyshphal. And they had no warning. Rannon had no warning!

"Two weeks," Vessoth said. "I'll agree to two—" He paused.

Abruptly, the milkstones changed their vibration rates, including the one in my chest. They began to pulse. A sense of intense danger swept over me.

"Something isn't right," Vessoth said.

"What?" Kamrack demanded.

I knew what wasn't right—my emotional response to a threat against Rannon. Somehow, being in this place let me listen in on Vessoth. It had to be through the milkstones, the connection between the ones in this artifact and the one inside me. Maybe this thing had even been created to serve as a kind of communication device. But that made it a sword with two edges. Vessoth could listen in on me as well, and my fear had just given me away.

For an instant, my panic spiked. If Vessoth realized who I was, he'd come for me with every weapon he could command. There'd be no chance to warn Nyshphal or derail his plans for attacking my home country. I had to shatter the connection, had to stop Vessoth from locating me.

I *felt* Vessoth cast his sorcerous net toward me, felt a sense of mental power I could hardly have dreamed of. He was coming, following a trail of energy that ended with the milkstone in my chest. In that moment, when total terror threatened to swamp me, I remembered something Queen Lavisa of the Indigo Llurns had said. She'd spoken of my sendahtia ability. She'd claimed that I was better at receiving than sending, and that mostly she picked up my emotions.

Emotions are the key!

Vessoth is homing in on them!

I closed my eyes, relaxed my body, purged my mind of feeling. Emotion was the enemy; I must conquer it. I became water without waves, a day without wind. I became a black room where no light shone. Inside of me, something raged to be free, shrieked to be free. It was not me, not Ruenn Maclang. I fought it with every ounce of strength I possessed. The connection broke. Just as Vessoth reached out to hammer me, it broke. I could not even allow a sense of victory to touch me. I was stone, forever.

The burning in my chest dissipated. I opened my eyes, looked down. The knot where the milkstone had pressed out against the skin was gone. The toir'in-or had subsided back beneath the flesh, and the other toir'inor, those suspended in the matrix of light around me, had quieted as well. The sphere itself was no longer opaque and I could see Stefan and Jelvin and the Six Captains of the Brotherhood standing and watching me from outside the sphere. I turned, strode toward them, stepped out into the normal world again.

They looked at me, their eyes wide. But the calm still possessed me.

"Well," I said. "Did I pass your test?"

CHAPTER THIRTY-FIVE

THE COUNCIL OF SIX DISAGREES

"What happened in there?" Owin Degan demanded. His flushed face had gone pale.

I shrugged in response. "I took your test. Don't know what else you mean."

Degan shook his head. "I've seen dozens of men tested. And never anything like that."

"Like what?" I asked.

"Lightning bolts," Degan said. "Hundreds of them striking within the sphere. Before it went black."

"And there was a humming," Sobrus the Klar added. "There's never been a sound before."

"I didn't see any lightning," I said. "And no blackness from inside. The sphere turned a darker gold is all. I heard the humming, though. What do you normally see?"

"Color changes," Degan said. "Flashing lights. But nothing like lightning."

"What else did you experience?" Duramos demanded of me.

My calm was fading. I had to fight anew to answer him civilly. "Heat," I finally said. "At one point I thought there were voices. Then the sphere cleared and I walked out here."

"What kind of voices?" Duramos asked suspiciously and I cursed myself for mentioning them.

"I couldn't make them out," I lied. "Look, what is this thing supposed to do anyway?"

Wulfe, the Human with the crew-cut hair, gazed at me speculatively. He spoke.

"The sphere is supposed to read emotions and magnify them. Fear becomes terror. Anger becomes rage. Too many of those who come to us with the thought of joining our ranks are complete slaves to their passions. You can never trust such men. Their passions get them killed. Or worse, get others killed."

"Or in moments of weakness they betray their companions," Sobrus the Klar added.

"Yes," Wulfe continued. "The Brotherhood survives because we stand together. Those who cannot control their emotions do not come back out of the sphere. Or they come out frothing with insanity."

"Then it looks like I passed," I said. "I'm alive. And no crazier than before."

"He didn't pass," Duramos snapped. "The sphere didn't function as it was supposed to. I say we can't trust him. He hasn't earned the right to join the Brotherhood."

Several members of the Council of Six turned irritated gazes on Duramos. Clearly, he was not popular.

"Perhaps," Wulfe said, "the sphere didn't function the same way because Baadon here is not like any being we've tested before."

Stefan added his own words to the issue. "I vouched for him. And he came out of the test alive and sane. By our rules, he *is* a member of the Brotherhood."

"Aye," Jelvin added.

Wulfe was the most important voice in what was to come, I thought. He was gazing around at the others. Duramos was shaking his head. Degan and Sobrus were nodding. Corlus gave no indication that he cared. Shadrack remained silent and still for a long moment before granting Wulfe a small nod.

"It's decided," Wulfe said.

He turned to look at me, offered his right arm. I offered mine in turn and we clasped wrists in a traditional Taleran version of the handshake.

"Welcome to the Brotherhood, Saar Baadon."

Duramos cursed, turned and stalked off, flinging a few words behind him. "Tregren will not like this!"

Wulfe chuckled. Degan and Shadrack joined him.

It didn't matter what Duramos or his captain said. They were overruled. I had become a full fledged member of the Brotherhood of the Skull Flag. I'd earned the trust of thieves and murderers. Soon, I might have to betray it.

Stefan and Jelvin came up to congratulate me, but of the six council members of the Brotherhood, only Wulfe lingered. His brown eyes seemed almost lazy as they studied me, but I doubted they missed much. Knowing that my adopted country of Nyshphal was due to be attacked soon, the goad of worry dug at me. But I also needed information, and Wulfe might be the man to supply it.

"How long has the Brotherhood been using this device?" I asked him, gesturing toward the toir'in-or sphere.

He seemed to consider whether or not to give an answer, but finally shrugged. "A few years," he said.

A few years. Well before Vessoth escaped his prison. But who knew how long the Snake God had been in contact with Kamrack.

"So it wasn't here when the Brotherhood first settled this island?"

"It was. But it was dark and silent. Just an ancient artifact with no purpose. Or so we thought. Tregren, the Captain you haven't yet met, was curious about the thing. He finally called in an ally of ours to look at it. That ally was quite excited. He explained to us what the artifact was, activated it for us. We've been using it since."

"An ally," I said. "You mean a sorcerer?"

"Yes. But why are you so curious?"

I smiled without showing any teeth. "I've experienced many strange things in my life, but nothing quite like that."

Wulfe laughed, as if at some cosmic joke that I did not share. "Oh believe me, my friend, there are far stranger things one can experience."

Before I could pursue the matter further, Wulfe turned to look at Stefan. "Captain," he said. "I know you and your men are looking for a bit of rest. But the Council is urging every crew to return to sea as quickly as possible and to bring back as many prize ships as they can. You were lucky to catch so many of the Six here. Most of us will be sailing ourselves within a day or two."

"What's going on?" Stefan asked.

"Our friends on Priminiphal are paying huge coin for ships at the moment. Who knows why, but they've almost doubled their rate."

Stefan arched an eyebrow. "I see," he said. "Many of my men still won't be happy at the hurry. They were looking forward to getting some grog in them and seeing their women. And spending some of the treasure they've earned."

"Treasure will spend as well in a month as it will today. As for the women, have the men not heard that time away equals more time in the hay?"

Stefan smiled faintly. "I'm sure that saying will be quite the comfort to them."

Wulfe laughed. "They'll live. Also, as soon as possible, get the smallest skeleton crew you can aboard the Fueirean prize and get it off to Priminiphal."

Stefan nodded.

"I'll volunteer for the prize crew," I said. "I'm kind of curious about this Priminiphal place."

Wulfe gave me a hard stare. "As long as you stay out of trouble. You don't want to go messing with that sorcery loving bunch. Their gold is good but that's the only thing I want from them."

"I wouldn't dream of misbehaving," I said.

CHAPTER THIRTY-SIX

PRIMINIPHAL

Fueire's Whisper was stripped of anything valuable and a skeleton crew of twelve was put aboard. I was one of the twelve. Jelvin commanded. We sailed east from Boneash Isle, with the sun rising in our faces. That sun was still green, but the gold of summer was coming. The ocean was heating and where a few weeks before the seas had been calm, now they were starting to awaken.

We were seeking a place whose exact location we did not know. Priminiphal was actually one of the floating sky islands, perhaps the oldest of them. But it had grown so heavy over the centuries from an accumulation of soil and from being hit, apparently, by iron meteorites, that the Vyn'ishad-or gas could no longer support it and it had settled to the surface of the ocean. Because it was not rooted, it moved slowly with the currents and one could never guarantee finding it in the same place twice in a row.

Fortunately, Priminiphal also never drifted far from the equator. And, the powers that be on the island put out navigational guides for those hunting it. We'd find the place. But how long would it take? Time ticked away on the planned attack on Nyshphal. That knowledge rode me hard, but I could do little other than chafe. Had there been a saddle bird or airship on Boneash Isle to be stolen, I would have tried to get word to Chalathar so Nyshphal could be warned. There hadn't been.

We knew there were saddle birds on Priminiphal. That was how I planned to escape once I accomplished my mission of precisely locating Kamrack and Vessoth. Now, I was even more desperate to find the two Asadhie so we could launch a preemptive strike against them. There'd be no attack on my adopted homeland if they were both dead.

Almost a week of precious time passed before we located the navigational buoys that pointed us toward the coast of Priminiphal. We picked them up in late afternoon from the glow globes attached to them. A wet night followed, with a line of squalls coming up one after another to drench us. But when morning came the skies cleared, and we saw the coast ahead of us.

There was no true harbor here. Instead, the entrance to a canal stood before us, one wide enough for half a dozen ships to pass each other at once. According to Jelvin, this canal extended all the way to Nakish-amora, the settlement originally established by the Indigo Llurns and appropriated by Kamrack the Bull and his army.

In seeing the canal, I felt sure it had not been built by the Llurns but must have been constructed by a much more scientifically advanced race—either the Asadhie themselves or some Asadhie-inspired popula-tion. Lavisa had mentioned the Llurns finding the ruins of older cities on Priminiphal when they arrived. Perhaps the inhabitants of those ruins had dug this great structure.

Whoever had built it must also have visited Boneash Isle, for the mechanism used at Boneash to draw ships in and out of the caldera was the same as that being used here in the Priminiphal canal. As a result, we had only to wait until men attached the appropriate cables to the *Fueire's Whisper*, and then were drawn along without any further effort on our part. This pleased me, as it gave me a chance to study the land we passed through.

It seemed a prosperous land. A steel wall about six feet high lined either side of the canal, but from the deck of the ship I could see over it. Close to the coast were many broad, open buildings that appeared to serve the needs of the fleet that Kamrack the Bull was gathering here. I saw ships in various states of construction or repair. And many more ships stood idly arranged along two of the lanes of the canal. It occurred to me that if someone were to block or destroy this waterway, much of Kamrack's great fleet would never be able to put to sea.

About a verlang in from the coast, we passed the last of the buildings and came into a section of cultivated land. Fields of cymer, a golden Tal-eran grain somewhat akin to wheat, alternated with plots of white honey-grain, redcorn, and vineyards filled with the purple of wine-grapes. Gar-dens bloomed with carsoli, whitethorn, and other herbs, or grew green with rows of taabers, beans and field peas. There were orchards filled with apple and pecan trees, and even a few dedicated to some kind of domesticated tipit, which I had never seen before.

Spaced between the planted fields, lime-green meadows fed herds of terval, stugah, taverel, and collex. Terval and stugah are bovines, cattle-like and oxen-like respectively. The taverel resembles a goat and is much prized for both its meat and its milk, from which a dense and fragrant cheese is made. The collex is a six-legged saddle animal, not much like a horse although it is used in similar ways.

Whenever the breeze shifted and the smells of all those growing things blew over me, I wanted to smile. I had a farm on Nyshphal, in a lovely place called Cathlin Valley, though I did not get a chance to visit it often. I wished to be there with Rannon, smelling the bright scents of burgeoning life rather than contemplating the dark odors of savagery and death.

Here, there was no escaping the latter—at least in my imagination—for I also saw while gazing out over the fields why this land prospered. It fattened on the backs of gray clad slaves who dug and weeded in the vineyards and gardens, and who herded the animals through their days. There were many such slaves, Human, Kaldi, Koro, Llurn, Ss'korra, Vhichang, and even Vlih. All worked with their heads down and shoulders slumped.

My fists clenched. I hated slavery. I'd been a slave. I remembered the daily humiliations, the daily violence. I remembered the anger, fear, depression. Worst of all, a slave's life does not belong to the slave but to the master. Could there be any greater violation?

Jelvin came up beside me at that moment. His one rosary bead eye studied the slaves just as mine did, and he clicked his beak twice, which is much the same gesture as a Human spitting in disgust. I glanced at him.

"Don't much care for slavers," he said.

"But does not the Brotherhood sometimes sell captives as slaves?"

"Aye." He nodded toward the fields where the slaves labored in the hot sun. "Some there could be ones the Brotherhood sold to these Priminiphal bastards. But Stefan doesn't take slaves. That's one reason I sail with him."

"What do you have against slavers?"

He gazed at me, double clicked his beak again. "My mother was a slave. Far south of here. I was born to it." He pointed to a particularly ugly scar on the right side of his beak, which looked almost like the letter 'Y.' "This is how slavers brand Vhichang," he said. "But when I was old enough I ran away. My mother was dead by then. Few slaves live long lives."

"I was slave once myself," I said. "Of the Klar."

"So you know."

I nodded. "You mentioned once that the Council of Six might be trying to usurp Stefan's captaincy. Is that because he doesn't take slaves? Do they feel they're losing out on gold?"

"That's a big part of it, I think. And because their masters here on Priminiphal keep telling them to bring more slaves. To be fair, though, it's not all of the Six. Mostly Tregren, the captain served by that bastard

Duramos. And Corlus, who traffics heavily in slaves. Probably Shadrack, the Ebon Llurn, as well. Hard to know about him for sure."

"Does Stefan have any friends on the Council?"

"Not friends, particularly. I think Wulfe rather likes him. He doesn't take slaves either, though he generally ransoms all his captives."

I changed the subject, or at least I'm sure it seemed that way to Jelvin. "What happens when we reach the other end of the canal?"

"The society here is highly stratified. The Bull-men form the core of the army's legions, with other races serving as archers and auxiliaries. Mostly the Klar handle the slaves. There's a kind of caste of…inspectors. Almost all of those are Human. They keep the records. A few of those will check out our ship, pay us if it meets their requirements. I'm sure it will. We'll turn the vessel over to them and bunk at a seaman's hostel there until we can catch a trade ship back to Boneash. It's usually not a long wait."

I studied Jelvin's face carefully as I said, "I won't be going back with you."

The Vhichang's one eye twinkled. "Captain Stefan said you probably wouldn't. He knew right away that you joined us for reasons having nothing to do with piracy. It took me a while but I came around to his way of thinking."

"Then why did you both support me for membership in the Brotherhood?"

He shrugged. "Reckon we both just liked you." He grinned. "Not sure why. You're an ugly son of a slut."

I grinned back. "For all you know, I might be the prettiest thing around where I come from."

He gave a fake shudder.

I turned serious, reached out and placed a hand on his shoulder. "Take care of Stefan. If Tregren and the others tried to replace him once, they'll try again. I wouldn't want to see him brought down."

"I'll do my best. But you have to tell me what it's all about. I won't tell anyone but Stefan. But I have to know. Maybe you even owe us that."

I nodded. "I do. Another thing you mentioned to me one time was the rumor about an Asadhie being on Priminiphal. The rumor is true. His name is Kamrack the Bull. And recently another Asadhie joined him. Vessoth. The Snake God. The army and fleet they've amassed are to be used in a bid to gain power over all Talera. The slavery you see here." I nodded toward the shore. "The brutally rigid society needed to control slaves. Kamrack and Vessoth want to export that way of life to every corner of the world."

"And you can stop them?"

"Not alone. I work with others. My mission is to find out where Kamrack and Vessoth are on Priminiphal. Then we'll hit them. Kill them if we can. Or at least disrupt their strategy."

Jelvin's beak gaped. "Attack Asadhie! That's suicide."

I shook my head. "We've got a plan."

His fists clenched on the ship's rail. "Would that I could be there," he said. "Such evil must be stopped."

I gazed at him. "Even if we manage to kill Kamrack and Vessoth, it won't be the end of the battle to save Talera from its past. If you mean what you say about the evil of the Asadhie, there may be a time when I'll call upon you for aid in that battle."

He turned toward me, offered his arm and wrist. I took them.

"Call away," he said. "But for now, at least let me tell you everything I know about this city of the Asadhie. Including," he smiled, "a little something that might help you in your quest."

CHAPTER THIRTY-SEVEN

NAKISH-AMORA

Early afternoon saw us reach canal's end. The inspectors that Jelvin had mentioned greeted us. They were officious but efficient. We turned the *Fueire's Whisper* over to them and a large quantity of gold went into Jelvin's pouch for the Brotherhood. Slaves rowed our small crew to shore and we found cots in a local hostel. Jelvin also managed to reserve us berths aboard a ship leaving the next morning for Boneash Isle. One of those berths was for me but I'd never be using it.

I'd learned as much as possible from Jelvin about the city lying before me. It still bore the name given to it by the Indigo Llurns—Nakish-amora—but I imagined it was much changed from its original form. It was two cities really, known as the Outer and the Inner, both of which nestled in a enormous crater well over a verlang across. That would be almost two miles in Earthly measurements.

The Outer City was an expansion beyond the original settlement and no doubt had been built to the specifications of Kamrack the Bull. Two types of buildings were found. The first were great square piles made from cyclopean blocks of gray stone, many threaded with metal ore. These stood five to six stories high. Some were barracks-like housing for Kamrack's massive army while others provided quarters for Priminiphal's numerous slaves.

The second kind of building was much smaller but more numerous. These were also square built, of the same materials, but stood only one or two stories high. They filled gaps between the more massive buildings and served a variety of purposes, from taverns, to markets, to brothels, to stables for riding animals, including some saddle birds; there are no individual homes in the Outer City. Between the various buildings ran wide, straight thoroughfares, which cut the city into rectangular blocks that would be easy to move troops through.

The Inner City lies at the center of the crater and is encircled by a fifteen foot wall. Inside is most of what was the original settlement of the Indigo Llurns. Jelvin had seen it once, though visitors are not generally allowed inside. He'd described a large, tree-like tower and various smaller domed buildings around it. The tower had to be the one grown and shaped by the Llurns from the seeds of carbaxus and ahmbr trees. The domed buildings were apparently government and military offices, as well as residences for the elite.

I'd probably have to enter the Inner City. It seemed the most likely place to find Vessoth and Kamrack. I tried one other tactic first. On Boneash Isle, during my test, the milkstone implanted in my chest had somehow allowed me to connect with Vessoth's consciousness. Now, I tried to do so again, deliberately, using what modest sendahtia powers I possessed. If this allowed me to locate Vessoth and Kamrack, I'd be able to complete my mission and escape much more easily.

Accessing the stone was not a problem, but I was unable to tap into anything. I didn't know if it were my own weak sendahtia skills, or whether the first time had been a fluke brought about by the amplification of the toir'in-or artifact in which the test took place. It seemed likely to be the latter, and I might still be able to locate Vessoth this way if he were close enough. That definitely meant finding a way into the Inner City. One question was how, and I had only hints as to a solution. Another question was whether I could get out again. Time was running out on my chance to find answers.

While Jelvin and the rest of the skeleton crew of the *Fueire's Whisper* addressed themselves to a few bottles of wine, I left the hostel and wandered the nearby streets. I was looking for something specific and soon found it.

Though there was a nighttime curfew for visitors to Nakish-amora, daytime wandering was permitted in the area around canal's end. To travel deeper into the settlement, particularly toward the Inner City, required special permission. Since I had no suitable reasons to request such permission, I had to find another way. And I had a plan, or at least the fragment of one that Jelvin had helped me develop.

A few streets down from the seaman's hostel, I stumbled upon the weapons shop I'd been hoping to find. It was still sunlight so there was little to do other than find a place to hide and wait for dark.

Once full night fell, I slipped free of my hiding spot and approached the shop's rear door. It was locked, but I was prepared for that. From a small pocket sewn into my left boot, I drew a pair of lockpicking instruments. Jelvin had suggested very strongly that I'd need such a skill in Nakish-amora, and he'd provided me with the tools and a few quick lessons.

It took longer to pick a lock in practice than I would have liked and nervous sweat drenched me before the door finally clicked open and I was able to slip inside the shop. While there had been enough ambient light outside the building from street lanterns to see what I was doing with the lock, inside it was pitch black.

I drew a small device called a striker from my pocket. This is a kind of lighter invented years ago by some Taleran genius. It's a small metal tube filled with rundal oil, a highly flammable liquid used in lanterns. A wick is inserted through an inner metal cap and the tube's outer cap has an attached flint and tiny metal spike. Popping the lid open sets sparks to the wick and you have flame. The wick is coiled down into the oil and has to be tugged upward as it shortens, but both oil and wick can be replaced when needed.

Hiding the light of the striker behind my hand, I began exploring the large shop. I'd noted that the city guard of Nakish-amora wore a kind of uniform consisting of a black steel cuirass with black gauntlets and black greaves to cover the legs. A type of helmet called a spangen completed their dress. This has a domed steel top with attached cheek and nose pieces. Since the guard is one of the few groups in Nakish-amora that has members of many races in it, I hoped to pass for one, especially with a helmet to cover most of my head.

Finding a table full of guard gear was easy; it took longer to find a set that fit my rather large frame. A bronze shield and a short sword completed my acquisitions. They seemed to be standard issue for the guards.

Shutting off the striker, I slipped to the door and through, and darted quickly into the shadows. Once it was clear I'd escaped the armory without being sighted, I straightened my shoulders and strode along the street as if I belonged there. A few souls passed me but paid no heed. A few real guards nodded and I returned the gesture. Security certainly seemed to be lax, which made some sense given that no one had challenged the rule of the Minotaurs here for a long time.

The comparative emptiness of the streets did not mean the city was quiet, however. Many of the barracks that housed Kamrack's army blazed with light and raucous merriment. The festivities were just kept indoors.

Approaching the Inner City, I became more cautious. I dared not try to enter through either of the two gates that pierced its wall. Even being dressed as a guard would not protect me from suspicion, for Jelvin had said that everyone who sought entrance into the central portion of Nakish-amora was required to have printed orders. Jelvin had also revealed another way to get into the Inner City, however. It required considerable stealth.

After making sure I wasn't observed, I ducked off the main thoroughfare and worked my way between buildings to the wall guarding the Inner City. Slowly, I began creeping along that wall, searching for the sign that Jelvin had told me about.

Every city has its crime and criminals, even one as rigid and controlled as Nakish-amora. Jelvin knew a back way into the Inner City because he was friends with someone involved in a smuggling ring moving blood drug and other specialty items in and out of the place. At a point well away from either of the main gates, in a wide but overgrown alley behind a public cohrnex, some smuggler years before had carved hidden steps up the outside of the wall. The only way to find them was to first locate the base step, which resembled no more than a crack in the lowest part of the wall.

Guided by the stench of the cohrnex, I quickly found the alley, and after some careful inspection located the steps. For each step except the first, a block of stone had been removed and reinserted into its original hole. One slid the blocks halfway out to make foot and handholds, then kicked them in again as you climbed up the wall.

Keeping only my original weapons, I stripped off my guard disguise and hid it. The guards in the Inner City were all Minotaurs and there was no way to pass for one. I crept up the wall, using the steps, and paused just below the lip until a patrol passed. A quick rush took me across in the dark. There were steps on the inside wall too but no time to use them. I let myself hang off the side by my hands before dropping into a crouch at the base. It wasn't a long fall when you were already over six feet tall.

No alarm sounded. It had been easy so far. That made me nervous, but I had no choice other than to push my luck. An old saying from Earth suddenly sprang into mind and I had to fight not to laugh semi-hysterically as I muttered to myself:

"You just gotta seize the bull by the horns."

After taking a long moment to regain my mental composure, I began working my way through the Inner City toward the center where the top of a great tower was just visible. The architecture around me was very different from that in the Outer City. Here, there were no wide, straight roads, only crooked ones. Most buildings looked like overgrown igloos, though built of stone, of course. From what Jelvin had told me, these were mostly private homes for Kamrack's advisors, bodyguards and sorcerer priests, as well as for the commanders of his armies and other important figures in his government.

The streets were even emptier here than outside the wall. I began to wonder if there were a curfew. Good for me if there was, unless I got caught violating it. Quickly, I found my way to the base of the central tower. While the tower might originally have been grown and shaped from interwoven carbaxus trees, that old Llurn workmanship had long since been overlain by baroque later construction. Great spires of obsidian and bronze had been added, supported by thick steel girders. Iron and brass work abounded, threaded through with mother-of-pearl and lapis lazuli. The whole thing had the dark and sinister cast of some monstrous beetle's exoskeleton.

Only one door pierced the tower and it was guarded by six Minotaur giants with axes in their hands. Far above me on the side of the building, though, were a series of stained glass windows, placed almost randomly. Perhaps there was my entrance; I began to climb.

The Baadon body, with its long limbs, was well adapted to climbing, as I'd already learned. Getting to the windows wasn't hard—footholds and handholds were plentiful—but the first few I came to were either too small or were placed in areas where the guards could easily see them. I finally found a suitable one, large enough for even my frame, and hidden behind a spire away from the main entrance. Through a clear panel in the stained glass, I could see a distorted image of what lay inside. It was a large room, empty except for half a dozen round tubes that somewhat resembled coffins.

Taleran glass is thicker than Earthly glass. It doesn't shatter easily. I used my elbow to crack the glass away from the window frame and began slowly and carefully working the big pane free. Soon enough, I was able to slip through the window without raising any alarm.

Once inside, I found that the round "tubes" were actually a set of surrogate chambers like those used by Chalathar and other Asadhie. Only, these were laid on their sides instead of standing up straight. There were no surrogates in them but they weren't empty either. They bubbled with a bluish liquid, and something floated in each chamber.

Curious, I moved around the room, studying the contents of the tubes. The first held only an amorphous clump of flesh. The second contained a mass of tissue that had sprouted stumps where a Human's arms, legs, and head would be. Each form after that appeared more and more humanoid, until the last one, which was *clearly* Human, although its body seemed to be covered with pink jelly and the features of the face showed little definition. I realized what I was seeing. These chambers were full of clones, growing, developing clones. The last one even looked disconcertingly familiar, although I could not quite place it.

Moving away from the unsettling clones so as to calm my emotions, I stopped where a set of wooden stairs led downward into the tower. Once again, I decided to try and access my implanted milkstone to see if I could trace Vessoth and Kamrack. If the two Asadhie were in the Inner City, surely this tower was the most likely place to find them. But I had to be sure. Many lives depended on it.

Closing my eyes, I placed my left hand over my chest above where the stone was implanted. Focusing my mind inward, I tried to visualize the toir'in-or stone awakening. A fluttering began under my fingers, almost random at first, but steadying and speeding up until it thrummed like a baby bird's heart.

In the next instant, the connection I sought was made. Powerfully! No voices came this time, as they had during my 'test' on Boneash Isle, but once more an image formed in front of my eyes. Once more I was looking out from behind another being's face. It had to be Vessoth, and somewhere close to me. He was seated at a table, staring deeply into a chalice of red wine.

A reflection shivered on the surface of the wine. I leaned forward, eager to unmask the form the Snake God was wearing now. There were two reflections, I realized suddenly. One was Kamrack the Bull, standing behind and above the figure whose eyes I was seeing through. The other face was that of Ruenn Maclang.

CHAPTER THIRTY-EIGHT

DISCOVERED!

A flashing chill froze me to the marrow. My mind locked up and my heart started to hammer. Vessoth wore the body of Ruenn Maclang. My body! Or a clone of it.

Emotion had revealed me to Vessoth before so I tried to fight that which rose like a storm within me. Too late. Vessoth jarred back in his chair. His hand spasmed, sending the elaborate goblet that he held spinning across the table where he sat. The metal of the cup chimed on the wood; crimson wine sprayed like blood.

Vessoth's voice struck through to me. It was harsh, crackling with hate. "You!"

I strove to break the connection between us but could not. My emotions were too strong and Vessoth had his hooks in me. Mental force gripped my head like the crushing fingers of a behemoth.

"You again!" Vessoth snarled.

The Asadhie's rage came forging into my mind. He'd lost me the first time our thoughts had crossed this way; he seemed determined not to do so again. His emotions were a bludgeon beating against me. My left hand still rested on my chest, over the milkstone that had been implanted there. A flush of heat rose from the stone; a knot of proud flesh formed beneath my fingers. The stone had pulsed like a heart. Now it pounded, pounded, pounded. Pain radiated from it.

I no longer had any control over the toir'in-or. Vessoth owned it; surely he had put it in the Baadon body in the first place. His thoughts were channeling their way into me through the doorway of the milkstone. His khi was possessing mine. I was fighting; he was winning. And he knew it.

Nothing could keep Vessoth's threats out. They flowed straight through to me, filled with gloating. "Tear you! Crush you! End you!"

The pain in my chest ratcheted up. Again I remembered scenes of milkstones exploding. Panic tried to take me. Vessoth was going to use the toir'in-or to rip me apart. Even if I'd been able to force my mind to calmness, it was too late for that to save me. Nothing could save me.

Except!

The lips curled back from the savage teeth that filled my mouth; the dark inside uncoiled. A snarl raged up through my throat, erupted into the air like a thousand scorpions with wings. If I could not win through silencing my emotions, let them roar free. If I could not have peace—let it be war.

The fingers of my left hand locked around the knot of flesh in my chest where the milkstone pulsed. With my right, I tore a knife free of its sheath at my belt. The stone burned like an oven; I held on, tugged down on the skin. Bringing the knife across, I sliced into the muscle above the toir'in-or. The blade was sharp but Baadon's skin was tough. I had to press hard, had to saw the knife back and forth. Blood welled, then sprayed. A new pain joined the old but both were consumed in hate.

The stone revealed itself through a slime of blood, through threads of flesh. It gleamed like the sun, brighter and more multifaceted than any diamond. My fingers closed over it, yanked it free with a faint sucking sound. It cauterized the flesh around it as I pulled it loose, leaving the wound clean. Still, the thing cooked in my hand. I hurled it away.

Steps led down at one side of the room where I stood. I threw the stone toward them and it hit and bounced, went tinkling away. The milkstone's glow was still visible and in the next instant the glow suddenly expanded. A pulse of intense white light blinded me and I threw up my hands to block it.

An explosion followed. The whole building rattled. Acrid smoke swirled up the steps into the room where I stood. Dust rained down from everywhere. But my connection to Vessoth was obliterated.

For the nonce, the rage seemed to have been cast away from me with the stone, and now a terrible urge to flee swept me. The steps were no longer an option. Piles of fallen material choked them. I rushed to the window, swung through onto the side of building. Guards shouted from inside the tower, from outside, from everywhere. I'd never be able to climb down and get back to the wall to escape into the Outer City. Even if I could, where would I go? I started climbing higher.

The thought that surged to the fore was that I had to get a message to Chalathar and the Indigo Llurns before being captured. We'd hoped I'd be able to get the information on Vessoth's and Kamrack's location and escape aboard a saddle bird or flyer. That wasn't going to happen. But we'd planned against that eventuality.

I found a spire of the tower to hide behind and took off my sword sheath. Sewn onto the back of the sheath was a long, leather pouch. I uncapped it and pulled out three thin tubes wrapped in paper. Each was about a foot long and had a fuse coming out of one end. The tubes were filled with gunpowder I'd manufactured myself while still at Yteril, the settlement of the Indigo Llurns.

What I'd made was a kind of firework—a gunpowder rocket. If they worked, they'd shoot well up into the air before exploding in a bright burst of color. Before I'd left Yteril, we'd agreed that the Llurns would keep constant watch via saddle birds over Priminiphal. If escape proved impossible, I'd send up a message instead. The watchers would call in an immediate attack at the point of the signal.

Finding a notch in the ironwork in which to insert the three rockets, I drew out my striker, fired it up and lit the fuses. Sparks sizzled down onto the tower's roof. I ducked behind the spire to hide in case things didn't go as planned.

The fuses burned slowly. An agonizing moment passed while I waited. Then came a shsshing sound, followed an instant later by another. The dark sky overhead blinked twice with crimson firework bursts. The third rocket hadn't fired but still I felt like cheering. I restrained myself. Though the flashes seemed bright to me, they weren't very high up and I couldn't know if they'd been intense enough for an observer on a saddle bird to see.

Only time would tell. Meanwhile, I couldn't try to escape now, even if it had been possible. Vessoth and Kamrack had to be kept here, in the Inner City. Or else our attack would be wasted. That meant they'd have to think they'd caught the one and only spy in their midst.

Checking on the third rocket showed that the fuse had burned out upon reaching the cylinder. A dud apparently. I broke it apart and scattered it so it wouldn't be recognized for what it was. Then I climbed down to another of the tower's stained glass windows and kicked it in. As I swung inside, two Minotaur guards came charging into the room from a stairwell, their axes drawn. My hands went up in surrender, my sheathed sword dangling from the fingers.

"I'm the man you're looking for," I told them. "I have words to share with your lords Kamrack and Vessoth."

One of the guards stepped to my side, his axe up and ready to shear off my head should I try anything. The other snatched the sword and sheath from my hand with a snarl.

"Take care of that," I told him. "I'm going to want it back."

CHAPTER THIRTY-NINE

THE SNAKE AND THE BULL

The guards bound my hands behind me and led me down through the tower to the throne room of Kamrack the Bull. Vessoth was there as well. The two of them seemed to be aware that an intruder had been caught.

Though I noted it only in passing, the room to which I was taken was large and circular. Light globes illuminated the walls, which were inlaid with mother-of-pearl and striped with friezes whose content I made no attempt to discern. Chairs and a table rested at one side of the room, the table filled with dirtied silver plates and cups. At the other side stood a high throne and in it sat Kamrack.

Kamrack made the archetype upon which all Minotaurs were based. He stood nearly eight-feet-tall, with heavy, broad features, a thick beard at his chin, and massive curling black horns. I paid him little mind, for in a somewhat less ostentatious chair to his right sat Vessoth in the form of Ruenn Maclang. I let my gaze burn upon him. My hatred rekindled, became a livid thing inside of me.

In the instant that he saw me, Vessoth's eyes widened and he sat bolt upright in his chair. In the next instant he threw himself to his feet. His fists were clenched, his lips a thin line. The rage in his face was palpable.

"You!" he snarled. "How came you here?"

Kamrack interrupted any response I might have made. He sounded surprised. "You know this spy?"

Vessoth turned to his fellow Asadhie. "As do you," he snapped. "This is Baadon. Who your fhaze described to—" He paused abruptly and gazed around, then continued, "This is not for all ears to hear."

Kamrack frowned, but nodded. He called to the two guards who'd escorted me into the room. "Did he have weapons on him? Or anything else?"

The guard who held my sword answered. "He had only two daggers, My Lord. And this." He held up the blade.

"Give me the sword," Kamrack ordered, holding out his hand.

The Minotaur warrior nodded and strode forward. He paused only once to bow, then handed the weapon to his master. Kamrack examined the sword sheath. He found the pouch on the back but there was nothing in it. Next, he drew out the blade. It glittered in the light.

The Asadhie nodded as he examined the Llurn sword's workmanship. "A fine weapon," he said. He resheathed it and offered it to Vessoth, then spoke again to the two guards. "Leave us."

The guards obeyed and as they exited the room I let my gaze rest once more on Vessoth. It felt like looking in a fun house mirror. The "reflection" was basically mine but with distortions. The expression in the eyes was not right. The mouth seemed constantly distorted into a moue of distaste. The face was paler, for while I had always spent time in the sun, Vessoth clearly did not.

Vessoth was staring at me as well, over my sword, which Kamrack had passed to him. Very deliberately, the Snake God offered me a sneer. "Trash," he stated, and tossed the weapon aside to clang on the floor.

That small unreasonable act brought my internal rage boiling quickly to the surface. I took a step toward the Asadhie who wore Ruenn Maclang's body, with Baadon's lips curled back into a snarl over shark-like teeth. Vessoth did not retreat but his face paled even further.

"Enough!" Kamrack snapped.

I glanced toward the giant Minotaur. He was looking at Vessoth rather than at me, and a look of irritation had engraved itself across his broad features. It appeared that he, too, had disliked Vessoth's insult of the Llurn sword. He was, at least, a warrior, with a warrior's respect for weaponry. Perhaps the alliance of these two Asadhie was not as cemented as I'd thought.

Kamrack's face settled back once more into calmness and he asked: "So, Vessoth. The guards are gone. Tell me how you know this spy. How 'we' are supposed to know this spy."

"It's Baadon—one of my surrogates before I was imprisoned and they were taken from me. He was given to the one who calls himself Chalathar. But according to your fhaze, the Baadon body now carries the khi of Ruenn Maclang."

Surprise flickered across Kamrack's face as he glanced at me. "Are you sure? The last we heard of that one and Chalathar, they'd gotten themselves trapped without recourse to sorcery on one of the Sky Isles. The force we sent to hunt them should have been sufficient. How could he have come to be here?"

"I don't know," Vessoth said. "But we haven't heard from the troops we sent on that hunt. And I know this body. It *is* Baadon. Call your fhaze.

Let him identify for sure whether or not this is the being he saw with Chalathar."

Kamrack nodded. His eyes closed for a moment, then reopened. "He's on the way," he said.

So, I thought, the fhaze survived the sword wound I'd dealt him. I wondered what he looked like now. Surely he had not kept the form of my friend Rence. A moment later, I found out.

A Nokarran came from a hallway to one side of the room. He was big, as all Nokarrans tend to be, but his size was the only typical thing about him. His niveous fur marked a shade I'd never seen among his people. But that snow-white coloration was no sign of an albino. His piercing eyes were startlingly blue.

"Tregren," Kamrack said. "Have a look at this captured spy. Is he the same being you saw with the traitor Chalathar?"

Tregren! That name. I'd heard it. But where? Then I remembered. He was one of the six captains who ruled the pirates of Boneash Isle. He was the only one I'd not met, because he was absent on the day I had my test for membership in the Brotherhood. I imagined he'd been recovering from a sword wound I'd administered to him inside the Hael planetoid. Seems I'd been extremely lucky on my test day. It also explained many things about the Brotherhood to find that one of their leaders was truly a shapeshifting fhaze who served Kamrack and Vessoth.

Tregren strode over to stand in front of me. His eyes studied me as if I were a smudge of dirt on the freshly polished leather of his boots. I had known he was arrogant; I saw that he was also vain. To make a contrast against his white fur, he wore blood-red leathers threaded with gold, and slits in the leather emphasized his musculature. Jewels flashed on every finger of his hands, and at his ears. I wondered how long slaves had spent brushing and oiling his fur so that it glistened.

Vanity and arrogance did not mean he was a weakling, however. An exquisite rapier of Tyzinn steel hung sheathed at his waist, and it had clearly seen plenty of use. His hand rested on the blade's hilt but he did not draw it as he gazed at me. I stared back.

"You seem to have a penchant for turning up when and where you're not wanted," he finally said.

I shrugged. "It's good to have a skill."

A faint smirk curled his lips.

"Apparently," I added, "a diet of steel didn't permanently disagree with you."

"Survival is one of *my* skills," he replied.

"So far at least," I agreed.

His smirk grew. He turned his head and glanced back at Kamrack. "This is he," he said. "Ruenn Maclang. Though I don't know how he got here. At least not yet."

Kamrack nodded. Tregren stepped around me. I heard him take up a position at my back, waiting, no doubt, like a trained hound for his next orders. Vessoth approached me next, his expression full of gloating. I did not appreciate seeing such a look on what was essentially my own face.

"Finally," Vessoth said. "Your crimes have brought you helpless before me."

"My only 'crimes' have been to oppose you and your wife Vohanna's tyranny."

He slapped me. Tension surged into my muscles; my teeth clenched. I took a step toward him and he ducked back quickly in startlement. But the tip of a sword pressed suddenly against me from behind and that provided enough incentive for me to swallow my rage. I'd had my spine severed once; I did not care to repeat the experience.

Vessoth approached even closer. "You will die here," he said. "Die in agony. I will take great pleasure in the watching. And then I will replace you."

Tension ached in my arms. I imagined my hands going around his throat, strangling him slowly despite the face that he wore. But it was no more than imagination. For the moment he might as well have been back on the moon of Nimeru. To touch him would be to die myself, and with my hands bound behind me I could never kill him before Tregren ran me though.

"No one will buy you as Ruenn Maclang for long," I finally grated out. "It doesn't matter what you look like on the outside."

"Oh! Will they not? Or do you perhaps fear that I'll replace you all too easily? Perhaps even in the arms of your loving wife?"

For a moment, anger surged through me again. Then I thought more carefully about what he'd said. To imagine that my queen would be fooled in such a matter. It was ridiculous. I laughed out loud.

"Try that with Rannon," I said, "and you'll be wearing your intestines for a hat."

Vessoth's green "Ruenn Maclang" eyes went deathly cold. He drew himself up. His hands lifted and black embers began to bleed from his fingers. I could see the outline of milkstones pressing out against the skin of his palms. When Vessoth had fled Nimeru, he'd been weak. Most of his toir'in-or stones had been taken from him during his imprisonment. It looked as if he'd found replacements for those stones, and he almost surely had the power to rip me apart with sorcery alone.

"I'm going to kill you," he said.

I prepared myself.

"Let me do it," a voice said from behind me.

Tregren!

Vessoth looked past me, over my shoulder. "You already failed once," he snapped at the fhaze.

"I admit I was overconfident," Tregren replied. "He surprised me. That won't happen again. I'll make him suffer."

The black light bleeding from Vessoth's hands began to dissipate, but still a frown molded his features. He glanced back over his own shoulder toward Kamrack. "It's dangerous to wait," he said. "We should kill him now. He's proven himself slippery before. I don't want to take any chance on him escaping."

Kamrack nodded. "You're probably right. But…it would be glorious to see. I missed their fight on Hael. I could have a second chance to watch two blademasters face each other. And here, we could make sure that even if Maclang wins, he does not *win*."

Vessoth shook his head and snarled an oath under his breath, but he lowered his hands and turned away from me to stalk back to his chair. Tregren came up to stand on my left. He was looking at Kamrack, who seemed to be musing upon something.

Finally, the big Asadhie looked directly at his servant. "Prepare yourself, Tregren. In one dhaur you'll meet this being who is enemy to us all in our private arena. Do not fail to kill him this time."

Tregren bowed. "Your will be done, My Lord."

CHAPTER FORTY

KILLING TIME

The guards returned after some signal from Kamrack and escorted me to a small, bare room in the tower that could serve as a cell. Only a dhaur passed before they fetched me again and took me down a set of wooden stairs into a large underground room. I recognized it immediately as an arena—a circular area, paved with marble, with blood drains in strategic places. The guards pushed me roughly into the center of the area and left me there, with my hands still bound behind me.

Dark thoughts bloomed and roiled within me, but I held them in check by telling myself that I'd soon have a chance to gain some measure of revenge. To distract myself, I gazed around. Tiers of seats rose on three sides of the arena. On the fourth side rested only a single throne of dark gray basalt. Even as I noted the king's chair, Kamrack came in from the wings of the arena and seated himself. Four more Minotaur guards followed, carrying an elaborate throne of wood. They placed it to the right of Kamrack's throne and Vessoth soon arrived to seat himself pretentiously upon it.

The six guards retreated into the nearby tiers, and Tregren, the fhaze, came out from the wings and crossed into the arena to approach me. He wore a chest plate and greaves of boiled gray leather, and a gold-hilted rapier hung at his right side. He carried a second sword, my own Llurn blade, which had so recently been taken from me.

With no expression on his face, Tregren stepped around behind me. I heard his footsteps pause. For a bare instant I felt the tip of a sword press against my back, at almost the exact point where a blade had once stabbed into Ruenn Maclang and paralyzed him. I tensed, fearing in that instant that Kamrack had rethought his decision and either intended to have me executed, or paralyzed again.

The sword tip finally removed itself; I felt my wrists grasped and twisted. Steel slid between my palms to caress the ropes binding my hands. Those ropes fell away. Tregren stepped back, but not before allowing himself the pleasure of slicing the sword lightly across the pad of flesh below my right thumb. Blood flowed in response. I let it run, hoping it would clot quickly, but rubbed at my wrists to urge feeling back into my hands.

Tregren strode to a point several feet in front of me and stopped. My sword hung from his left hand. He drew his own blade into his right, then lifted both arms in command. As if in answer to the fhaze's order, long steel poles began to ascend from previously unnoticed holes in the floor all around the arena. As the poles reached a height of about five feet, pairs of twin blades unfolded up and down their entire lengths and began to spin. In an instant, we were surrounded by a wall of whirring death.

"Good way to make sure no one runs from a fight," I said. It occurred to me, also, that anyone who was forced back into those whirling fans, or merely misjudged their location, would be badly hurt.

Tregren smiled but made no other response to my observation. He tossed the Llurn blade at my feet, gestured for me to pick it up. I did not move other than to lift my right hand to my mouth and suck at the still bleeding cut the fhaze had gifted me with.

"Well," the fhaze said after a moment. "Take up your sword. Let us begin."

Now that battle was nearly upon me, I felt my training reasserting itself over my roiling emotions. For a moment, the rage inside me was under control. I deliberately waited another moment, then lowered my right hand and wiped it on my breeks. The bleeding had mostly stopped; Baadon's blood clotted faster than a Human's normally would. No doubt, Tregren had hoped to slicken my grip on the sword. I didn't intend to let that happen.

"Do you think things will end any differently for you this time?" I asked.

A smirk curled Tregren's pantherish lips. "You were lucky last time. You know it. The same won't happen again."

I shrugged, but still made no move to pick up the sword. Once more I wiped my hand on my breeks, and this time only the faintest smear of crimson came off on the leathers.

Tregren's lips thinned. "Don't think you can anger me into behaving foolishly the way you did Dharus when you first joined the crew of *The Painted Maid*. He was nothing compared to me."

"So you know about *The Painted Maid* and Dharus, do you? What about Emig? He was quite the swordsman but he didn't fare well against me." I shrugged my shoulders. "I suppose, though, that he did about as well as you did the first time."

He made no response to my barbs, but only said: "I believe you are familiar with a certain artifact found in the stronghold of the pirate brotherhood. I used it to contact a friend of mine. Through his sources, he was able to enlighten me about everything that has occurred with you since you first set foot in the tavern at Drin's Landing. Beating Dharus means nothing. His knowledge of the blade was miniscule. Emig was good. But I'm the one who trained him."

"And what about before Drin's Landing?" I asked. "What do you think I was doing then?"

"I don't care how you escaped from that Sky Island. Chalathar must still be there. Or be dead. If he were anywhere close, Kamrack and Vessoth would have detected the signatures of his toir'in-or. Without him, you are nothing. Now…pick…up…your weapon."

I looked away from Tregren for a moment, gave final consideration to my hand. The bleeding had stopped. Glancing back toward the fhaze, I reached out with a booted foot and hooked the toe into the basket hilt of the Llurn blade. I kicked the sword up into the air and caught it, then stood casually at ease.

Surprised by my action, Tregren took an abrupt step backward and brought his own sword to an on guard position. I stepped forward, swung my blade out to tap against his. I let him feel the strength in my arm.

"The last time we fought," I said, "you had multiple blades and I still beat you. This time will be even easier. And much quicker."

"We'll see," he said, and lunged toward me with his blade straight out for the kill.

I parried hard, knocking his sword to the side. A swordsman is trained to do one of two things after blocking an attack—riposte, or step back to give yourself room to work your own blade. My blade was out of line for any riposte. Tregren expected me to step back. I didn't.

As the fhaze's lunge brought him toward me, I stepped sharply into his attack. My left hand shot out and grabbed him by the throat. The fingers tightened like a vice around his windpipe. He gasped; his eyes widened. I saw his Nokarran features go fluid and knew he was about to shift shape to escape my grasp. I head butted him.

Tregren's features were already starting to flow. My forehead hammered brutally into that semi-liquid face. Blood and a clear serum sprayed. For an instant, the fhaze was stunned and unable to continue his transformation. In that instant, I brought my sword back around and thrust it into his side just where the plates of his armor met.

Deeply, deeply the blade buried itself—until the sharp tip burst through on the other side of his body. The fhaze's form convulsed around the blade, and I lost control over the hateful spirit living inside of me. I drew the sword back, twisting it as I pulled it free. Tregren's mouth opened to scream. But a gruel of blood and vomit and pale ichor purled out instead of any sound.

I hacked across with the sword, chopping almost completely through his neck. His head flopped to one side; his eyes goggled. A hiss of air escaped like steam from the gaping hole above his chest. A writhing mass of liquid-black tentacles erupted from that same hole. Even as they slapped out to grab me, I stepped back, rose onto my toes and cleaved my sword down through the fhaze's body, splitting him from neck to waist.

Gore splattered; nodules of pink-white flesh rose and burst along the edges of the awful wound, sending out tendrils of gristle that linked quickly with each other. It was as if some invisible spider were building a web at breakneck speed. I heard screaming, coming as if from inside my head. My sendahtia skills were weak but even I could pick up the agony of the fhaze as it tried to knit itself back together. It did not trouble me.

Oddly enough, the monstrous thing still held its gold-hilted sword in a recognizably Nokarran right hand. I plucked the blade away, kicked out with a booted foot. The thing went flying backward into the madly whirling fans that encircled our battlefield. Shreds of tissue and serum sprayed everywhere. I took a step toward that barricade myself and whipped Tregren's sword across that spinning wall toward Vessoth, who was just starting to rise from his chair in shock.

Vessoth's hands darted up. His palms were full of black. *Milkstones.* Dark flame smote forth from those toir'in-or, slagging Tregren's rapier into a spatter of molten metal before it could reach him. Vessoth shrieked in rage. He shrieked through Ruenn Maclang's throat; his contorted face was *my* face. I wanted to noose my hands around that throat. I wanted to smash that face.

I took several steps back, then launched myself in a dead run directly toward the spinning wall that blurred around me. At nearly the last instant, I leaped, putting every ounce of strength I had into it. I went up, up—and over. In Ruenn Maclang's body, I could never have made it. In Baadon's body I had room to spare.

I landed in a crouch, exploded out of that toward Vessoth. He thrust his hands out. A blast of black light churned toward me. I dodge to one side, felt the wind of his attack whip past me. Triumph curved my mouth as I lifted my blade for the strike that would cut the Snake God down.

I'd forgotten Kamrack. He too was an Asadhie. Even as my blade hacked toward Vessoth's face, Kamrack's axe seemed to materialize in the sword's path. The axe was not a real weapon but some kind of projection. Yet, my blade struck it and rebounded as if it were true steel. Stinging pain rushed up my arms, but the cry I unleashed was of frustrated rage.

In that moment, Vessoth had me. His hands were already sketching quivers of black arrows in the air. He pushed them toward me; I could not avoid them. Despair hit, and fled just as quickly. I would die when the sorcerous arrows struck, but I had to take Vessoth along. That was all that was important, to kill this source of all my rage. I lunged forward. The arrows flashed toward me…and winked abruptly out of existence.

The shock of it froze me. And Vessoth. For an instant we were face to face and I did nothing. Kamrack did not freeze. With a howl, he hurled his real axe toward me. I saw it coming from the corner of an eye, got my sword up to deflect it. The power behind the throw drove me backward, though, and in that instant Vessoth turned and ran.

I was left facing Kamrack. He stared up at the ceiling, as if he could see through the stone there into the distant sky. It seemed that a faint rumble came from above us. But perhaps it was only my imagination.

"We are under attack!" Kamrack shouted.

Attack! *Yes*! Euphoria swept me. My signal had been seen. Queen Lavisa's people. Chalathar and my friends. Anyone else they'd been able to recruit. They were striking now. And for this moment…any Asadhie sorcery was cancelled.

Kamrack seemed to realize this at the same instant. He spun toward the wall behind his throne, ripped down an axe that hung there as decoration. When he spun back, his furious gaze found his guards. He pointed the axe at me while shouting to them. "Kill the spy! I must see to blunting the attack."

There were six of the guards. Bull-men all. They came swarming toward me with their weapons drawn. I knew what had happened to Vessoth and Kamrack's sorcery. The Evrisanie had happened. The Llurns had filled some of their zeppelin-like airships with the small creatures; they'd flown them down into the city of Nakish-amora. Such strength those small beings had when they were grouped together. No toir'in-or sorcery could work in the face of their sendahtia powers.

But the guards who charged toward me were not sorcerers. Their weapons were steel and iron. The Evrisanie could do nothing about that.

CHAPTER FORTY-ONE

PURSUIT

Fight or flee! There was only one choice for me. Vessoth was running, seeking escape. He must not be allowed to gain it. I had to catch him, stop him, kill him—while the Evrisanie dampening effect held sway over the power of the toir'in-or stones. I turned away from the rushing guards and tore after Vessoth.

I caught only a glimpse of the Snake God as he reached the top of the wide set of steps leading up from the arena area. I followed, sheathing my gory sword so I could run faster. At the top of the stairs, two corridors extended. Neither had a door. The echoes of racing footsteps came from the corridor on the left. I burst along it only to find more stairs at the end.

Up and up we went. Before me came the speeding sound of Vessoth's steps; behind I heard the thud of the guards' boots as they hammered in pursuit. I was gaining on both. The stairs ended at a corridor. Four doorways loomed in either wall along that hallway. And I could no longer hear Vessoth's footsteps.

I paused in an agony of indecision. Had Vessoth continued straight down the corridor or turned through one of the four doorways? I had to make a selection. Quickly. The Minotaur guards had fallen back but they'd reach this point in seconds. I'd have only one chance to get it right. I opened my mind, trying in desperation to call upon what little sendahtia powers I possessed. Queen Lavisa had said I was better at receiving than sending. Could I make use of that talent now?

An impression came through. *Second door on the left.* It seemed to glow red in my mind, as if with blood and murder. But was this a true sensing or merely a wishful hunch? There was no time to consider. I turned through the second door, passed quickly through a small room into another corridor, one which rapidly narrowed as I raced along it. The way angled upward and the narrowing had to mean that we were climbing very high in the tower. If Vessoth were indeed in front of me, he was running out of escape room.

The corridor ended abruptly—at a wall. Frustration, rage, despair flashed through me. I'd lost Vessoth. I cursed the decision to trust in some power other than flesh or steel. I'd have to retrace my steps, probably have to fight my way through Kamrack's guards before I had a chance to make another choice and try to catch up to the Snake God. By then it would surely be too late.

I lifted both hands, pounded them angrily against the offending wall. Dust pattered down. The wall...shifted slightly. My eyes widened. I threw my weight against one side of the wall and it rotated outward. I stumbled through into a large room. It was a place I recognized. A half dozen Asadhie surrogate chambers were scattered about. To one side was a stairwell clogged with debris as if from an explosion. This was the room where I'd first entered the tower. The stairwell was the one I'd thrown a milkstone down before it blew up.

I spun toward the window whose glass I'd broken out to get into this room. Vessoth stood there. But he was trapped. Some of his own people must have bolted iron bars across the window from the inside as a temporary measure. The Asadhie sorcerer wanted out but was stymied by the bars. He'd been at work on the bolts before I entered. Now he stopped work, drew a sword into hands that shook.

I smiled an awful smile, kicked back with one boot against the secret door that had let me into this room. It closed. And unless the Minotaur guards knew the secret, or stumbled upon it as I had, they'd not be able to reach us here. Vessoth knew it as well as me. He lifted a hand, sketched a rune in the air. It died aborning. His magic was gone, smothered by the collective energy of the Evrisanie. Of such small things is victory made.

I shook my head at Vessoth. "Nowhere to go," I gloated. "No escape."

He backed away from the window, into a corner. He lifted the sword, as if it would be of use to him. "How did you... How did you...steal my power?" he asked, his voice trembling.

"You'll never know."

"Please! Please. I surrender. Imprison me again. Anything. Just don't kill me."

I shook my head a second time. "It would never be possible to trust you. For the safety of all Talera, you have to die. I stepped toward him, my own sword ready.

"Do not move, Scum!" came a gruff voice from outside the window.

I turned slightly, keeping an eye on Vessoth while simultaneously glancing toward the speaker. For an instant, a deep sense of relief flushed over me. At the window, with a crossbow in his hand pointed into the room, was a man I recognized. It was Gallas, a member of Nyshphal's

Imperial guard, which also served as a police force under the leadership of Rajan Critus. His presence meant that my brother Bryce had been able to contact Nyshphal and get some help for this attack.

I started to turn further toward Gallus and speak, but he hefted his crossbow and snarled at me to, "Stand!" I realized the truth in that instant; he didn't recognize me. Well, of course. He'd never seen me in the Baadon form.

Did that mean?

"My lord," Gallus said. "Are you all right?" He was looking at Vessoth, speaking to the Snake God who wore the visage of Ruenn Maclang, the visage of the man who'd recently become Gallus's king.

"I am all right, soldier," Vessoth said. "Thanks to you. But now." He gestured in my direction. "I want you to kill this scum for me."

CHAPTER FORTY-TWO

WHO LIVES AND WHO DIES

"That's not Ruenn Maclang!" I said abruptly to Gallus. "That's Vessoth, the sorcerer who you were brought here to stop. He only wears the outward form of Ruenn Maclang."

"Do not listen to him, soldier," Vessoth snapped. "*He* is the sorcerer. Have you ever seen a being like him? Strike while his sorcery is weakened. Strike for Nyshphal. For your Queen, Rannon. For me, your lord."

"Have you ever known Ruenn Maclang to need someone else to do his killing for him?" I asked Gallus. I pointed at Vessoth. "*This* is the creature who threatens your Queen and your homeland. Put down your crossbow and let me finish him."

Gallus hesitated, but how long would that last? And if I attacked Vessoth, Gallus would surely shoot me. I played the only other card I held.

"If he is truly Ruenn Maclang," I said. "Ask him to name you. He can't. But I can. I know you serve in the Imperial Guard under Rajan Critus. I know other things as well about you. He knows nothing."

The doubt grew in Gallus's eyes. His gaze shifted between me and Vessoth, though his crossbow did not waver. Finally, he asked Vessoth:

"So, what is my name? I've spoken more than once to Ruenn Maclang. I believe he will remember me."

Still, Vessoth tried to bluff. "I...I know it. But at this moment I cannot think." He jabbed a finger in my direction. "This sorcerer. He attacked my mind. I fought him off but there's still...confusion. But surely you can *see* who I am? Surely you recognize me as your emperor?"

A thrill struck through me at Vessoth's words. I had him.

"Gallus," I said softly. "You know that Ruenn Maclang has never called himself 'emperor.' He does not even like it when others do. This being is *not* Ruenn Maclang. Lower your weapon and I'll prove it to you.'"

For another moment, Gallus considered. Then: "If you are indeed Ruenn Maclang," he said to Vessoth. "Tell me about your Queen."

"My Queen?" Vessoth seemed taken aback. "She… I…love her. Of course. She is beautiful."

"How do you *feel* about her?" Gallus demanded.

"I do not understand," Vessoth protested. "I have told you that I love her. What more can I say? She has lovely black hair. We chose each other."

Gallus shifted his gaze to me. I smiled and spoke: "Rannon Jystral has hair as dark and fine as silk. And eyes bluer than sapphire. But none of that truly matters to Ruenn Maclang. Without her, his life would be empty. He would not be a man, but a beast."

Gallus nodded at my words and abruptly lowered his weapon. I was watching him, but was not so foolish as to have ignored Vessoth. The Snake God was trapped without the toir'in-or sorcery that he'd depended on for his entire long life. That sorcery had armed him against his enemies, had armored him against danger, had allowed him to escape at will into another body. It had maintained his very life.

Now the power of the milkstones had abandoned him. For a weapon, he had only the blade in his hands. With a desperate scream, Vessoth lunged toward me, thrusting the sword toward my unprotected side. I'd expected it, was ready for it.

No doubt, Vessoth had practiced with swords—perhaps in the very body I now wore. But practice is not the same as battle. Vessoth was no bladesman. In his panic, his attack was clumsy. I twisted to my right, easily avoiding it. My left arm swept downward, locking around his and trapping his weapon arm against my side. My hand crushed his wrist. He screamed again, with pain this time. As if under its own power, my sword lifted and the tip pressed up against the soft pad of flesh just behind the sorcerer's chin.

I looked down upon the Snake God, who wore the stolen form of Ruenn Maclang. He looked up at me. His green eyes filled with terror; his mouth quivered with it. I thought of all the horrors visited upon my beloved Nyshphal by this being and his wife, Vohanna. My hands trembled with the urge to slay him.

"Please!" Vessoth whimpered.

I did not count my own pain. But so many others had suffered. My brother, Bryce. Ahrethane and Diken Graye. Shai. These still lived with their pain, but too many of my friends had been brutally tortured and murdered at the behest of this fiend. He deserved death.

Flesh is weak; steel is strong. I pushed a little harder on the sword where it pressed beneath his mouth, and a pearl of red blood appeared at the very tip of the blade.

"Please! Please! Please!" Vessoth begged. "Punish me. Imprison me. Please do not kill me!"

I thought of Rannon. She had nearly been lost to me. A howling rage tore up through my soul. I wanted to ram my sword through Vessoth's skull, to tear his head from his body. But the man inside of me could not quite do it. The khi of Ruenn Maclang could not slaughter even this monster in brutal cold blood.

No, Ruenn Maclang could not.

But Baadon could.

And the black thing that lived inside of me twisted and tore free. It was Baadon's hand that suddenly pressed upward on the sword. The tip slid through soft meat, thrust through the mouth, through the tongue. Blood sprayed from between Vessoth's lips. But the sword drove on, through the palate into the brain. A shriek died in Vessoth's throat. His eyes bulged. His whole body shuddered, spasmed violently. I held him until he stilled, then drew the blade slowly out of the awful wound and let Vessoth and his purloined body slump to the floor.

I glanced toward the window, toward Gallus. He looked distinctly ill. But before I could speak, a crashing sound came from the corner of the room behind me. I spun about to see the panel door to the secret passage smash inward. Two Minotaur guards came through, but not by choice. They were being driven.

Chalathar and Jubyl appeared, weapons gleaming and slashing. Before I could take more than a step in that direction, the battle was over. The Minotaurs lay dead or dying upon the floor, and Chalathar turned in my direction. He smiled. I returned it. He saw the other body that lay on the room's floor. His eyes widened and he knelt quickly beside that body. His hand touched the throat, held for an instant and fell away. He looked up at me.

"Dead," he said.

"It was Vessoth," I said. "How he manage to acquire a clone of me, I don't know."

Chalathar nodded.

A small popping sound caught everyone's attention. We looked at Vessoth's corpse. Half a dozen knuckle-sized boils appeared suddenly on the dead sorcerer's body, one in the forehead, one in each palm, and three in a line across the upper chest. The boils broke open as we looked on. Six toir'in-or milkstones extruded themselves from the puckered wounds and fell out on the floor. Their whiteness was clouded with swirls of gray/black, like milk gone moldy. Chalathar scooped them up and tucked them into a pouch at his belt, then rose.

"Jubyl!" a voice called from beyond the barred window.

We all turned. An Indigo Llurn stood there beside Gallus.

"My lord," he said. "The enemy is recovering from their surprise. They've started to bring up ballistas. Our airships will be in danger soon."

Jubyl glanced at Chalathar, then snapped out an order. "All right. Time to go." He started past me toward the window.

"Wait!" I said. "What of Kamrack?"

Chalathar shook his head. "We fought our way through most of the tower. No sign of him. Did you not see him?"

"He went one way and Vessoth went the other. I followed Vessoth."

Again Chalathar nodded. "Well, no time now. Without Vessoth, Kamrack's claws have been trimmed. He was not the catalyst behind their plans anyway, and we can't risk losing our entire force in this attack."

My fists clenched, but I knew he was right. I turned away, toward the window. Jubyl worked there at the bolts holding the iron bars in place. I strode over to him and, in a fit of pique, reached down to grasp the bottom row of the bars. With a tremendous wrench, I tore them free and tossed them aside.

For a moment, silence claimed the room. Then activity resumed. I did not take part. With the act of tearing lose the bars, all the rage that had nestled within me dissipated. I felt suddenly adrift, like a rudderless raft in a wild current.

Half a dozen more of Chalathar's and Jubyl's men had come out of the secret passageway now. Chalathar called them to him, gestured at the body of Vessoth. "Bring this one," he ordered.

I stepped to one side as the men picked the corpse up, carried it to the window, and passed it through to others. Jubyl was outside, calling for ropes to be lowered from the airship that hung just above our tower. I looked back for Chalathar. He had paused to examine the surrogate chambers placed around the room. He slapped one of them, called again to his men.

"Take this as well."

I watched, but with only the faintest curiosity, while Chalathar rushed quickly to each of the remaining chambers and pressed his fingers against various runes engraved along their sides. Each chamber he so touched, snapped open. A blue mist curled up from within them. It smelled of ozone and something else that was sweetly-sick.

Chalathar rushed to me. He gestured toward the window but I didn't move. He gave me a push and I turned and slipped through onto the roof. The Asadhie sorcerer followed. Outside it was cacophony—with the shriek of saddle birds, the whistle of arrows flashing, the roar of war-cries breaking the sky. Jubyl's men had been using God's Fire against the city, a concoction of oil and pitch mixed with sulfur. It clings and burns where it touches. I heard explosions and saw smoke and fire below us. Yet, the fight seemed distant from me.

The corpse of Vessoth was already being hauled up toward the Llurn ship overhead. More ropes had been attached to the surrogate chamber and it started to sway upward as well. A rope ladder provided a way for living men and women to reach the deck and I took it at Chalathar's urging. Chalathar followed after grabbing a clay pot of God's Fire from a nearby warrior and hurling it through the window into the room we'd just quitted. Flames roared up.

The "deck" of the Llurn airship consisted of a big, oval-shaped gondola woven from thick reeds. Just above us, hooked on with stout cables, was the great bag filled with Vyn'ishad-or gas. I couldn't see the pilot but as soon as everyone was aboard, the ropes that anchored us to the tower were cut and the ship's prow lifted.

Large propellers on the gondola's stern, driven by the muscle power of crewmen, provided directional control. These were cranked down for maximum lift, and a lot of ballast had already been discarded in the form of weaponry that had been used against our enemies. We began to climb. But the process was slow. Looking over the side, I wondered dispassionately if it would be enough, and in time.

The enemy had indeed gotten themselves organized. Perhaps Kamrack had been part of that. Several massive ballistas had been hauled into the Inner City of Nakish-amora by teams of Minotaur warriors. These were far larger than the ones we'd used on *The Painted Maid*, larger even than the ones arming the air battleships of the Nyshphalian navy.

The other three Llurn vessels were already too high for even these great enemy weapons to strike. But our ship was not. As I looked on, the ballistas were cranked to their highest angle and aimed in our direction. They fired.

A dozen forty pound arrows came climbing toward us at incredible speed. Their heads were wickedly barbed and would tear us open if they hit. I watched them close with us but no fear stirred within me. A mild curiosity still seemed to be my only emotion.

Around me, men and women clutched at the rails of the ship or clutched at each other. I heard curses and murmured prayers. Bargains were struck with many gods. The arrows closed in. Deep breaths were drawn and held. The arrows faltered. They fell away. Cheers erupted.

None of it touched me.

CHAPTER FORTY-THREE

BLEAK SEASON

Nakish-amora began to fall behind us as we rose into a cloud dotted sky. The emerald of that sky was rapidly fading. We were finally in the summer passage, that time when the sun turns from green to gold and ushers in the hot days of the Taleran year. In many places it is a call to festival. But not here. Not now.

A few enemy saddle birds had lifted to attack our small fleet but they were beaten off by a host of our own war-birds and their riders. My friends Diken and Valyan were among those riders. There were others who I recognized from Nyshphal, and many faces of those I did not know. In the short time they'd had, Queen Lavisa and Chalathar had raised a small army. I'd likely have been dead by now if they'd not.

Slowly, in the aftermath of danger, the crew of the airship drifted away to their duties. I was alone at the rail when Shai came to speak with me. She grasped my shoulder with a smile on her lean warrior's face.

"Glad you survived, my friend," she said.

I nodded. "And you. Have you seen Bryce?"

"He's on one of the other ships. The last I saw of him, he was fine."

I nodded again.

Chalathar joined us. He smiled at Shai; he studied me.

"Are you all right?" he asked.

I shrugged. "I feel…empty."

Shai frowned. Chalathar vented a small sigh.

"I'm not surprised," the Asadhie sorcerer finally said. "You've been running on hate for a long time. First for Vohanna. Then for Vessoth. That hate no longer has a target. Too, it seems that being in the body of Baadon has…changed you."

I glanced at him. "Changed me?"

"Have you not felt it?"

I looked away from his gaze.

His voice softened. "I lived with hate myself for many long years. Sometimes still it possesses me. But I have learned how, most times, to let it go. Baadon was once inhabited by Vessoth; if anyone were a child of hate, it would be he. Even without Vessoth's khi within that body, there must have been some residue left. I should have realized this. You've been resisting it. And resisting well. But you are not like us. You've had no experience at switching forms. And switching to *that* body had to be particularly difficult given your history with Vohanna and Vessoth."

Chalathar's words made me grit my teeth; my fists clenched. I forced them to relax and took a deep breath. "It started getting worse after I joined the pirates," I finally said. "My thoughts grew constantly black, constantly attuned to slaughter. It felt good. Now, it's as if something inside of me is…sated. But it's not gone." I met the sorcerer's gaze. "I'm afraid of it. I don't know how long I can control it. Or who it might turn on now that Vessoth is dead."

Chalathar reached out and placed a hand on my shoulder. I winced, as if my skin had been scraped raw.

"I have a cure for what ails you, my friend."

"What cure?" I asked.

"Two cures really. The first is to get you out of this body and back into your own."

I shook my head. "You said it takes a year to grow a clone. My body won't be ready for a long time yet. I don't know if I can make it."

"It does take a year. But we have one clone of Ruenn Maclang that's already fully grown."

"What?" I asked, startled.

Shai, too, looked confused.

Chalathar gestured toward the surrogate chamber that we'd taken on board from Kamrack's tower.

"I looked at that," I said. "It may be a clone but it's not mine."

"To the contrary," Chalathar replied. He motioned for us to follow as he walked over to the chamber.

I joined him and stood looking in through the glass lid at the body beneath. When I'd first seen the form inside this chamber, it had been covered by a pink, jelly-like substance. That had mostly dissipated, leaving me with a better view of the thing. It certainly resembled a Human and was about the size of Ruenn Maclang, but it did not look like me.

I gazed in confusion at Chalathar. "Not me," I said.

"It's the caul," the sorcerer replied. "Clones grow with a thick layer of tissue over their forms to protect them. Believe me, when the caul is removed, this will be the body of Ruenn Maclang."

A spear of hope blazed suddenly within me. Was it possible? I could barely tolerate the Baadon form anymore. But until this moment, I'd expected to have to wear it for many more months.

"How?" I asked, trying to manage my hopes before they rose higher and were dashed. "If it takes a year to grow a clone, how did Vessoth and Kamrack manage to grow several in such a short time? It was only weeks ago that the fhaze stole my body."

"I've asked myself that," Chalathar said. "I don't know the answer for sure. Either they managed to get a sample of your flesh long before we thought they had. Or, they found some way to accelerate the cloning process. I suspect the former. But, whichever is the answer, the proof that they succeeded lies before us."

"Is this...." I gestured toward the clone. "Is it...clean?"

"You mean, has it been implanted with milkstones so they can influence it?"

"Yes. Or anything else they may have done to...alter it."

"I don't think so. But I won't know for sure until I can examine it using my own toir'in-or stones. I've asked Jubyl to drop us off on one of the small floating islands that lack a population of Evrisanie. We'll take this chamber with us and I'll open a gate back to the Hael planetoid. If everything is fine with the clone, I'll complete your retransference there."

I stood stunned, but nodded.

Inside, I hoped.

And feared.

CHAPTER FORTY-FOUR

RETURN TO FORM

Chalathar opened the door to his surrogate room within the Hael planetoid, and Shai, Valyan, Diken, and I carried the chamber holding the clone of Ruenn Maclang within. Bryce followed and closed the door.

I'd seen this room once. It was nowhere near as large or as beautifully appointed as the surrogate room on Nald where Chalathar had transferred my khi *into* the body of Baadon. It held only a dozen surrogate chambers, some filled, some empty, and the walls were barren rock. But there was a black altar much like the one on Nald, and Chalathar carried his toir'in-or within himself. Those stones would provide the power needed to transfer my khi back from Baadon into the form of Ruenn Maclang.

At least I hoped so.

We placed the surrogate chamber on the floor and Chalathar unlocked it and opened the lid. I reached within and picked up the limp and empty clone and laid it on the altar. I could see a thick caul of nearly translucent tissue completely covering the body. Chalathar used a knife to cut this away, and the face of Ruenn Maclang was revealed to all. Chalathar had been right. It was my face—one that I desperately wanted back.

Hope warred with terror inside me. Chalathar interrupted the battle. "To complete the transference, it would be best for Ruenn and me to be alone. If the rest of you will wait outside."

The others nodded, turned to go. Diken gave me a smile. Bryce and Valyan each touched my shoulder before leaving. Chalathar followed them out for a moment, leaving me alone in the presence of two bodies that belonged to me. In the form of Baadon, I studied the clone. It was almost, but not quite, the Ruenn Maclang I remembered. There were no scars, for one thing. Ruenn had earned scars. I wondered if I would miss them.

The Baadon form—tall, fast, immensely strong—was a body built for violence. It had served me well in its own way. I would not miss it.

Chalathar reentered the room and approached. "Are you ready?"

I thought of unfinished business and unanswered questions. Kamrack still lived and still had an immense army, though Chalathar believed that he would not act without the goading of Vessoth. Too, we still did not know what had happened to my old, crippled body. Had Vessoth ever actually gotten his hands on it? If so, it was probably still hidden away in Nakish-amora. Or, had it been destroyed by Chalathar's booby-traps on Nald?

The Minotaurs who'd invaded Chalathar's home base on Nald had abandoned it again. They'd left it gutted, and though we'd searched it we'd found no signs of any bodies, not mine, and not that of Rence, whose whereabouts remained a mystery. None of this, of course, was within my power to do anything about.

I met Chalathar's gaze. "More than ready," I replied.

He led me toward one of the empty surrogate chambers standing upright around the room. The front of the casket-like structure opened as he pressed at some of the engraved symbols extending down the side. I stepped within.

"It'll be over soon," Chalathar said, before shutting the door.

A snick came as the chamber sealed. A puff of cool air misted across me, faintly blue and with a scent like rain. A lassitude began to coat my muscles as Chalathar returned to the altar to stand beside the clone. For a moment longer, though, my thoughts were fully awake. I recalled the agony of my transference into Baadon. I wondered if it would be as bad, or worse, to go back. I hoped not, but in truth would have borne even greater pain to return once more to who I was.

The lassitude finally reached my mind. Through blurring eyes, I watched Chalathar's hands sketching bright runes in the air over his altar. The body of Ruenn Maclang began to glow and twitch. My eyes closed.

And opened again.

Something was wrong. I was looking up at a ceiling rather than out from the surrogate chamber where I stood. Then I realized what that change of viewpoint meant. I sat up abruptly. A dozen feet away stood the chamber with Baadon's body in it.

I turned. Chalathar stood beside me, smiling. I grinned back, grinned hugely.

"I was expecting it to hurt," I said.

"Easier to come home than to leave," he remarked. Then, as he had done after my first transference, he brushed his fingers through the air in front of my face. A glowing oval appeared, resolved itself into a kind of mirror. I saw myself. I saw Ruenn Maclang—the same dark brown hair, the same sharp features and green eyes. Even the scar that I'd carried along the line of my left jaw since my early days on Talera was back. I gazed at Chalathar with wonder.

"The scar! How?"

He chuckled. "All your scars. At least all the ones I knew about. A minor rearranging of a few skin cells. Simple with a toir'in-or stone. I couldn't have your lovely wife wondering what strange things I allowed to happen to you while you were in my company. She is not to be trifled with."

"No, she is not," I said, and hopped off the altar.

Chalathar caught me as I staggered and nearly fell. "Careful," he said. "It took you a while to get used to the Baadon body; it'll take a while to adjust back to your own."

I laughed. "I've got time." And I did. Whatever had been steadily weighing down my thoughts and mood while I wore the shell of Baadon was gone. I felt free, as I'd not felt in a very long while.

"Here," Chalathar said, handing me some clothes. "Put these on and we'll start on the second part of the cure I promised you."

"Rannon," I said, while slipping into leather boots and breeks and a long-sleeved cotton shirt of forest green.

"Yes," Chalathar agreed. "I've already sent Bryce and your other friends through a gate to Nyshphal. They'll be waiting for you there. With your queen."

Joy leaped inside of me. My whole body trembled with eagerness. Then a thought occurred and I leashed my joy again for a moment. There was something I had to know before returning to my love. It was something that had been promised me. I met Chalathar's gaze until his own smile faded.

"You owe me a story," I said. "A true story."

Chalathar sighed. "Yes. I do. And I *need* to tell someone. But while I originally wanted Shai to hear too, I don't think I'm quite ready to share it all with her. I'll ask you to keep another secret. At least for now."

"If I can," I agreed. "If it does not harm those I love."

Again Chalathar sighed, then nodded. "That will have to do, I suppose."

He closed his eyes for a moment, opened them again and began to speak. His voice was low, oddly inflected. It hardly sounded like the being who had become my friend. Perhaps, in many ways, it was not.

CHAPTER FORTY-FIVE

ASADHIE GENESIS

"Understand," Chalathar said. "Most of what I tell you I did not witness myself. The tale begins far away in time and distance. For much of it, I know only pieced together bits from many sources."

He looked at me. "There are no stars in the sky of Talera but you come from the world of Earth. You've seen them. I've seen them myself. We know that the stars are all suns with planets of their own. There are many millions of them in a great cluster that Earth's Humans call the Spine of Heaven, or the Milky Way."

"Yes," I said.

"Outside the Milky Way are two smaller clusters of stars. Far away and dim."

I nodded. "I've heard them called the Magellanic Clouds."

"Well, the story of Talera now, begins there, and then. It begins with a race called the Sembrini, who dwelt in one of those clusters. I do not know what these beings looked like. I've never seen an image of them. They were highly advanced and peaceful. But they were lonely. They knew of no other intelligences like theirs. And so they made for themselves a companion race. They took a primitive species known as the Selkrie and raised them to sentience, offering them the glory of the suns. It was an act of good intent, and of great hubris.

"The Sembrini wanted fellowship and love; the Selkrie preferred hate. In time, the created went to war with the creator. The Sembrini were not prepared for such violence. They fled rather than fight. The Selkrie followed.

"It was the Sembrini who created the toir'in-or stones. The Selkrie mastered them as well. They used toir'in-or power to smash every symbol of Sembrini existence they could find. The Sembrini fled to the Milky Way. There, they found many other intelligent races. They realized there'd been no need to create the Selkrie. But it was too late.

"The Sembrini wanted only to befriend the new races they met. The Selkrie came to conquer and destroy. It was a group of Selkrie who made

Talera, who brought here all the disparate plants and animals and beings that inhabit it today. Those Selkrie used this world as a playground. You know of them as the Asadhie. The original Asadhie."

"But you are not of that Asadhie," I said. "Nor were Vohanna and Vessoth."

Chalathar shook his head. "Despite their hatred of the Sembrini, the Selkrie so often tried to ape every behavior their creators exhibited. They also took a primitive and savage species and raised them to sentience. *We* were their servants, their slaves, their occasional confidants. I believe, mostly, we were a kind of pet. And they were not particularly solicitous of the things they owned."

"What did the Selkrie look like?" I asked.

"To us, they were tall pillars of white light. Not quite flesh, not quite pure energy. Except, of course, when they chose to house themselves in the surrogate bodies they cultured like fungi in their laboratories."

"Bodies such as...?"

"Such as this one," Chalathar said, indicating his own form. "Most of the surrogates you have seen were created by the Selkrie. Vessoth and Vohanna managed to create others in a much more brutal fashion—through surgery and the bloody sacrifice of their subjects."

"And your own race," I said. "I saw both Vohanna and Vessoth inhabiting shapes that looked like...some large hybrid of an insect and a mollusk. Are those your native forms?"

"Yes."

Chalathar lifted his palms toward me. I saw the gleam of milkstones burning there. The stones begin to flash on and off, and for an instant behind his flesh, as if I were looking through a window smeared with grease, I saw the life force that inhabited him. He had scaled wings of glittering gold, and a dozen crimson tentacles as thin as whips. His black body and head were almost mantis-like, and upon the head bulged a dozen diamond-shaped eyes the color of smoky gin. In the next instant, the glow of the milkstones dimmed and the being before me was just Chalathar again, with pale eyes of the same gin color and hair of reddish-blond.

"My true form," the sorcerer said. "Just as that," he gestured toward the body that I wore once again, "is yours."

"How did your race take over from the original Asadhie?" I asked.

"We didn't. One day, the Selkrie just left. We don't know why they went, or where. They took nothing with them that we could see. They left us behind without a thought or a word, without instruction or guidance.

"As a being is treated, so often he or she comes to treat others the same. We are a long lived race. For a long time after the Selkrie left, we did nothing. Some of us still do nothing. But others of us had learned at least something of what it meant to be gods. We did not have the power over the toir'in-or that the Selkrie had, but we had more than any other race on Talera. We assumed the mantle of the Asadhie.

"Pale shadows of our masters, we might have been, but still we sought to make ourselves rulers of this world. We turned Talera into our battlefield and our playground. The God War that you have heard of was an example of such hubris. It exhausted us, destroyed many of us. It irrevocably changed many others. I was so changed."

Chalathar's voice softened further, verging upon a whisper. And he did not look at me now.

"Other than long life, my species also has the ability to…hibernate, if you will, to enter a trance state where thousands of years might pass without our reckoning. Most of us who had played at games of empire during the God War chose to hibernate afterward. I was one.

"When I woke again, in this age we live in, I saw that some of my people had changed not at all. Vessoth and Vohanna and others liked them still craved only power and destruction. I came to see that the God War had never ended. It had merely paused. That is when I became that which I am now. But it does not matter that I have tried to stop the horror. I am still a member of a vain and savage race, a race of created monsters who should never have existed."

Chalathar fell silent. I knew his story was over, but could scarcely imagine what I might say in response to his pain. I managed only: "We are all savages. All monsters on the inside."

Chalathar looked up at me and smiled, rather wistfully, I thought. "I know," he said. "All we can ever strive to do, is to not be a monster on *this* day. Old wisdom, but I fear it has lost much of its meaning for me."

I grasped his shoulder. "We can also, on our weak days, reach out to others for help in combating our monster."

He nodded, gave a large sigh. "You're right. Will you go now out of this room and find Shai. She should be in the corridor. Ask her to join me. Perhaps it *is* time I shared this all with her."

"Perhaps it is."

"After you speak to her, I'll open a gate for you. Right into the throne room in Timmuzz, where your love awaits."

"I appreciate that," I said. "But not directly into the throne room. Can you put me in one of the gardens on the castle grounds?"

"I can. Why?"

I grinned. "Someday I'll tell you. Or Rannon will."

He chuckled, spread his hands and bowed his head slightly. I grasped his wrist, turned and exited the chamber. As Chalathar had predicted,

Shai was waiting in the corridor. She spun around as I came out and smiled broadly to see me back in the old form of Ruenn Maclang. I thought, though, there was a little disappointment on her face that I was not Chalathar. Her love for him was clear.

"He asked for you to join him inside," I said.

Her smile broadened. She offered her wrist and hand to me in the Taleran fashion. Much to her surprise, I laughed and hugged her. A moment later, she was striding briskly as she entered Chalathar's surrogate room.

A gray sphere of mist formed in the corridor before me. I stepped into that sphere gate and let it take me to Rannon.

CHAPTER FORTY-SIX

HOMECOMING

As I'd requested, the gate opened by Chalathar deposited me in one of the many gardens that grow within the wall surrounding Jystral Palace. Two guards saw me appear and drew their swords before they recognized me. As soon as they did, both dropped to a knee and bowed their heads to their king.

"Up, warriors," I said. "You don't need to kneel before me."

They rose, but stood there uncertainly. I strode to them, grasped each on the shoulder. "Go if you will," I told them. "Tell your queen that her husband will be behind you in just a moment. I have one thing to do first."

"Can we help you, My Lord?" one guard asked.

I grinned at him. "I believe I can manage on my own."

With matching nods, the two men hurried off. I glanced around the garden. Beds of blue and crimson hysis grew thickly. Goldenswords waved in the breeze and honeywhisper moss draped a few samphur and tharspa trees. A Taleran bird pecked at the berries of a hanris bush. In one corner, near the wall, a few moonroses bloomed.

Quickly collecting what I'd come to collect, I strode purposefully toward the steps leading into the palace. Many guards and other people were about. They bowed or curtsied as I passed. I acknowledged them all.

A great staircase rose in the center of the palace and extended up to the third level, which is where the throne room lay. That staircase was of black marble veined with silver and inlaid with fossilized bone. The railings were green glass. I had seen it many times and paid no heed to its beauty. In stepping off the stairs, I did pay heed to the engraved doors of gold and white that marked the entrance I sought. Men opened those doors and I went through.

At one time, the doors had opened into another waiting area and a short hallway with a guard cubicle at the end just before a final and smaller set of doors. Rannon had done away with the waiting area and cubicle, and the inner doors were already thrown wide. I went through them into the throne room of Rannon Jystral, Empress of Nyshphal.

During the reign of Rannon's father, this room had been an ostentatious illustration of wealth and power, meant only for the highest of state functions, those having to do with war and empire. After Hurnan Jystral's death, I had seen the room splashed with blood, with fire blackened walls and battle-slain corpses. That damage had been undone and Rannon had transformed the space into one that welcomed her people on any business, large or small.

Tall windows stood open in the walls to the left and right, pouring in sunlight and fresh air. Carpets softened the hard marble floors, and padded benches were arranged where supplicants could wait in comfort. While in those benches, the men and women of Nyshphal could see the kind of justice their queen dispensed. Of the old days, only the snowwood throne of her father remained. That was a choice of the people, who are often comforted by such signs of continuity and tradition.

Many people filled this great room now. I had eyes only for Rannon. Gray-cloaked guards stood scattered about her. Maids waited in case they should be called. Bryce, and Valyan and Diken Graye stood close to my wife, having brought her word that I would soon be arriving. Rannon was conversing with the three of them when the hubbub quieted and she turned to see me approaching.

She smiled, and the world receded. My wife had taken to wearing her hair up since becoming Empress of Nyshphal, but it was down now, as it had been when I'd first met her. The silken flag of it hung black and soft across her shoulders. And she wore a gown instead of the scarlet battle leathers I'd so often seen her in. That gown was sewn from ivory silk, pleated and draped. She was heartbreakingly beautiful. I walked to her, though I wanted to run. I went to one knee and held up that which I'd gathered in the garden.

"This time I remembered to bring flowers," I said.

Her blue eyes brightened with tears that threatened to fall. But a deep, wilding smile curved her pale face. She took the flowers, a bouquet of blue hysis that were nearly the same color as her eyes, with a moonrose in the center.

Her words followed her actions. "As you promised."

A signal from Rannon brought a maid to her side. She handed the flowers to the young woman. "Put these carefully in a vase," she said. "And bring them here to the throne room to sit in a window."

The maid nodded, took the flowers, stepped back. Rannon reached down, wrapped her hands in the front of my shirt. She pulled me to my feet and we came into each other's arms. We kissed long and passionately there in front of everyone. I imagine most of the watchers were smiling, though I did not see it.

When the kiss broke, leaving us both nearly breathless, Rannon whispered. "Good to see you, husband."

"And you, Saysa," I managed.

Rannon took a deep breath, then gazed around the room. "Please, everyone," she said. "Will you give us a few moments?"

The room cleared quickly, with many smiles that I *could* see. Rannon took my hand, drew me over to one of the windows overlooking rose-stuccoed Timmuzz. She kissed me again before leaning back against the wall next to the window.

"I wasn't sure I'd get you back in one piece," she said. "But you look to have come through it with no new scars." She reached up and ran a finger along the old scar that curved along my jaw. An impish smile twisted her lips. "Have you, perhaps, been doing nothing more than relaxing these long months since I've seen you?"

"Very little of that, Saysa. But it's a rather long story."

"I want to hear it."

"Later," I said, leaning to kiss her again.

She kissed me back, her breath warm. One hand stroked my face, the other captured one of *my* hands and brought it down to rest upon her stomach. When she at last drew back from the kiss and leaned once more against the wall, she kept my hand held tightly in that place. I felt it, a small bulge in her belly that had never been there before.

My eyes widened. I gasped, looked up into Rannon's eyes.

"You're—" I did not finish. I did not need to.

"Yes," she said.

"How long?"

"Only a few months. I think it happened just before the battle of Teleur. During that time when we were making love so often because we weren't sure how long we had together. I'm just beginning to show. Hardly anyone knows. But there's no doubt."

I covered my mouth to keep from whooping with joy. I could not control the size of my smile. Rannon smiled also as she stroked my face.

"It'll be a child of two worlds," she said. "Your Earth and my Talera."

I did not look away from my wife, but through the glass of the window I could feel the heat of Talera's golden summer sun on my shoulders. And I knew that Earth had no part of me anymore.

"No," I said quietly. "A child of one."

COMPLETE CAST OF CHARACTERS

Major Characters

Maclang, Ruenn: An earthman who has made a place for himself on Talera. An American born in 1888. Tall. Lean. A swordsman with green eyes.

Maclang, Bryce: Ruenn's grey-eyed younger brother. Although he was once corrupted by Vohanna's sorcery, he seems to be recovering his original self.

Jystral, Rannon: Queen of the island empire of Nyshphal, and Ruenn's wife.

Vohanna: (Deceased). An Asadhie, supposedly one member of the alien race that created Talera. She hoped to conquer Nyshphal and make it the center of an empire, but her evil was brought to an end in the book, *Witch of Talera*.

Vessoth: Another Asadhie. Vohanna's husband. He was once imprisoned inside the moon of Nimeru by an alliance of other Asadhie, but escaped during the events of *Wraith of Talera*. He is also known as the Snake God.

Chalathar: A mysterious warrior who was finally revealed in *Witch of Talera* to be an Asadhie, supposedly a member of the race who created Talera. Unlike most Asadhie, Chalathar wants to end the constant strife that torments the planet.

Ahrethane: Once a druidess of the forest, she has been irrevocably changed after coming into contact with Asadhie milkstones.

Supporting Characters

Graye, Diken: A Human mercenary. A friend of Ruenn's. Dark eyed. Male.

Jask: A Klar, which is a reptilian race. He and Ruenn fought together in *Swords of Talera* to free his people from tyranny. He became High-Council of the Klar kingdom of Talen.

Jystral, Kuurus: Younger brother of Rannon. He allied himself to Vohanna in an attempt to gain control of Nyshphal, but was arrested for his crimes at the end of *Witch of Talera*.

Critus, Rajan: Commander of the Nyshphalian Imperial guard, which also serves as a police force. Human male.

Tiersal, Valyan: A member of a race called the Emerald Llurns, who were genetically modified from Humans in the past to have emerald skin and yellow eyes. He is a close friend of Ruenn's.

Koremos, Durhain: Nyshphalian noble who helped kidnap Rannon in *Swords of Talera*. He was exiled for that crime. Gray eyes. Handsome.

Daik, Oleg, &Taren: Three members of Ruenn's crew aboard the air battleship, *Khiang*.

Munt: A young man, a war-orphan who serves on Ruenn's battleship, *Khiang*. His name, which he chose himself, is taken from a term meaning monkey.

Ostt, Cailif: Pilot for Ruenn Maclang's air battleship, the *Khiang*. Human male.

Rence: A Human warrior who has joined Chalathar's fight to bring peace to Talera. His eyes are described as "mescal colored," a very light clear brown.

Shai: A warrior woman with light brown eyes. She has also joined Chalathar's effort to bring peace to Talera.

New Characters in Gods of Talera

Basinj: A Human male with a peg-leg and twisted arm who serves Chalathar. Primarily a cook.

Corlus: A very fat Vhichang who is missing half his beak. One of the Six Captains who lead the Brotherhood of the Skull Flag.

Darmin: A male Vhichang warrior who serves Chalathar. Carries a wooden handled axe resembling a long tomahawk.

Degan, Owin: A Human male, one of the Six Captains who lead the Brotherhood of the Skull Flag.

Dharus: A Nokarran male. The original First Mate of *The Painted Maid*.

Gallus: A Nysphalian soldier in the Imperial Guard. Human male.

Jelvin: A one-eyed Vhichang pirate. Male.

Khene: A Nokarran pirate aboard *The Painted Maid*. Male.

Lann: An Indigo Llurn warrior. Female.

Lyra: A Human female. Once a slave girl, she was brought to Chalathar's home base because she learned too much about his operation. Generally serves as a housekeeper and cook's helper.

Semish: A paunchy Kaldi who serves Chalathar. Captured and tortured while on a dangerous mission, Semish lost his nerve for combat. Now a gardener.

Sobrus: A Klar, one of the Six Captains who lead the Brotherhood of the Skull Flag. This is an unusual role for a female Klar.

Stefan: Captain of *The Painted Maid*. Human male.

Teltshirn, Shadrack: An Ebon Llurn, one of the Six Captains who lead the Brotherhood of the Skull Flag. Male.

Tesluc: A red-furred Ss'Korra female who serves Chalathar. A warrior.

Tregren: A Nokarran with the unusual combination of white fur and blue eyes. A member of the Council of Six that rules the Brotherhood of the Skull Flag. There is much more to him than meets the eye.

Tuunshin: A Kaldi female who serves as Chalathar's phoros (doctor).

Vokule, Jubyl Versath Miesh: A youthful warrior prince of the Indigo Llurns. Male.

Vokule, Lavisa Mersath Tanishmora: Queen of the Indigo Llurns, mother to Jubyl.

Wulfe: A Human, one of the Six Captains who lead the Brotherhood of the Skull Flag. Has a crew cut, an odd haircut for Talera.

Zene: A Nokarran warrior in Chalathar's forces. Apparently killed by a shapeshifter, who replaced him.

www.ingramcontent.com/pod-product-compliance
Lightning Source LLC
Chambersburg PA
CBHW031430250626
47155CB00004B/1693